STORIES FROM A
MING COLLECTION

UNESCO COLLECTION OF REPRESENTATIVE WORKS
CHINESE SERIES

STORIES FROM A

MING COLLECTION

TRANSLATIONS OF CHINESE SHORT

STORIES PUBLISHED IN THE

SEVENTEENTH CENTURY

by

CYRIL BIRCH

GROVE WEIDENFELD
NEW YORK

Published by Grove Weidenfeld
A division of Wheatland Corporation
841 Broadway
New York, NY 10003-4793

ISBN 0-8021-5031-4

Library of Congress Catalog Card Number 68-44187

Manufactured in the United States of America

Printed on acid-free paper

First Evergreen Edition 1968

13   15   16   14   12

CONTENTS

To My Wife

Introduction

THROUGH the long history of China, every age seems in retrospect to have deposited its own distinctive form of tribute in the vast storehouse of her civilization. We think of the later centuries of the Chou period as the Age of the Philosophers. With the name of the T'ang dynasty we associate Tu Fu, Li Po and others of China's greatest poets. So, down the centuries, one form after another of creative expression has offered itself to men. The Ming was the last of the native Chinese dynastic houses. Its founder drove the Mongols out of China in the fourteenth century; the last of the line saw the Dragon Throne fall to the Manchu invaders in 1644. The centuries of Ming rule were not an age of gold. No doubt the highest ambition of the men of the time, in many things, was to avoid falling too far short of the achievements of their illustrious ancestors. But if there was one art of all others which found fresh favour in this age it was the art of fiction.

The six stories I have translated in this volume formed part of a collection entitled *Stories Old and New*, published in Soochow in the early 1620s. The writer of the preface to the collection had no misgivings as to its quality:

> To such a high stage of advancement have the arts been carried under the aegis of our Imperial Ming, that there is no school but has flourished, and in popular literature the writing has often reached a standard far above that of Sung. Those who reject the style of such work as unfit for comparison with the writings of the T'ang period are making a mistake. The eater of peaches need not reject the apricot. Fine linen, silk gauze, plush, brocade, each has its proper occasion. To hold that Sung writing should model itself on that of T'ang is to hold that T'ang should model itself on Han, and Han in turn on the times of the *Ch'un-ch'iu* and the Warring States; the logical conclusion being to confine all within the scope of a solitary brush-mark by the divine Fu-hsi [the legendary ruler reputed to have discovered mystic diagrams on the back of a tortoise, which prompted him to the invention of writing]. Which is an impossible position.

7

In general terms, T'ang writers fashioned their phrases to appeal to the cultivated mind; Sung writers used the colloquial to accord with the rustic ear. Now the cultivated minds of this world are few, the rustic ears many; and fiction lends itself more to the popularizer than to the stylist. Make a trial of the story-tellers of today, with their extempore descriptions: they will gladden you, startle you, make you weep for sorrow, make you dance and sing; some will prompt you to draw your sword, others will make you want to bow in reverence, or strangle yourself, or give money. The coward will be made brave, the profligate pure, the miser generous, the dullard ashamed. Although a man from his childhood days intone the *Analects of Confucius* or the *Classic of Filial Piety*, he will not be moved so swiftly nor so profoundly as by these story-tellers. Can such results be achieved by anything but popular colloquial writing?

The latter half of the sixteenth century was the age of the *Chin P'ing Mei*, the great novel which was partly a development from, partly a reaction against the artificial romances, often pornographic, which enjoyed a vogue among a section of the literati of the day. Wu Ch'eng-en, author of the satirical novel which Arthur Waley has translated under the title *Monkey*, died less than forty years before the publication of the *Stories Old and New*. The most completely developed version of *The Men of the Marshes* (Pearl Buck's *All Men Are Brothers*) and several editions of the *Romance of the Three Kingdoms* date from the end of the Ming period.

With rebels within the frontiers, and aggressive tribes without, it was only in the region of Chiang-nan, 'south of the Yangtze', that peace reigned at this time. It was here that men of leisure and of literary inclinations assembled and flourished. Members of the gentry, poets and painters, scholars who had despaired of success in the examinations or had for other reasons turned their back on a career in the bureaucracy: it was among such men that the taste for the lighter forms of literature grew, and among such men that the reading, writing and publication of colloquial fiction became something of a craze.

Feng Meng-lung, who compiled and published the *Stories*

Old and New, belonged to this Chiang-nan society. He was born
in Soochow in 1574. His official career was of the sketchiest. After
obtaining his first degree he must have taught school for some
considerable time, for (presumably in middle age) he qualified
for selection as a 'senior student', in accordance with the Ming
system whereby certain salaried graduates from local establish-
ments, men of sufficiently long standing, were sent to the capital
to take the preliminary examinations for the third degree and to
enter the Imperial Academy for training. Up to this time, no
doubt, Feng's teaching salary had kept him alive, but had needed
to be augmented by the proceeds from his prolific output of
fiction and plays.

In 1634, at the age of sixty and ten years after he had published the *Stories Old and New*, Feng was at last able to enter
the bureaucracy as Magistrate of Shou-ning, a district in Fukien.
He held this office for four years, during which his administration was easy-going but free from corruption and he earned
the name of an honest official. He earned also, however, the comment in the local gazetteer that he 'honoured literary pursuits
above all': the obvious inference being that he devoted no more
of his time to official business than he could possibly avoid. His
companions were men of like interests—poets like Yüan Hung-
tao, playwrights like Yüan Yü-ling, besides a host of dilettantes.
A nineteenth-century scholar gives an illuminating account of
a good turn which Feng once performed for Yüan Yü-ling:

As soon as Yüan had completed his play *Hsi lou chi* he showed
it to Feng Meng-lung. The latter read it through, then put
it down on the table without expressing an opinion. Yüan
took his leave considerably disconcerted. It so happened
that Feng had just come to the end of his supplies of food,
but when his wife informed him of this he replied, 'Don't
worry, the great Yüan is going to feed us this evening.'
His household took this for boasting. But when Yüan returned
home, he spent the day in worrying, until at nightfall he
suddenly called for a lamp and set off to see Feng, taking with
him a hundred gold pieces. Reaching Feng's gate he found it
still open, and on asking a servant the reason for this he was
told, 'My master has a candle in his hand at this moment,

awaiting your arrival.' Startled, Yüan hastened into the house. Feng greeted him with the words, 'I was convinced you would come. Your play is excellent, but it is one act short. This act I have now added.' The act was the one entitled *Ts'o meng*. Yüan was filled with reverence for Feng Meng-lung.

Literature in its less esoteric forms was Feng's dominant passion. He wrote plays, poems, collections of anecdotes, accounts of contemporary events, and handbooks on the card-game *ma-tiao*, which was probably an ancestor of mahjongg. But his original writings were few in proportion to the great number of works by other men which he edited and revised. These included several novels of great length as well as the pieces contained in *Stories Old and New* and in companion collections.

For the stories of the type I have translated here were not the work of Feng Meng-lung, nor indeed of any one man whose name is known to us. They go under the generic title of *hua-pen*, 'prompt-books'. Feng collected these prompt-books, of widely-varying ages, some from earlier collections, some existing only in manuscript form. No doubt many of the pieces which came into his hands still had the form in which they had originally been written down. They were in fact verbatim records of the performances of the street-corner story-teller, made either by the story-teller himself for the benefit of his colleagues or apprentices, or by enthusiasts, men of letters who wanted a more permanent record of the story-teller's work.

The story-teller was a popular figure of the market-place as early as the T'ang dynasty, but it was in the twelfth and thirteenth centuries, the Southern Sung period, that he really came into his own. Many of Feng Meng-lung's prompt-books dated from that time, and originated in the capital of the day, Lin-an, the present Hangchow. The artists of Lin-an developed the techniques of oral narration to a fine art. Singing does not seem to have been an integral part of the technique, nor was there necessarily accompaniment by any musical instrument other than a drum or a 'waking-board', used to reinforce a point or to rouse the somnolent. But—to come down to recent years—there is a record of one man who 'in one breath' could produce seven distinct sounds to represent in realistic fashion the screams of a pig in the successive stages of its slaughter. The story-tellers formed societies, such as the Hsiung-pien-hui or 'Society for Eloquence'; but each man was in fact a specialist in one or other of the main fields: historical romances, expounding the Buddhist scriptures, or fiction proper, which included stories of love and of crime.

Again according to the preface to our collection, the story-teller's audience included, if indirectly, even so august a figure as the Emperor Kao-tsung himself. When, in 1163, he 'relinquished his task of government, and rested on the support of all under Heaven, he took pleasure, in the hours of relaxation which his long life of virtue had ensured for him, in perusing prompt-books. He ordered his eunuchs to procure him a new story every day, and if the story pleased him, its author would be richly rewarded with money. In consequence of this the eunuchs were always on the look-out for strange tales of former days and for the tittle-tattle of the countryside. Then they would commission men to elaborate this material into stories to present to the Emperor for his delectation. But once read, the stories were discarded, so that in the end many disappeared from view in the recesses of the palace, and not more than one or two out of ten ever became current among the people.'

It is our great debt to Feng Meng-lung that he rescued so many of these stories from oblivion and ensured their survival to the present day. We know that he reprinted some stories from earlier collections with hardly a word altered. The pieces are full of the traces of oral performance. There is always some kind of preface, often a prologue-anecdote as a kind of curtain-raiser or as a time-filler while the audience assembled and settled itself. There is a certain amount of reiteration of the action, obviously for the benefit of late-comers. There are constant injunctions to the audience to 'clean its ears' and 'listen to this one', and a flow of technical phrases which enabled the story-teller to keep the strands of his complicated plot distinct in the minds of his hearers: 'let us say no more about him, but rather go on to tell how . . .'; 'our story forks at this point . . .' and so on. And of course, every so often the narrative is punctuated by a little jingling verse which points a moral, comments on the action or more vividly realizes a scene for the audience.

Yet, though the stories are far from being Feng's own work, there is apparent in many of them the outlook which he and the men of his circle must have shared. One story displays a fine contempt for official values by eulogizing the poet Liu Yung, who treasured the regard of the *filles de joie* more highly than that of his bureaucratic colleagues. Often we find the viewpoint of the man who has retreated from official life into the magical and contemplative consolations of Taoism. The bureaucracy in general fares badly in the stories. In *The Restitution of the Bride* (translated under this title by E. B. Howell) the meanness and corruption of official life are vividly painted: the hero is the liberal T'ang statesman P'ei Tu, who stands out as the sole virtuous man amid a crowd of petty bullies, toadies and intriguers. At the peak of his career, he discovers that the only course open to him, as an honest man, is withdrawal from public life.

At the same time, there is evident a sneaking admiration for the successful man, in such a story as *Wine and Dumplings*, which I have translated. The hero is a man (of undisputed merit) who rises to the top, not by a hard grind in the examination halls, but by a lucky chance—clearly, those who professed to scorn official honours were not above a certain amount of wishful thinking. An amusing facet of the scholar's mentality is revealed in the fourth story of the collection: after an unhappy love affair a woman's fidelity to her dead lover, and her care for the child she has borne him, suffice to wipe out the disgrace of the fact that they were not married; but the gossip of the neighbours ceases only when the illegitimate son makes good as highest-placed candidate in the final examinations.

In general, though, the stories belong less to the scholar-official class than to the wider semi-literate public of their day. It was for the benefit of this wider public that they used the simple colloquial style. The strong didactic element is also directed at this public, which is urged to observe sexual morality, to practise loyalty in friendship, to reverence the heroes of old, to accept the doctrines of retribution, to put its trust in benevolent spirits and to beware of demons. 'Glory and decay, poverty and riches, pass and re-pass like a rolling ball'—many maxims of this kind flatter the common man and encourage him to accept his lot. But be that as it may, a glance through *The Canary Murders* will confirm the essential realism of the stories, and confute the charge that has sometimes been laid, that they present an idealized picture of the life of their time.

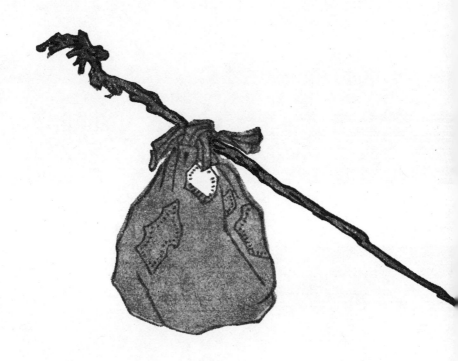

The Lady Who Was a Beggar

THE twelfth and thirteenth centuries were the period of the Southern Sung dynasty when the Chinese court, driven south across the Yangtze by the Chin Tartars, established a new capital at Lin-an (present-day Hangchow). The magnificence of Lin-an is attested a little later by Marco Polo, who knew the city as Kinsai and declared that it made Venice look like a fishing-village. To this city where the arts already flourished flocked men of talent from the old northern capital, Kaifeng, and from nearby Soochow and Chin-ling (Nanking), until Lin-an must have seemed indeed a worthy centre of the civilized world.

The school of story-telling which was at work in Lin-an at this time made a speciality of tales of love. These were of two sorts, cautionary tales and romances. *The Lady who was a Beggar* is a typical Lin-an romance, with its happy ending in the reunion of parted lovers. But it is very much more than just another 'chance reunion' romance. It is a frontal attack on the vice of snobbishness, of which the central figure Mo Chi is the personification. The story's moral is driven home not by injunctions and asides, but by the high realism of every step of the action. Watch the behaviour of Jade Slave, the heroine, when her husband bows before her begging forgiveness for the wrong he has done her. No doubt in many a story of less sincere quality she would grant her forgiveness with a calm, sweet smile. But not here. Not before she has spat in his face and roundly berated him.

THE LADY
WHO WAS A BEGGAR

That side the wall, the branches—this side, the broken blossoms,
Fallen to earth, the playthings of every passing breeze.
The branches may be bare, but they will put out more flowers—
The flowers, once adrift, may never regain the trees.

THIS is the 'Song of the Rejected Wife', by a poet of former
times. It likens the position of a wife to that of the blossom on the
branch: the branch may be stripped of its blossom, but it will
bloom again in the spring; the flowers, once they have left the
branch, can never hope to return. Ladies, if you will listen to me,
then serve your husband to the extent of your powers, share with
him joy and sorrow, and follow one to the end. Unless you wish
to lay up repentance in store, do not scorn poverty and covet
riches, do not let your affections wander.

Let me tell you now of a famous statesman of the Han dynasty
whose wife, in the days before he had made his name, left him
because 'though she had eyes, she did not recognize Mount
T'ai'. In vain did she repent in later years. Who was this man,
you ask, and where did he come from? Well, his name was Chu
Mai-ch'en, he was styled Weng-tzu, and he came from the region
of Hui-chi in the south-east. Of poor family, he had as yet
found no opening, but lived, just himself and his wife, in a
tumbledown cottage in a mean alley. Every day he would go into
the hills and cut firewood to sell in the market-place for the few
cash he needed to carry on existence. But he was addicted to
study, and a book never left his hand. Though his back was bowed
down under a weight of faggots, grasped in his hand would be a
book. This he would read aloud, rolling the phrases round his
mouth, chanting as he walked along.

The townspeople were used to him, they knew Mai-ch'en was
here with his firewood as soon as they heard the sound of intoning. They all bought from him out of sympathy for a poor

19

Confucian; moreover, he never haggled but simply took whatever you wanted to give him, so that he never found his firewood difficult to sell. But there were always gangs of idlers and street-urchins ready to make fun of him as he came along, intoning the classics with a load of faggots on his shoulders.

Mai-ch'en never noticed them. But one day when his wife went out of doors to draw water, she felt humiliated by the sight of these children making fun of Mai-ch'en with his burden. When he came home with his earnings she began to upbraid him: 'If you want to study, then leave off selling firewood, and if you want to sell firewood then leave studying to others. When a man gets to your age, and in his right senses, that he should act like that and let children make fun of him! It's a wonder you don't die of shame.'

'I sell firewood to save us from penury', replied Mai-ch'en, 'and I study to win wealth and esteem. There is no contradiction there. Let them laugh!'

But his wife laughed at this. 'If it's wealth and esteem you're after, then don't sell any more firewood. Who ever heard of a woodcutter becoming a mandarin? And yet you talk all this nonsense.'

'Wealth and poverty, fame and obscurity, each has its time,' said Mai-ch'en. 'A fortune-teller told me my rise would begin when I had passed fifty. They say you can't measure out the ocean with a gallon can—don't you try to measure my mind for me.'

'Fortune-teller indeed!' said his wife. 'He could see you were simple and deliberately made fun of you. You should pay no heed to him. By the time you're fifty you'll be past even carrying firewood. Death from starvation, that's what's in store for you, and then you talk about becoming a mandarin! Unless, of course, the King of Hades wants another judge in his court and is keeping the job vacant for you!'

'Chiang T'ai-kung was still a fisherman on the River Wei at the age of eighty,' replied Mai-ch'en, 'but when King Wen of Chou found him he took him into his chariot and honoured him as counsellor. Kung-sun Hung, a Chief Minister of the present dynasty, was still herding swine by the Eastern Ocean at the age of fifty-nine. He was turned sixty when fate presented him to the present Emperor, who made him a general and a marquis. If I

begin when I am fifty I shall be some way behind Kan Lo,[1] but
in front of the two I have just mentioned. You must be patient
and wait a while.'

'There's no need to ransack all the histories,' said his wife.
'Your fisherman and swineherd were full of talent and learning.
But you, with these useless books of yours, you'll still be the same
at a hundred. What is there to hope for? I was unlucky enough
to marry you, and now, what with the children following you
about and poking fun at you, you've taken my good name away
too. If you don't do as I say and throw those books away, I'm
determined I won't stay with you. We'll each lead our own life,
and then we shan't get in each other's way.'

'I am forty-three this year,' said Mai-ch'en. 'In seven years'
time I shall be fifty. The long wait is behind us, you have
only to be patient for a little longer. If you desert me now in
such a callous fashion you will surely regret it in years to
come.'

'The world's not short of woodcutters,' his wife rejoined.
'What shall I have to regret? If I remain with you another seven
years it will be my corpse as well as yours that is found starved
by the roadside. It will count as a good deed if you release me
now, for you will have saved my life.'

Mai-ch'en realized that his wife had set her heart on leaving
him and wouldn't be gainsaid. So he said, with a sigh, 'Very well,
then. I only hope that your next husband will be a better man
than Chu Mai-ch'en.'

'Whatever he's like he could hardly be worse,' returned his
wife, whereupon she made two obeisances and went joyfully out
of the house and away without so much as looking back.

To relieve his distress, Chu Mai-ch'en inscribed four lines of
verse on the wall of his cottage:

> Marry a dog, follow a dog,
> Marry a cock, follow a cock.
> It was my wife deserted me,
> Not I rejected her.

By the time Chu Mai-ch'en reached his fiftieth birthday the
Han Emperor Wu-ti had issued his edict summoning men of
worth to serve their country. Mai-ch'en went to the Western

Capital, submitted his name and took his place among those awaiting appointment. Meanwhile his abilities were brought to the notice of the Emperor by a fellow-townsman, Yen Chu. Reflecting that Chu Mai-ch'en must have intimate knowledge of the people of his native place and of their condition, the Emperor appointed him Prefect of Hui-chi, and he rode off to take up his appointment.

Learning of the impending arrival of the new Prefect, the officials of Hui-chi mobilized great numbers of men to put the roads in order. Among these coolies was Chu Mai-ch'en's marital successor; and at this man's side, attending to his food, was Mai-ch'en's ex-wife, barefoot and with matted hair. When the woman heard the din of the approach of the new Prefect and his suite, she tried to get a glimpse of him—and saw her former husband, Chu Mai-ch'en.

Mai-ch'en also, from his carriage, caught sight of her and recognized his ex-wife. He summoned her and seated her in one of the carriages of his suite.

At the official residence, the woman did not know where to put herself for shame. She kotowed and poured out a confession of her faults. Mai-ch'en ordered her second husband to be summoned to his presence, and it did not take them long to bring him in. He grovelled on the floor, not daring to raise his eyes. Mai-ch'en burst out laughing: 'A man like this—I don't see that he is much of an improvement on Chu Mai-ch'en?'

His ex-wife went on kotowing and confessing. She had eyes but no pupils and had not recognized his worth; she would wish to return as humble slave or concubine; as such she would serve him to the end of her days. Chu Mai-ch'en ordered a bucket of water to be brought and splashed on the floor. Then he told his wife: 'If this spilt water can go back into the bucket, then you can come back to me. But in memory of our childhood betrothal, I grant you waste land from my demesne sufficient to support yourself and your husband.'

When the woman left the residence with her second husband the passers-by pointed her out to each other: 'That's the wife of the new Prefect!' Humiliated beyond measure, when she reached her piece of land she jumped in the nearby river and drowned herself.

There is a verse in evidence of all this:

The general Han Hsin, starving, was looked after by a washer-
woman,
But this poor scholar is deserted by his own good wife.
Well aware that spilt water cannot be recovered
She repents that in time past she would not let him study.

A second poem maintains that to despise poverty and esteem
only wealth is a commonplace in this world, and not limited to
such a woman as the wife of Chu Mai-ch'en:

> *Using success or failure as the sole gauge of merit*
> *Who can discern the dragon lying hidden in the mud?*
> *Do not blame this woman for her lack of perception,*
> *More than one wife in this world has kicked over the traces.*

After this story of a wife rejecting her husband, let me tell one
now about a husband rejecting his wife. It was equally a case of
scorning the poor and adulating the rich, at the expense of justice
and mercy alike, so that all that was gained in the end was a name
among all and sundry for meanness and lack of feeling.

It is told that in the Shao-hsing reign-period of the Sung
dynasty (1131–1163), although Lin-an had been made the
capital city and was a wealthy and populous district, still the
great number of beggars had not diminished. Among them was
one who acted as their head. He was called the 'tramp-major',
and looked after all the beggars. Whenever they managed to beg
something, the tramp-major would demand a fee for the day.
Then when it was raining or snow lay on the ground, and there
was nowhere to go to beg, the tramp-major would boil up a drop
of thin gruel and feed the whole beggar-band. Their tattered
robes and jackets were also in his care. The result was that the
whole crowd of the beggars were careful to obey him, with bated
breath like a lot of slaves, and none of them dared offend him.

The tramp-major was thus provided with a regular income, and
as a rule he would lend out sums of money among the beggars
and extort a tidy interest. In this way, if he neither gambled
nor went whoring, he could build up a going concern out of it.
He depended on this for his livelihood, and never for a moment
thought of changing his profession. There was only one draw-

back: a tramp-major did not have a very good name. Though he acquired land by his efforts, and his family had prospered for generations, still he was a boss of the beggars and not to be compared with ordinary respectable people. No one would salute him with respect if he showed himself out-of-doors, and so the only thing for him to do was to shut his doors and play the great man in his own home.

And yet, distinguishing the worthy from the base, we count among the latter only prostitutes, actors, yamen-runners and soldiers: we certainly do not include beggars. For what is wrong with beggars is not that they are covered in sores, but simply that they have no money. There have been men like the minister Wu Tzu-hsü, of Ch'un-ch'iu times, who as a fugitive from oppression played his pipes and begged his food in the market-place of Wu; or Cheng Yüan-ho of T'ang times who sang the beggar's song of 'Lien-hua lo', but later rose to wealth and eminence and covered his bed with brocade. These were great men, though beggars: clearly, we may hold beggars in contempt, but we should not compare them with the prostitutes and actors, the runners and soldiery.

Let us digress no longer, but tell now how in the city of Hangchow there was once a tramp-major by the name of Chin Lao-ta. In the course of seven generations his ancestors had developed the profession into a perfect family business, so that Chin Lao-ta ate well and dressed well, lived in a fine house and cultivated good land. His barns were well-stocked with grain and his purse with money, he made loans and kept servants; if not quite the wealthiest, he was certainly one of the rich. Being a man of social aspirations, he decided to relinquish this post of tramp-major into the hands of a relative, 'Scabby' Chin, while he himself took his ease with what he had and mingled no more with the beggar band. But unfortunately, the neighbours were used to speaking of 'the tramp-major's family', and the name persisted in spite of his efforts.

Chin Lao-ta was over fifty. He had lost his wife and had no son, but only a daughter whose name was Jade Slave. Jade Slave was beautiful, as we are told by a verse about her:

> Pure to compare with jade,
> Gracious to shame the flowers,

Given the adornments of the court
Here would be another Chang Li-hua.[2]

Chin Lao-ta prized his daughter as a jewel, and taught her
from an early age to read and write. By the age of fifteen she was
adept in prose and verse, composing as fast as her hand could
write. She was equally proficient in the womanly crafts, and in
performing on the harp or flute: everything she did proclaimed
her skill. Her beauty and talent inspired Chin Lao-ta to seek a
husband for her among the scholar class. But the fact was that
among families of name and rank it would be difficult to find
anyone anxious to marry the girl—no one wanted a tramp-major's
daughter. On the other hand, Lao-ta had no desire to cultivate a
liaison with humble and unaspiring tradespeople. Thus, while
her father hovered between high and low, the girl reached the
age of seventeen without betrothal.

And then one day an old man of the neighbourhood came along
with news of a student by the name of Mo Chi who lived below
the T'ai-ping Bridge. This was an able youth of nineteen, full of
learning, who remained unmarried only because he was an orphan
and had no money. But he had graduated recently, and was
hoping to marry some girl in whose family he could find a home.

'This youth would be just right for your daughter,' said the
neighbour. 'Why not take him as your son-in-law?'

'Then do me the favour of acting as go-between,' said Chin
Lao-ta; and off went the old man on his errand, straight to the
T'ai-ping Bridge.

There he sought out the graduate Mo Chi, to whom he said,
'There is one thing I am obliged to tell you: the ancestors of
Chin Lao-ta followed the profession of tramp-major. But this
was long ago: and think, what a fine girl she is, this daughter of
his—and what's more, what a prosperous and flourishing family!
If it is not against the young gentleman's wishes, I will take it
upon myself to arrange the whole thing at once.'

Before giving his reply, Mo Chi turned the matter over in his
mind: 'I am not very well-off for food and clothes just now, and
I am certainly not in a position to take a wife in the usual way.
Why not make the best of it and marry into this family? It would
be killing two birds with one stone; and I needn't take any notice
of ridicule.' Turning to the old man, he said, 'Uncle, what you

propose seems an admirable plan. But I am too poor to buy the usual presents. What do you suggest?'

'Provided only that you accept this match,' replied the old man, 'you will not even be called on to supply so much as the paper for the exchange of horoscopes. You may leave everything to me.'

With this he returned to report to Chin Lao-ta. They selected an auspicious day, and the Chin family even provided clothes for Mo Chi to wear at the wedding.

When Mo Chi had entered the family and the ceremony was over, he found that Jade Slave's beauty and talents exceeded his wildest hopes. And this perfect wife was his without the outlay of a single copper! He had food and clothes in abundance, and indeed everything he could wish. Even the ridicule he had feared from his friends was withheld, for all were willing to make allowances for Mo Chi's penniless condition.

When their marriage had lasted a month Chin Lao-ta prepared a generous banquet at which his son-in-law could feast his graduate friends and thus enhance the dignity of the house. The drinking went on for a week: but what was not foreseen was the offence which all this gave to the kinsman 'Scabby' Chin. Nor was Scabby without justification.

'You're a tramp-major just as much as I am,' said he in his heart, 'the only thing is that you've been one for a few generations longer and have got some money in your pocket. But if it comes to ancestors, aren't yours the very same as mine? When my niece Jade Slave gets married I expect to be invited to drink a toast—here's a load of guests drinking for a week on end to celebrate the first month, but not so much as a one-inch by three-inch invitation-card do I receive. What is this son-in-law of yours—he's a graduate, I know, but is he a President of a Board or a Prime Minister as well? Aren't I the girl's own uncle, and entitled to a stool at your party? Very well,' he concluded, 'if they're so ready to ignore my existence, I'll go and stir them up a bit and see how that pleases them.'

Thereupon he called together fifty or sixty of his beggars, and took the lot of them along to Chin Lao-ta's house. What a sight—

Hats bursting into flower, shirts tied up in knots,
A rag of old matting or a strip of worn rug, a bamboo stick
    and a rough chipped bowl.

Shouting 'Father!', shouting 'Mother!', shouting 'Benefactor!',
what a commotion before the gate!
Writhing snakes, yapping dogs, chattering apes and monkeys,
what sly cunning they all display!
Beating clappers, singing 'Yang Hua',[3] the clamour deafens the
ear;
Clattering tiles, faces white with chalk,[4] the sight offends the eye.
A troop of rowdies banded together, not Chung K'uei[5] himself
could contain them.

When Chin Lao-ta heard the noise they made he opened the
gate to look out, whereupon the whole crowd of beggars, with
Scabby at their head, surged inside and threw the house into
commotion. Scabby himself hurried to a seat, snatched the
choicest of the meats and wines and began to stuff himself,
calling meanwhile for the happy couple to come and make their
obeisances before their uncle.

So terrified were the assembled graduates that they gave up at
once and fled the scene, Mo Chi joining in their retreat. Chin
Lao-ta was at his wits' end, and pleaded repeatedly, 'My son-in
law is the host today, this is no affair of mine. Come another day
when I will buy in some wine specially for you and we will have
a chat together.'

He distributed money among the beggar band, and brought
out two jars of fine wine and some live chickens and geese,
inviting the beggars to have a banquet of their own over at
Scabby's house; but it was late at night before they ceased their
rioting and took their leave, and Jade Slave wept in her room
from shame and rage.

That night Mo Chi stayed at the house of a friend, returning
only when morning came. At the sight of his son-in-law, Chin
Lao-ta felt keenly the disgrace of what had happened, and his
face filled with shame. Naturally enough, Mo Chi on his part
was strongly displeased; but no one was anxious to say a word.
Truly,

> *When a mute tastes the bitterness of cork-tree wood*
> *He must swallow his disgust with his medicine.*

Let us rather tell how Jade Slave, conscious of her family's disrepute and anxious that her husband should make his own name for himself, exhorted him to labour at his books. She grudged neither the cost of the works, classical and recent, which she bought for his use, nor the expense of engaging tutors for learned discussion with him. She provided funds also for the entertaining that would widen her husband's circle of acquaintances. As a result, Mo Chi's learning and reputation made daily advances.

He gained his master's degree at the age of twenty-two, and ultimately his doctorate, and at last the day came when he left the great reception for successful candidates and, black hat, doctor's robes and all, rode back to his father-in-law's house. But as he entered his own ward of the city a crowd of urchins pressed about him, pointing and calling—'Look at the tramp-major's son-in-law! He's an official now!'

From his elevated position Mo Chi heard them, but it was beneath his dignity to do anything about it. He simply had to put up with it; but his correct observance of etiquette on greeting his father-in-law concealed a burning indignation. 'I always knew that I should attain these honours,' he said to himself, 'yet I feared that no noble or distinguished family would take me in as a son-in-law, and so I married the daughter of a tramp-major. Without question, it is a life-long stain. My sons and daughters will still have a tramp-major for their grandfather, and I shall be passed from one man to the next as a laughing stock! But the thing is done now. What is more, my wife is wise and virtuous, it would be impossible for me to divorce her on any of the seven counts.[6] "Marry in haste, repent at leisure"—it's a true saying after all!'

His mind seethed with such thoughts, and he was miserable all day long. Jade Slave often questioned him, but received no reply and remained in ignorance of the cause of his displeasure. But what an absurd figure, this Mo Chi! Conscious only of his present eminence, he has forgotten the days of his poverty. His wife's assistance in money and effort are one with the snows of yesteryear, so crooked are the workings of his mind.

Before long, Mo Chi presented himself for appointment and received the post of Census Officer at Wu-wei-chün. His father-in-law provided wine to feast his departure, and this time awe of the new official deterred the beggar band from breaking up the party.

It so happened that the whole journey from Hangchow to Wu-wei-chün was by water, and Mo Chi took his wife with him, boarded a junk and proceeded to his post. After several days their voyage brought them to the eddies and whirlpools below the Coloured Stone Cliff,[7] and they tied up to the northern bank. That night the moon shone bright as day. Mo Chi, unable to sleep, rose and dressed and sat in the prow enjoying the moonlight. There was no one about; and as he sat there brooding on his relationship with a tramp-major an evil notion came into his head. The only way for him to be rid of life-long disgrace was for his wife to die and a new one to take her place. A plan formed in his mind. He entered the cabin and inveigled Jade Slave into getting up to see the moon in its glory.

Jade Slave was already asleep, but Mo Chi repeatedly urged her to get up, and she did not like to contravene his wishes. She put on her gown and crossed over to the doorway, where she raised her head to look at the moon. Standing thus, she was taken unawares by Mo Chi, who dragged her out on to the prow and pushed her into the river.

Softly he then woke the boatmen and ordered them to get under way at once—extra speed would be handsomely rewarded. The boatmen, puzzled but ignorant, seized pole and flourished oar. Mo Chi waited until the junk had covered three good miles before he moored again and told them that his wife had fallen in the river while gazing at the moon, and that no effort would have availed to save her. With this, he rewarded the boatmen with three ounces of silver to buy wine. The boatmen caught his meaning, but none dared open his mouth. The silly maidservants who had accompanied Jade Slave on board accepted that their mistress had really fallen in the river. They wept for a little while and then left off, and we will say no more of them. There is a verse in evidence of all this:

> The name of tramp-major pleases him ill;
> Hardened by pride he casts off his mate.
> The ties of Heaven are not easily broken;
> All he gains is an evil name.

But don't you agree that 'there is such a thing as coincidence'? It so happened that the newly-appointed Transport Commissioner for Western Huai, Hsü Te-hou, was also on his way to his post; and his junk moored across from the Coloured Stone Cliff just when Mo Chi's boat had disappeared from view. It was the very spot where Mo Chi had pushed his wife into the water. Hsü Te-hou and his lady had opened their window to enjoy the moonlight, and had not yet retired but were taking their ease over a cup of wine. Suddenly they became aware of someone sobbing on the river bank. It was a woman, from the sound, and her distress could not be ignored.

At once Hsü ordered his boatmen to investigate. It proved indeed to be a woman, alone, sitting on the bank. Hsü made them summon her aboard, and questioned her about herself. The woman was none other than Jade Slave, Madam Chin, the wife of the Census Officer at Wu-wei-chün. What had happened was that when she found herself in the water her wits all but left her, and she gave herself up for dead. But suddenly she felt something in the river which held up her feet, while the waves washed her close to the bank. Jade Slave struggled ashore; but when she opened her eyes, there was only the empty expanse of the river, and no sign of the Census Officer's junk. It was then that she realized what had happened: 'My husband, grown rich, has forgotten his days of hardship. It was his deliberate plan to drown his true wife to pave the way for a more advantageous marriage. And now, though I have my life, where am I to turn for support?'

Bitter reflections of this kind brought forth piteous weeping, and confronted by Hsü's questioning she could hold nothing back, but told the whole story from beginning to end. When she had finished she wept without ceasing. Hsü and his wife in their turn were moved to tears, and Hsü Te-hou tried to comfort her: 'You must not grieve so; but if you will agree to become my adopted daughter, we will see what provision can be made.'

Hsü had his wife produce a complete change of clothing for the girl and settle her down to rest in the stern cabin. He told his servants to treat her with the respect due to his daughter, and prohibited the boatmen from disclosing anything of the affair. Before long he reached his place of office in Western Huai. Now it so happened that among the places under his jurisdiction was

Wu-wei-chün. He was therefore the superior officer of Mo Chi, who duly appeared with his fellows to greet the new Commissioner. Observing the Census Officer, Hsü sighed that so promising a youth should be capable of so callous an action.

Hsü Te-hou allowed several months to pass, and then he addressed the following words to his staff: 'I have a daughter of marriageable age, and possessing both talent and beauty. I am seeking a man fit to be her husband, whom I could take into my family. Does any of you know of such a man?'

All his staff had heard of Mo Chi's bereavement early in life, and all hastened to commend his outstanding ability and to profess his suitability as a son-in-law for the Commissioner. Hsu agreed: 'I myself have had this man in mind for some time. But one who has graduated at such a youthful age must cherish high ambitions: I am not at all sure that he would be prepared to enter my family.'

'He is of humble origin,' the others replied. 'It would be the happiest of fates for him to secure your interest, to "cling as the creeper to the tree of jade"—there can be no doubt of his willingness.'

'Since you consider it practicable,' said Hsü, 'I should like you to approach the Census Officer. But to discover how he reacts, say that this plan is of your own making: it might hinder matters if you disclose my interest.'

They accepted the commission and made their approach to Mo Chi, requesting that they should act as go-betweens. Now to rise in society was precisely Mo Chi's intention; moreover, a matrimonial alliance with one's superior officer was not a thing to be had for the asking. Delighted, he replied, 'I must rely entirely on you to accomplish this; nor shall I be slow in the material expression of my gratitude.'

'You may leave it to us,' they said; and thereupon they reported back to Hsü.

But Hsü demurred: 'The Census Officer may be willing to marry her,' said he, 'but the fact is that my wife and I have doted on our daughter and have brought her up to expect the tenderest consideration. It is for this reason that we wish her to remain in her own home after marriage. But I suspect that the Census Officer, in the impatience of youth, might prove insufficiently tolerant; and if the slightest discord should arise it would be most painful to my wife and myself. He must be prepared to be patient in all things, before I can accept him into my family.'

They bore these words to Mo Chi, who accepted every condition.

The Census Officer's present circumstances were very different from those of his student days. He signified acceptance of the bethrothal by sending fine silks and gold ornaments on the most ample scale. An auspicious date was selected, and Mo Chi itched in his very bones as he awaited the day when he should become the son-in-law of the Transport Commissioner.

But let us rather tell how Hsü Te-hou gave his wife instructions to prepare Jade Slave for her marriage. 'Your step-father,' Mrs Hsü said to her, 'moved by pity for you in your widowhood, wishes to invite a young man who has gained his doctorate to become your husband and enter our family. You must not refuse him.'

But Jade Slave replied, 'Though of humble family, I am aware of the rules of conduct. When Mo Chi became my husband I vowed to remain faithful to him all my life. However cruel and lawless he may have been, however shamefully he may have rejected the companion of his poverty, I shall fulfil my obligations. On no account will I forsake the true virtue of womanhood by remarrying.'

With these words her tears fell like rain. Mrs Hsü, convinced of her sincerity, decided to tell her the truth, and said, 'The young graduate of whom my husband spoke is none other than Mo Chi himself. Appalled by his mean action, and anxious to see you reunited with him, my husband passed you off as his own daughter, and told the members of his staff that he was seeking a son-in-law who would enter our family. He made them approach Mo Chi, who was delighted by the proposal. He is to come to us this very night; but when he enters your room, this is what you must do to get your own back. . . .'

As she disclosed her plan, Jade Slave dried her tears. She remade her face and changed her costume, and made preparations for the coming ceremony.

With evening there duly appeared the Census Officer Mo Chi,

all complete with mandarin's hat and girdle: he was dressed in
red brocade and had gold ornaments in his cap, under him was
a fine steed with decorated saddle and before him marched two
bands of drummers and musicians. His colleagues were there in
force to see him married, and the whole procession was cheered
the length of the route. Indeed,

To the roll and clang of music the white steed advances,
But what a curious person, this fine upstanding groom:
Delighted with his change of families, beggar for man of rank,
For memories of the Coloured Stone Cliff his glad heart has no
    room.

That night the official residence of the Transport Commissioner was festooned with flowers and carpeted, and to the
playing of pipe and drum all awaited the arrival of the bridegroom.
As the Census Officer rode up to the gate and dismounted, Hsü
Te-hou came out to receive him, and then the accompanying
junior officers took their leave. Mo Chi walked straight through
to the private apartments, where the bride was brought out to
him, veiled in red and supported by a maidservant on either side.
From beyond the threshold the master of ceremonies took them
through the ritual. The happy pair made obeisances to heaven
and earth and to the parents of the bride; and when the ceremonial
observances were over, they were escorted into the nuptial
chamber for the wedding feast. By this time Mo Chi was in a state
of indescribable bliss, his soul somewhere above the clouds. Head
erect, triumphant, he entered the nuptial chamber.

But no sooner had he passed the doorway than from positions
of concealment on either side there suddenly emerged seven or
eight young maids and old nannies, each one armed with a light
or heavy bamboo. Mercilessly they began to beat him. Off came
his silk hat; blows fell like rain on his shoulders; he yelled
perpetually, but try as he might he could not get out of the way.

Under the beating the Census Officer collapsed, to lie in a
terrified heap on the floor, calling on his parents-in-law to save
him. Then he heard, from within the room itself, a gentle
command issued in the softest of voices: 'Beat him no more, our
hard-hearted young gentleman, but bring him before me.'

At last the beating stopped, and the maids and nannies,

tugging at his ears and dragging at his arms like the six senses tormenting Amida Buddha in the parable,[8] hauled him, his feet barely touching the ground, before the presence of the bride. 'What is the nature of my offence?' the Census Officer was mumbling; but when he opened his eyes, there above him, correct and upright in the brilliance of the candle-light, was seated the bride—who was none other than his former wife, Jade Slave, Madam Chin.

Now Mo Chi's mind reeled, and he bawled, 'It's a ghost! It's a ghost!' All began to laugh, until Hsü Te-hou came in from outside and addressed him: 'Do not be alarmed, my boy: this is no ghost, but my adopted daughter, who came to me below the Coloured Stone Cliff.'

Mo Chi's heart ceased its pounding. He fell to his knees and folded his hands in supplication. 'I, Mo Chi, confess my crime,' he said. 'I only beg your forgiveness.'

'This is no affair of mine,' replied Hsü, 'unless my daughter has something to say. . . .'

Jade Slave spat in Mo Chi's face and cursed him: 'Cruel wretch! Did you never think of the words of Sung Hung [9]? "Do not exclude from your mind the friends of your poverty, nor from your house the wife of your youth." It was empty-handed that you first came into my family, and thanks to our money that you were able to study and enter society, to make your name and enjoy your present good fortune. For my part, I looked forward to the day when I should share in your glory. But you—forgetful of the favours you had received, oblivious of our early love, you repaid good with evil and threw me into the river to drown. Heaven took pity on me and sent me a saviour, whose adopted daughter I became. But if I had ended my days on the river-bed, and you had taken a new wife—how could your heart have been so callous? And now, how can I so demean myself as to rejoin you?'

Her speech ended in tears and loud wails, and 'Cruel, cruel!' she continued to cry. Mo Chi's whole face expressed his shame. He could find no words, but pleaded for forgiveness by kotowing before her. Hsü Te-hou, satisfied with her demonstration of anger, raised Mo Chi to his feet and admonished Jade Slave in the following words: 'Calm your anger, my child. Your husband has now repented his crime, and we may be sure that he will never again treat you ill. Although in fact your marriage took place some years ago, so far as my family is concerned you are newly-wed; in all things, therefore, show consideration to me, and let an end be made here and now to recriminations.' Turning to Mo Chi, he said, 'My son, your crime is upon your own head, lay no blame on others. Tonight I ask you only to show tolerance. I will send your mother-in-law to make peace between you.'

He left the room, and shortly his wife came in to them. Much mediation was required from her before the two were finally brought into accord.

On the following day Hsü Te-hou gave a banquet for his new son-in-law, during which he returned all the betrothal gifts, the fine silks and gold ornaments, saying to Mo Chi, 'One bride may not receive two sets of presents. You took such things as these to the Chin family on the previous occasion, I cannot accept them all over again now.' Mo Chi lowered his head and said nothing, and Hsü went on: 'I believe it was your dislike of the lowly status of your father-in-law which put an end to your love and almost to your marriage. What do you think now of my own position? I am only afraid that the rank I hold may still be too low for your aspirations.'

Mo Chi's face flushed crimson, and he was obliged to retire a few steps and acknowledge his errors. There is a verse to bear witness:

> *Full of fond hopes of bettering himself by marriage,*
> *Amazed to discover his bride to be his wife;*
> *A beating, a cursing, an overwhelming shame:*
> *Was it really worth it for a change of in-laws?*

From this time on, Mo Chi and Jade Slave lived together twice as amicably as before. Hsü Te-hou and his wife treated Jade Slave as their own daughter and Mo Chi as their proper son-in-law, and Jade Slave behaved towards them exactly as though they were her own parents. Even the heart of Mo Chi was touched, so that he received Chin Lao-ta, the tramp-major, into his official residence and cared for him to the end of his days. And when in the fullness of time Hsü Te-hou and his wife died, Jade Slave, Madam Chin, wore the heaviest mourning of coarse linen for each of them in recompense for their kindness to her; and generations of descendants of Mo and of Hsü regarded each other as cousins and never failed in friendship. A verse concludes:

Sung Hung remained faithful and was praised for his virtue;
Huang Yün divorced his wife and was reviled for lack of feeling.[10]
Observe the case of Mo Chi, remarrying his wife:
A marriage is predestined: no objection can prevail.

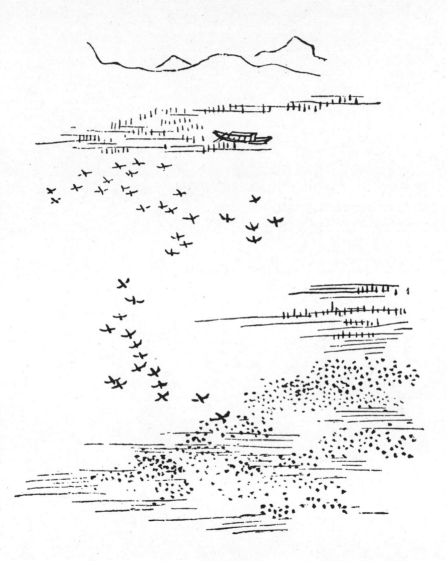

The Pearl-sewn Shirt

The Pearl-sewn Shirt is not only the longest of all the *Stories Old and New*. It is also the best, and the best-known. It is a product of the Ming story-tellers, and was probably written down not very long after the events narrated took place (1466 is the date on a bill of divorcement in the story). That these events, or something very close to them, did take place in actual fact is more likely than not. There is very little of the material of the prompt-books for which no basis can be found in real-life happenings.

The story belongs to the type of the cautionary tale, illustrating the unhappy effects of illicit passion. Similar tales survive from the Lin-an story-tellers of three centuries earlier, but none, I think, penetrates so deeply into the tragedy of the broken marriage. This sense of tragedy comes through despite the story-teller's obvious relish for his seduction scene, and despite the tacked-on happy ending. The 'cunning stratagem' by which the seduction of the heroine is achieved is an important feature of the plot of many stories. In the present case, the progress of the scheme occupies over a third of the total length of the story. The episode is reminiscent of Hsi-men Ch'ing's seduction of P'an Chin-lien in the novel *Chin P'ing Mei*, which is likewise assisted by the stratagem of an old and unscrupulous go-between. But the stratagem of *The Pearl-sewn Shirt* is far more involved and far more subtle. As for the happy ending, this will no doubt be the feature of the story hardest to swallow for the English reader. Clearly, a polygamous society offers a welcome increase of scope when it comes to the manufacture of plots for love stories.

In this as in almost all the prompt-book love stories, the personages belong to the lower merchant or minor official classes. Many stories centre round travelling vendors. These men were the only members of humbler, non-official society to have occasion to travel—apart from soldiers and bandits, who seldom figure in the love stories. It is thus inevitable that vendors should dominate plots which rely on movement. *The Pearl-sewn Shirt* demands the absence from home of the husband, Chiang Hsing-

39

ko, and coincidental meetings between Chiang, away from home, and Ch'en Ta-lang, who has seduced Chiang's wife in his absence. Another meeting is required at a later stage between Chiang and his wife, now divorced. These meetings on journeys are possible because Chiang and Ch'en are travelling vendors, whilst Chiang's ex-wife marries a district magistrate, a man also subject to a life of movement.

Although complex, the plot is set out with great clarity. Scrupulous care is taken that even the coincidental meetings shall appear to be within the bounds of probability. For instance, if Chiang Hsing-ko is not to be recognized, first by his wife's paramour when he meets him on a trading trip, and secondly by his wife's second husband the magistrate, it is essential that he should be under an assumed name. Now, it is not likely that a travelling vendor, depending on an established family connection, should change his surname. So, care is taken to make Hsing-ko's father pass him off as his nephew of different surname, in order to forestall jealousy. This is done at the beginning of the story, and seems superfluous, until later we find Hsing-ko already equipped with a pseudonym. Also, Chiang Hsing-ko's illness in Kwangtung, which is behind the whole scheme of his wife's seduction (to the extent that this would not have succeeded without his prolonged absence, nor would the lady have been so vulnerable), this illness is perfectly well accounted for by the rigours of travelling and his busy efforts to re-establish old connections, which have made him neglect his food. The fever is not fortuitous, but arises naturally from the action.

It is improbable that *The Pearl-sewn Shirt* is no more than a straightforward account of an actual incident. In any case, flawless continuity and verisimilitude of detail are the concern of the art of fiction and not of real life. Either they are the product of one man's supreme narrative talent, or, as seems more likely, they are the result of the telling of the story, time and again, to an audience well accustomed to listening to story-tellers and consequently highly critical. This would be the sort of thing that happened: the story-teller reaches the point where Chiang Hsing-ko meets his wife's lover. 'Why doesn't the lover realize who Chiang Hsing-ko really is?' asks a member of the audience. 'Because he is travelling under an assumed name' is the reply.

'Why?' returns the questioner. 'Because. . . .' The story-teller, his plot thickening, had to justify himself at every point, and when the story came to be written down in its present form all possible suspicion of his veracity had been countered, and the story-teller's possibly improvised explanations worked into the plot.

The real strength of the best of the love stories lies in their characterization. The author of *The Pearl-sewn Shirt*, in his portrayal of the hag Dame Hsüeh, uses all the means open to the novelist, from direct description to the examination of her impact on and reactions to the other personages in his gallery. She emerges as clever and cautious, grasping and unprincipled. But her character is not thus described in so many words. The author's direct description of her is limited to three comments. The first refers to go-betweens in general: 'Tell me, reader, when was there an old procuress who didn't covet money? How was Dame Hsüeh to remain unmoved at the sight of all this silver and gold? Her whole face creased into smiles. . . .' Only when she has herself given considerable evidence of her skill does the author describe her as 'quick of tongue, skilled in the art of persuasion'. The description is in any case redundant, since it is on account of this talent that she first appears on the scene. On her exit, when her stratagem has succeeded and the lovers reward her, the author comments again on her avarice: 'It was only for the sake of this unlawful gain that the old woman allowed herself to be involved in the affair.'

The part she plays in the action is of course enough in itself to give the outline of her character, her disregard for morality, her avarice, her cunning. The function of all the other writing about Dame Hsüeh is to round off and breathe life into the whole.

Small points of behaviour contribute. When we first meet her she is 'in her little yard, her hair dishevelled, grading her pearls. When she heard the knock at the door, she wrapped up the jewels and asked who was there.' In that one slight action of wrapping up the jewels, we are shown at once her guilty cautiousness and her avarice. The cautiousness comes out again in her reception of Ch'en: on his asking 'Can we talk here?', she takes the hint at once and bolts the door. She can drink: the complete old reprobate, she is described as 'a wine-jug, a wine-jar'.

Dialogue is a powerful means to depicting character. Dame Hsüeh being a kind of 'professional talker', we expect evidence of her skill with words. We see it in her clever flattery of Fortune, her hints, so delicate, of the husband's possible infidelity, the subtle and easy way in which she introduces the subject of love in her attempt to rouse the girl's passions, and in such self-justification as the following, spoken to Fortune: 'It was not mere bold presumption on my part (to introduce Ch'en Ta-lang to your bed). It was rather my pity for you, lady, spending each night alone in this springtime of your youth; moreover, I was concerned to save Mr Ch'en's life. The two of you are pre-destined from a former incarnation to come together; it has nothing to do with me at all.' Her use of 'four-character phrases' proclaims her an old gossip, in English life the sort of old woman who 'talks in proverbs'. She tells Fortune she is 'like flowers, like jade'; Chiang and his wife are 'like fishes in water, never apart by an inch or a foot'; she describes her son-in-law as 'carefree and gay from morn till eve'; the absent husband, she says, has plenty of opportunities for 'flowers in the breeze, moonlight on the snow' (amorous adventures).

The author shows us the old woman's cautious cunning in her reaction to Ch'en Ta-lang. She has a shrewd idea that he wants her help in some shady transaction, but hedges by protesting that she has no other trade but in jewels; she takes his bribe, but on the understanding that it will be returned if she cannot perform whatever it is he wants. We see her guilty conscience in her reaction to her eventual punishment: when the deceived husband called with his companions, 'blows fell like snow-flakes as they tore through the place. . . . Dame Hsüeh was conscious of her own misdeeds, and went into hiding.' Her thoughts on first meeting Fortune are a clue not only to the girl's beauty but also to Dame Hsüeh's lack of principle: 'She really has the looks of a fairy,' Dame Hsüeh thought to herself. 'No wonder Ch'en Ta-lang has fallen for her. If I were a man, I'd be just as infatuated.'

Lastly, Dame Hsüeh is shown to us in the way she appears to other personages in the story. We first see her through the eyes of Ch'en Ta-lang, whose one thought is to enlist her help in his campaign against Fortune's honour: 'Suddenly he thought of the jewel-seller Dame Hsüeh. . . . This old woman was skilled in the art of persuasion. Moreover she spent every day tramping the streets and alleys, and knew every household. He must talk things over with her, she'd be sure to have some suggestion.' To Ch'en, then, she is a knowing old bird. To the innocent, ingenuous Fortune she becomes a valued companion, full of sympathy and of worldly wisdom; and the servants all adore her for her ready wit.

There are the materials which establish, piece by piece, the character of the old woman. By the conscious or unconscious use of most of the resources open to the creator of fiction, the author has constructed a personage who really does seem to 'come to life on the page'.

THE PEARL-SEWN SHIRT

To amass wealth in office brings no honour,
Nor is there hope of living long past seventy.
When you are gone, who will preserve your fame?
The empty pageant of the world soon passes.

Do not despoil your youth by wild excesses,
Do not be deceived by wine and women.
Withdraw from puzzling over 'right' and 'wrong',
Accept your lot, content yourself with little.

THIS POEM, to the metre of 'The Moon on the West River',
urges us to keep quietly to our station in life and to find joy in the
acceptance of our lot. Do not let your spirit be destroyed and
your conduct ruined by the four vices of drink, lust, riches and
anger.[1] If you strive after happiness here you will fail to find it;
if you seek an easy gain you will lose. Think for a moment of these
four vices: none is so harmful as the vice of lust. The eye is
go-between for the passions, the heart is the seat of desire. At the
beginning, your heart is in a turmoil; at the end, you have lost
your soul. You may gain pleasure from some chance encounter
with a 'flower of the roadside', and it may be that no harm will
come of it. But when you begin to plan and scheme against the
code of society, you are seeking a moment's selfish gratification
at the expense of the life-long love and respect of others. How
would you feel, if your own charming wife or devoted concubine
should become the object of someone else's machinations? It is
well put in these words of a former poet:

Men's hearts may be blinded,
But the way of Heaven is unchanging.
Let me not defile the womenfolk of others,
And other men will not defile my wife.

I invite members of the audience to listen today while I
narrate the story-with-verses entitled 'The Pearl-sewn Shirt'.
You will see that retribution does not fail to come, and it will

45

give you a useful example to set before your sons and younger brothers.

Of this story I will show you first one personage only, Chiang Te, known as Hsing-ko, of Tsao-yang in the prefecture of Hsiang-yang, in the province of Hu-kuang. His father, Chiang Shih-tse, from boyhood on had covered the length and breadth of Kwangtung province as a travelling merchant. Bereft of his wife, Madam Lo, he now had no family beyond this boy Hsing-ko, who was just eight years of age. Chiang Shih-tse could not bring himself to part with the child, but neither could he put an end to his livelihood in Kwangtung. He gave every thought to his dilemma, but could find no solution but to take the eight-year-old boy along with him as a partner in his business, first teaching him some of the tricks of the trade. Although the child was so young, he was grown:

> Clear of brow, fine of eye,
> White his teeth, red his lip,
> Upright and dignified of step,
> Sharp and quick-witted in speech.
> Beyond the student in intelligence,
> Equal of a grown man in subtlety.
> People all called him 'pretty boy',
> Everyone praised him as a pearl without price.

Chiang Shih-tse feared the envy of others, and so he never in all his travels revealed that this was his own son, but passed him off as his wife's nephew, giving his name as 'Little Master Lo'.

Now the fact was that the Lo family were also in the Kwangtung trade, and indeed whereas the Chiang had only travelled there for one generation the Lo had been there for three. They were friends of long standing of all the innkeepers and dealers, who treated them more as members of their own families. And in fact, when Chiang Shih-tse had first begun to trade there, he had gone in the company of his father-in-law, old Mr Lo. But of late the Lo family had been forced to go to court to answer a whole series of unjust accusations. Their prosperity had waned and for some years past they had made no visits to Kwangtung. Thus there was no innkeeper or dealer who failed, when Chiang Shih-tse appeared, to ask after the Lo family with the most sincere concern. And this time, here was Chiang Shih-tse with a boy whom they discovered to be 'Little Master Lo'. Such a handsome child, too, and so smart to talk to. Everyone greeted him with delight, thinking back over the friendships of three generations, now to be continued into the fourth.

We will gossip no more, but tell how Chiang Hsing-ko made several trips in his father's company and proved such an apt and quick-witted pupil that soon he had mastered all the ins and outs of the business. His father was delighted with him. But who could have foreseen that when the boy was no more than sixteen years old his father was to die of a sudden illness? The one consolation was that he died during a brief stay at home, and thus escaped the misfortune of a wanderer's death.

Hsing-ko wept for a time, but had at last to dry his tears and attend to the funeral rites. It goes without saying that he prepared the body for burial and made the benefactions necessary to ensure the safe passage of the spirit into the next world. During the first forty-nine days of his bereavement, according to custom, he received the condolences of all members of both his father's and his mother's clans. Another who came to make offerings before the dead was a certain Mr Wang, a fellow-townsman, who was in fact the father of the girl to whom Hsing-ko was betrothed. Naturally he fell into conversation with the members of the Chiang clan, and the view was expressed that Hsing-ko was old beyond his years and had done very well in coping single-handed with his heavy task.

One thing followed another, until at length one of those present put a suggestion to Mr Wang: 'Since your daughter has reached womanhood now, why shouldn't you counter this sad occasion by completing the match, so that they can help each other, as husband and wife, through the days to come?'

Mr Wang was unwilling to assent, and before the day was out he took his leave. But the clansmen, after all the ceremonies of the interment were completed, came to urge their plan on Hsing-ko. He was at first unwilling, but after repeated exhortations he began to reflect on the loneliness of his position, and at last accepted their advice. He commissioned the original go-between to speak for him before the Wang family. But Mr Wang continued to oppose the plan. 'We have something of a dowry to prepare,' he said, 'and this cannot be done on the instant. More-over, the mourning period has not yet passed: such a wedding would go against the correct observance of the rites. If we are to discuss this marriage, let us do so after the first anniversary of his father's death.'

The go-between took back this reply, and Hsing-ko saw the justice of it and did not try to force the issue.

Time sped by like an arrow, and before one could realize it the anniversary had arrived. After Hsing-ko had made the offerings before his father's spirit-tablet, he put aside his mourning garments of coarse linen, and dispatched the go-between again to speak for him before the Wang family. Then at last the consent was given, and before many days had passed the six preliminaries were completed [2] and Chiang Hsing-ko had taken his new bride into his house. This is shown by a 'Moon on the West River':

> *Curtains of red replace the white of mourning,*
> *Not linen is worn, but brightly-coloured silks.*
> *The rooms are gay, festooned, ablaze with candles,*
> *The nuptial cup is ready, the feast prepared.*
>
> *Why fix your envy on an ample dowry?*
> *A wife of charm and beauty is more precious.*
> *The joys of 'cloud and rain' tonight will bring*
> *Felicitations in the days to come.*

Now, the new bride was the youngest daughter of Mr Wang. Her child-name was 'Third Eldest', and since she was born on the seventh of the seventh month, a day of festival,[3] she was also called 'Fortune' Third. Her two elder sisters, whom Mr Wang had already given in marriage, were both exceptionally good-looking. They were the toast of Tsao-yang, and indeed there was a jingle which ran:

> *The world is full of beauties,*
> *But the Wang girls have no flaw.*
> *Better to be husband to one of these*
> *Than the Emperor's son-in-law.*

It's often said that 'if you don't get on in your business, it's only for a time; if you don't get on with your old woman, it's for life!' In so many families of high or noble rank, a bride is chosen simply on account of her pedigree or her ample dowry, and the betrothal is arranged without distinction of fair or foul. Later, when the bride turns out to be of outstanding ugliness, yet must be brought forward to meet the entire clan assembled, it means great embarrassment for her parents-in-law. The husband, moreover, his heart filled with dismay, will be forced into illicit amours and wild conduct. The trouble is that it is the ugliest women who are most adept at keeping their husbands in order. If he takes the same attitude as she, there will be quarrels; if, on the other hand, he gives way to her just once or twice for appearance's sake, she will begin to get above herself. Faced with all these unpleasant possibilities, Chiang Shih-tse, when he heard that Mr Wang had been blessed with a succession of fine daughters, had sent gifts while his son was yet an infant and secured the youngest daughter as his son's betrothed.

And now, as the bride entered her new home, she proved indeed to be full of grace and beauty—for that matter, she was twice as lovely as either of her elder sisters. Indeed,

> *Hsi-shih, in the palace at Wu, would not compare,*[4]
> *Nan-wei, the beauty of Ch'u, would have to retire,*[5]
> *As worthy to be worshipped, with incense and bowing,*
> *As the 'Moon and Water Kuan-yin' herself.*[6]

Chiang Hsing-ko's own talents and ability were of a high order. Clearly, when he had married this beautiful wife, they made a pair like figures of jade, carved and polished by finest craftsmanship. A happy husband and a devoted wife, they excelled other married couples ten times over. After the 'third morning' of their marriage, they changed into clothes of lighter hue, and Chiang, paying no attention to outside affairs on the pretext of regulating his household, spent all his time upstairs alone with his wife. From dawn to dusk they devoted themselves to pleasure. In truth, walking or sitting they were never apart, in dreams at night their souls were together.

'Days of hardship are hard to get through, the happy times go quickly by'—that has always been so. Summer ended and winter began, and already the period of mourning for Chiang Hsing-ko's father was completed. We will not speak of how Hsing-ko set up his father's spirit-tablet and left off mourning; but of how one day he reflected that the trading in Kwangtung which his father had carried on during his lifetime had been neglected now for more than three years. A large number of trading credits were there waiting to be collected. That night he talked things over with his wife, and told her he wanted to make the journey. At first his wife agreed that he should go. But then she talked of all the roads he would have to travel: husband and wife so much in love, how could they bear separation? Without her knowing it, tears streamed from her eyes. Hsing-ko was just as reluctant to leave her, and after both of them had grown very melancholy, he gave up the idea. This happened more than once.

'Night follows day, day follows night', and two more years passed by unnoticed. And now Hsing-ko was determined to go. Unknown to his wife he quietly collected his things together away from the house, and chose an auspicious date. He only told his wife about it five days beforehand. 'They often talk about "sitting and eating the mountain away"! The two of us, husband and wife, must set up the family business, or we'll find ourselves with nothing to eat or wear. It's the second month now, the weather neither too cold nor too hot. If I don't set out now, when shall I be able to?'

His wife, realizing that she could no longer hold him back, could only ask: 'When will you be coming back from this journey?'

Hsing-ko replied: 'I've no alternative but to go off now. But whatever happens I'll come back after a year, even if it means I have to spend longer away the next time.'

His wife pointed to a cedar in front of the house: 'When this tree comes into bud next year, I shall be watching for your return.'

When she finished speaking her tears fell like rain. Hsing-ko dried them with the sleeve of his gown, but without his noticing it his own cheeks grew moist. Both of them were filled with regret at parting, and no words can suffice for the affection they showed for each other. When the fifth day arrived, husband and wife spent the whole night in talking and bitter weeping, and try as they might they could not sleep.

When daylight came Hsing-ko rose and made his preparations. He entrusted to his wife the safe-keeping of all the family jewels and valuables. He was to take with him only the money which was his trading capital, his account-books, and some bedding and spare clothing. These things, together with certain gifts which he had made ready, were neatly folded and packed. Of the two house servants he took only the younger one with him, leaving behind the older man to attend to the wishes of his wife and to look after the day-to-day running of the house. There were also two serving-women whose duties were confined to the kitchen, and two young girls, one named Light Cloud and the other named Warm Snow, who would be Fortune's personal maids and had instructions never to leave her side.

Having given all his orders, Hsing-ko said to his wife, 'You must wait for me with patience. The district is full of worthless young idlers, and you are a beautiful woman. Do not stir up trouble with them by standing gazing by the door.'

'You may set your mind at ease,' replied his wife. 'But go now quickly, and quickly return.'

And hiding their tears they took leave of each other. Indeed,

> *The thousand sorrows of this world*
> *Arise from parting, in life or by death.*

As Hsing-ko began his journey all his thoughts were of his wife, and he travelled on paying no attention to the passing scene until, after many days, he reached the province of Kwang-tung, where he found himself an inn. Here he was visited by all his old acquaintances. He distributed the gifts he had brought with him, and feasts were held in honour of his return. In this way two or three weeks passed before he had a moment to himself. Now Hsing-ko, even at home, had never been of very strong physique, and the rigours of his journey were now followed by a period of irregular eating and drinking. He contracted a recurrent fever which lasted all the summer. In the autumn it turned to dysentery. Every day he had doctors take his pulse and give him medicine to regulate his condition, but it was the end of autumn before he was fully recovered. All this time he had been obliged to neglect his business, and it became plain that to return home within the year was out of the question. Indeed,

> *All for a useless fly's-head of profit*
> *He cast aside his happy marriage and his bed of love*

Homesick though he was, as the time went by he forced himself to put such thoughts out of his head.

We will say no more of Hsing-ko on his travels, but go on now to tell how his wife Fortune, back at home, had indeed for months on end obeyed her husband's injunctions, neither looking out of the window nor venturing down the stairs. Time sped by like an arrow, and before one could realize it the year was approaching its close. In every home there were noisy celebrations as braziers were lit, fire-crackers exploded, family feasts held and all kinds of games played. The time was a sad one for Fortune, thinking of her absent husband. On this particular night she was feeling very lonely, exactly as described by a poet of former times:

> Winter ends, but not her sorrow,
> Spring returns, but not her husband.
> Daybreak finds her pining, lonely,
> No wish to try on her new dress.

The next day was the first of the first month, New Year's Day. The two little maids, Light Cloud and Warm Snow, made every effort to persuade their mistress to watch the scene in the streets outside from the front portion of the house. The point was that the Chiang residence consisted of two wings, front and rear, which were interconnected. The front wing gave on to the street; the sleeping quarters were in the rear wing, and it was there that Fortune normally spent all her time. But this day she could not resist the promptings of her maids. In the end she made her way through a side chamber to the front portion of the house. She ordered that a shutter be taken down and a curtain substituted, and she took up her position behind the curtain and looked out.

What a commotion on the streets that day! 'So many people everywhere,' said Fortune, 'yet I can't see any sign of a fortune-teller among them. If we saw one, we could have him in and ask him for news of my husband.'

'It is New Year's Day,' replied Light Cloud. 'People just want to enjoy themselves, no one is bothered about hearing fortunes.'

'Leave it to us!' exclaimed Warm Snow. 'Give us five days, and we will guarantee to produce a fortune-teller for you.'

On the morning of the fourth day of the month, after breakfast, Warm Snow had gone downstairs to relieve herself. Suddenly she heard outside a knocking sound, clop-clop, made by the thing known as the 'announcer', which is part of the stock-in-trade of the blind fortune-teller. Warm Snow couldn't even wait to finish what she was doing, but gathering in the waist of her trousers rushed out on to the street and halted the blind man. Then without pausing for breath she whirled round and flew upstairs again to inform her mistress. Fortune ordered that he be given a seat in the visitor's room downstairs, and when she had been informed of his fee she went down to hear his pronouncements.

The blind man selected a diagram, and she asked what was its use. By this time the kitchen women had heard that something was afoot and had come hurrying in, and they explained to their mistress, 'This is the diagram for questions about those absent on journeys.'

'Is it a lady asking about her husband?' asked the blind man.

'That's right,' said the women.

'When the green dragon Jupiter rules the world, the sign of wealth becomes active,' said the fortune-teller. 'If the lady is asking about her husband, he is on his way home. Gold and rich stuffs fill his chests, nor wind nor wave disturbs him. The green dragon belongs to the element wood, and wood flourishes in the spring. His homeward journey began about the time of 'spring beginning', and he will not fail to be here by the end of this month or the beginning of the next. Moreover, he will bring with him wealth in abundance.'

Fortune instructed her servant to give the man three silver cents and see him off the premises; then, filled with joy, she returned to her upper room. This sort of thing is exactly what is meant by 'gazing at plum-blossom to slake your thirst' or 'drawing a cake to satisfy hunger'. People generally find that if they don't entertain expectations, things don't bother them; once start expecting, and all kinds of silly idle dreams come crowding in and make the time pass with painful slowness. Just because she put faith in what the soothsayer had said, Fortune now found her every thought directed towards her husband's return, and from this time onwards she spent much of her time in the front portion of the house, gazing out from behind the curtain.

This went on until the beginning of the second month, when the cedar began to come into bud. Still there was no sign of her husband's return. Remembering his parting vow, Fortune grew more and more uneasy, and now went down several times a day to look out for him.

Obviously, trouble was in store for her, she was fated to meet her elegant young man. Indeed,

If the affinity is there, they will overcome a thousand-mile separation;
If the affinity is absent, they will not meet though face to face.

And who was this elegant young man? He was not as it happened a man of that region, but was from Hsin-an near Hweichow. His name was Ch'en Shang; but his child-name having been Ta-hsi-ko, 'Big Happy Boy', this was altered later to Ta-lang, 'Big Fellow'. He was twenty-three, and a very handsome specimen. Though he might not have surpassed Sung Yü and P'an An,[7] he would certainly not have fallen short of them. This 'Big Fellow' was another orphan. He had got together a capital of two or three thousand ounces of gold and made annual visits to Hsiang-yang, trading in rice and beans and such. His lodgings were outside the city-wall, and this particular day he had chanced to come into the city with the intention of picking up any letter from home that might be waiting for him at Manager Wang's pawnshop on Market Street. This pawnshop was directly opposite the Chiang home, and this was why he happened to be passing.

And how was he dressed, you ask? On his head was a many-tufted 'mane-hat' in the Soochow style, and he wore an undress robe of Huchou silk gauze of a fish-belly white shade. It was precisely the way in which Chiang Hsing-ko had been in the habit of dressing, and when Fortune saw him in the distance she told herself that her husband had returned. She raised the curtain and fixed her gaze upon him.

Ch'en Ta-lang looked up to find a beautiful young creature staring fixedly at him from an upper room. Imagining that she must have taken a fancy to him, he responded with a wink.

But—who could have dreamt it—both were in error. Fortune, realizing that this was not her husband, blushed scarlet for shame, hurriedly banged the shutter to and flew to the rear of the house. There she rested herself on the edge of the bed, her heart palpitating violently.

As for Ch'en Ta-lang, the truth was that the lustre of the woman's gaze had lifted the soul from his body. Returning to his lodgings, he could not for a second dismiss her from his thoughts. 'My wife, at home,' he said to himself, 'is a pretty woman, but how could one begin to compare her with this beauty? If only I could get some love-token to her—but I have no means of entry. If I could spend one night with her, I should have justified my existence in this world even though it cost me the whole of my capital.'

He sat and sighed. But then suddenly he thought of the jewel-vendor, Dame Hsüeh, in the alley off the east side of Market Street. He had done business with her in the past. This old woman was skilled in the arts of persuasion. Moreover she spent every day tramping the streets and alleys and knew every household. He must talk things over with her, she'd be sure to have some suggestion.

All that night he tossed and turned, and got through the time somehow. The next day he rose at dawn, announced that he had business to attend to, and called for cold water and washed and combed his hair. He took out a hundred ounces of silver and two large bars of gold, and rushed off into the city. They say of this kind of thing,

> To secure a life of ease
> You must work yourself to death.

On entering the city Ch'en Ta-lang made straight for the East Alley off Market Street and pounded on Dame Hsüeh's door. Dame Hsüeh was in her little yard, her hair dishevelled, grading her pearls. When she heard the knocking on the door she wrapped up the pearls and asked, 'Who is it?' But as soon as she heard the words 'Ch'en of Hweichow' she hastened to open the door and invite him in. 'I'm not yet washed and so I won't presume to receive you formally,' she said. 'What noble errand is it, sir, that brings you out at this time of the morning?'

'I have come specially to see you,' replied Ch'en, 'and was afraid of missing you by coming later.'

'Perhaps you have some jewels or trinkets you want me to dispose of?' asked Dame Hsüeh.

'I want to buy some jewels,' said Ch'en Ta-lang. 'But there is also a bigger deal I want you to undertake for me.'

'I'm afraid I'm not familiar with any trade other than this one,' said Dame Hsüeh.

'Can we talk here?' asked Ch'en, whereupon Dame Hsüeh bolted the front door and invited him to take a seat in a little private room.

'What are your instructions, sir?' she inquired.

Satisfied that there was no one else about, Ta-lang drew the silver from his sleeve, unwrapped it and placed it on the table. 'I can mention it, godmother, only when you have agreed to accept these hundred taels of silver,' he said.

Not knowing what was behind this, Dame Hsüeh was reluctant to accept it. 'You must not despise it as too little,' said Ch'en, and he hurriedly brought out two gold bars as well, shining yellow, and placed these also on the table. 'Please accept these ten taels of gold in addition,' he said. 'If you will not accept them, godmother, I shall take it as a deliberate refusal to help me. Today it is I who seek your help, not you who seek mine. This big deal I mentioned is not something beyond your capabilities. That is why I have come to you. And even if you are unable to bring it off, this money is still yours to keep. There is no question of my coming back to retrieve it and then never having anything further to do with you. There is no meanness of that kind about Ch'en Ta-lang.'

Tell me, members of the audience, when was there an old procuress who didn't covet money? How was Dame Hsüeh to remain unmoved at the sight of all this silver and gold? At this point her whole face creased into smiles, and she said, 'Please do not misunderstand me, sir. Never in my life have I taken a single cash from anyone unless all was clear and above-board. I shall accept your instructions now, and so for the time being I will take charge of this money; but if I fail to do what you wish, I shall return it to you.'

With these words she placed the gold with the silver in its packet and wrapped the whole lot up together; then calling out, 'This is very bold of me,' she took it off to secrete it in her bedroom. Hurrying out again, she said, 'I shall not presume to thank you yet, sir; but tell me now, what kind of business is this that I may be able to help you with?'

'There is a certain gem, a talisman,' replied Ch'en Ta-lang, 'which I am most anxious to procure. You have nothing like it here. It is only to be found in a particular household on Market Street. I beg of you, godmother, to go and borrow it for me.'

The old woman began to laugh. 'You're making fun of me again. I've lived in this alley for more than twenty years, but never have I heard of any talisman on Market Street. Tell me, sir, whose family does it belong to, this gem?'

'Who lives in the big double-storeyed house across the street from the pawnshop kept by my fellow-townsman, Manager Wang Three?' asked Ta-lang.

The old woman thought for a moment, then said, 'That house belongs to Chiang Hsing-ko, a man of this town. He himself has been away, travelling, for more than a year now. Only his wife is at home.'

'That is precisely the person from whom I wish to borrow this talisman I speak of,' said Ta-lang, and he drew his chair up close to the old woman and revealed to her his heart's desire, thus and thus.

But when he had finished speaking the old woman shook her head impatiently. 'This is a matter of the gravest difficulty,' she said. 'It is not yet four years since Chiang Hsing-ko married this wife of his. The two of them were like fish and water, never apart by a foot or an inch. Now that he has had to go away, the lady never descends her staircase, so great is her chastity. And since Hsing-ko has this peculiarity of being easily roused to anger, I have never yet crossed his threshold. I don't even know what the lady looks like, so how am I to undertake this business for you? As for what you have just given me—I have not the good fortune to be able to make use of it.'

At this Ch'en Ta-lang flung himself down on his knees, and when the old woman tried to get him to rise he clutched with both hands at her sleeves and pinned her to her chair so that she could not move. 'God-mother,' he began to mumble, 'Ch'en Ta-lang's life is in your hands. You must not fail to think out some cunning stratagem which will enable me to possess her and thus save my poor life. When the thing is done there will be another hundred taels of gold for your reward; but if you turn me down, there is nothing for me but to die this minute.'

The old woman was too terrified to think, and could only consent. 'All right, all right,' she said again and again, 'don't tear me to pieces. Please rise, sir, and I will tell you what I think.'

At last Ch'en rose to his feet, and said, hands folded respectfully before him, 'Please inform me at once, what is your cunning plan?'

'This affair must be allowed to run its natural course,' said Dame Hsüeh. 'As long as it succeeds in the end, there must be no counting of months and years. If you are to set me a time limit, I can hardly undertake it for you.'

'Provided it really does succeed,' said Ch'en, 'what does it matter if I have to wait a day or two. But where is our stratagem to start?'

'Tomorrow, after breakfast,' began the old woman, 'not too early and not too late, I will meet you in Manager Wang's pawnshop. You, sir, must bring along a good quantity of silver, giving out that you have some business with me. There is of course some point to all this. If I can get these two feet of mine through the Chiangs' doorway, then, sir, you are in luck. But you must hurry straight back to your lodgings. Don't loiter about in front of her doorway or people will see through our game and the whole plan will be ruined. If I can devise an opening of some kind I shall of course report to you.'

'I shall follow your instructions to the letter,' said Ch'en Ta-lang; and with a great shout of assent he joyously opened the door and left. Truly,

Before Hsiang Yü is destroyed or Liu Pang enthroned [8]
Already they build their altars and salute their generals.

Nothing further is to be said of that day. When the next day came Ch'en Ta-lang dressed himself in a fine suit and took out three or four hundred taels of silver, which he placed in a large leather case. This he had a boy take up on his back and bring along to Wang's pawnshop on Market Street. Ta-lang noticed that the windows of the house opposite were all shuttered tight, and assumed that the young lady was not there, but at the rear.

He greeted the shopkeeper with folded hands, and requesting a wooden stool seated himself before the doorway. He looked down the street to the east, and before very long there was Dame Hsüeh approaching, in her arms a wicker basket.

Ch'en Ta-lang called to her to stop. 'What have you got in that basket?' he asked.

'Jewels and head-ornaments,' replied Dame Hsüeh. 'Do you want any, sir?'

'Just what I'm looking for,' said Ch'en.

Dame Hsüeh entered the shop and greeted its owner; then, with a cry of 'Ho la!', she threw open her basket. Inside it were a dozen or so packets of pearls together with a number of little boxes. The boxes contained ornaments for the hair, each one embellished with artificial flowers and kingfisher feathers, skilfully wrought and dazzling to the eye. Ch'en Ta-lang selected some strings of pearls, those of the greatest size and whiteness, and added to the pile an assortment of hairpins and earrings. 'I'll take all these,' he said.

The old woman eyed him for a moment, then said, 'If you want them, have them. The only question is whether you're prepared to pay the price for them.'

Ch'en realized what she was up to, and opening his purse he drew out bar after bar of gleaming white silver which he stacked high. 'Look at all this silver!' he shouted. 'Don't tell me it won't buy this stuff of yours?'

Already seven or eight of the loafers of the neighbourhood had strolled across and were in position before the shop watching the proceedings.

'It was only my little joke,' countered the old woman. 'How should I presume to doubt a gentleman like yourself? But you must be careful with all this silver. Please put it back. All I ask is that you pay me the fair price.'

And so they started, one asking a high price and the other offering a low one, with all the distance of heaven from earth between them. The old woman wouldn't budge a fraction from the price she asked; whilst Ch'en Ta-lang, for his part, had the things in his hand and wouldn't let go, nor would he raise his offer. With deliberate intent, he went out of the shop and stood there letting the jewels sparkle in the sunlight as he picked them over one by one, pronouncing this one genuine and that one false, and estimating their weight and value. Before long he had attracted the whole town, and the air was filled with cries of admiration.

'If you want to buy them, buy them,' Dame Hsüeh was yelling, 'and if you don't want them put them down. What's the idea, just wasting people's time like this?'

'Of course I want to buy them,' said Ch'en; and the two of them fell back into their wrangling over the price. Truly,

A simple squabble over paying the price
Startles the flower-like, jade-like one.

The hubbub across the way drew Fortune Wang unthinking towards the front part of the house, where she opened a window and peeped out. There were the jewels gleaming and flashing, a beautiful sight. And there also were the old woman and her customer, still unable to agree on the price. And so Fortune ordered her maid to call the old woman across and let her have a look at her things. Light Cloud accordingly crossed the street and tugged at Dame Hsüeh's sleeve. 'My mistress would like a word with you,' she said.

The old woman deliberately feigned ignorance. 'Whose family are you?' she asked.

'The Chiang family, across the way,' replied Light Cloud.

The old woman thrust out her hand towards Ch'en Ta-lang and snatched back her goods, which she hurriedly wrapped up again. 'I haven't the time to bother with you any longer,' she said.

'All right then, I'll give you a little more,' said Ch'en.

'No, I'm not selling,' said the old woman. 'How long do you think I could stay in business with the sort of price you are offering?'

As she was saying this she was putting the jewels back in her basket, which she then locked up as before and took up in her arms ready to leave.

'I'll carry it for you, old lady,' said Light Cloud.

'No need,' replied Dame Hsüeh; and without once looking back she went straight to the house across the way. Ch'en Ta-lang, secretly delighted, gathered up his silver and took his leave of the shopkeeper, and made his way back to his lodging. Indeed,

> *His eyes behold the flag of victory,*
> *His ears hear the tidings of joy.*

Light Cloud led Dame Hsüeh upstairs, where she greeted Fortune. At the sight of the girl, the old woman said to herself, 'She really has the looks of an angel. No wonder Ch'en Ta-lang has fallen for her. I'd be bowled over too, if I were a man.' Aloud, she said, 'I have long been aware of your virtuous reputation, lady, and have lived in regret that I was not destined to make your acquaintance.'

'What is your name, old lady?' asked Fortune.

'My name is Hsüeh,' replied the old woman. 'I live just round in East Alley, so I am your neighbour.'

'Why wouldn't you sell those things of yours just now?' Fortune went on.

'If I never sold them,' replied the old woman with a smile, 'why should I bother to bring them out? But what a fool, that stranger down in the road there—a fine-looking man, but no idea what things are worth.'

And with this she opened her basket and took out hair-ornaments and earrings, which she offered for the lady's inspection. 'Lady,' she cried, 'just look at these ornaments. Think how much it costs for the workmanship alone! If I were to take such a ridiculous price as he was offering, how should I be able to go back and report such a loss to my employer?' Holding up some strings of pearls, she went on, 'Top-grade goods like these! He must have been dreaming!'

Fortune asked her the prices asked and offered, and said, 'Indeed, the truth of the matter is that you were asking too little!'

'Ah,' replied the old woman, 'but you are a lady of good family, and widely-versed in these things. You have ten times the understanding of a man.'

Fortune ordered her maid to serve tea, but the old woman protested, 'I will not trouble you so. I have an important matter of business which will take me to West Street, and I have already spent so long squabbling with this stranger—truly, "a deal that doesn't come off interferes with your work". May I trouble you to keep this basket here for me for the time being, if I lock it? I shall leave you for the moment but be back shortly.'

Thereupon the old woman took her leave. Fortune ordered Light Cloud to accompany her downstairs, and then she went off towards the west.

Fortune had fallen in love with the things she had been shown, and was impatient for the woman to return so that she could buy them from her. For five whole days she made no appearance. On the afternoon of the sixth day there was a sudden heavy shower, and before the sound of the rain had ceased they heard a heavy banging on the door. Fortune ordered her maid to open it, and there was Dame Hsüeh, half-drenched, in her hand a tattered old umbrella. As she entered the house she chanted,

> ' "*When it's fine you don't care to go—*
> *You wait till it pours with rain!*" '

She left her umbrella at the foot of the stairs and went up. After offering her best wishes, she said, 'I'm afraid I failed to keep my promise the other day, lady.'

'Where have you been these last few days?' asked Fortune when she had promptly returned her greeting.

'My youngest daughter has been blessed with the birth of a little boy,' replied the old woman. 'I went over to have a look at him, and stayed for a few days. I only left this morning, and on the way back I was caught in the rain. I managed to borrow an umbrella from some friends, but it was a tattered one—haven't I been unlucky?'

'How many children have you, old lady?' asked Fortune.

'Only one son, and he already married,' she replied, 'but I have four daughters. This one is my fourth. She is the concubine of Manager Chu Eight of Hweichow, who has the salt shop outside the North Gate.'

'So many more daughters than sons,' said Fortune, 'you really ought to look after them! There's no shortage of husbands in this town—why did you let her go to an outsider as a concubine?'

'Ah, lady, you don't understand,' the old woman replied. 'This particular outsider is a most generous man. Although she is only a concubine, the point is that his first wife stays in his private apartments whilst my daughter lives at the shop, surrounded just the same with servants and everything she wants. Every time I go there he treats me with all the respect due to an elder, and is never remiss in any way; and now that my daughter has given him a son things are even better.'

'Then it's a blessing for you that you have married her so well,' remarked Fortune.

At this point Light Cloud brought in tea, and as they drank the old woman went on, 'With this rain today I can do no business. If it is not too impudent of me, I wonder if I might have a look at your hair-ornaments? It would be a great thing for me to make a note of some really clever designs.'

'They're only very ordinary, I must ask you not to laugh at them,' said Fortune. She took a key and unlocked a chest, and brought out a large collection of jewelled hairpins and necklaces and so on, one piece after another.

Dame Hsüeh praised them beyond measure: 'With rare pieces like these, lady, I'm afraid you won't have any time for these things of mine.'

'You're just being polite,' said Fortune. 'I was on the point of asking your prices.'

'You are a connoisseur, lady,' said the old woman, 'there is no call for me to waste my breath.'

Fortune cleared away her things and brought out Dame Hsüeh's basket, which she placed on the table. Offering the key to the old woman, she said, 'Please open it up, old lady, and let me have a good look at them.'

'I'm afraid you will see through them,' said the old woman. She opened the basket and brought out piece after piece. Fortune assessed the value of each, and was never far out. The old woman didn't argue at all, but cried delightedly, 'Now this is really fair to one. Even if I get a few cash less than I could have done, I don't mind at all.'

'There's only one thing,' said Fortune, 'I can't lay hands on all the money just now. The only thing I can do is offer you half now, and pay off the rest in full when my husband comes home, which will be within the next few days.'

'There's no harm in letting it wait for a few days,' said Dame

Hsüeh. 'But I have given way a good deal on the prices, and I should like you to pay me in finest sterling.'

'There's no difficulty about that,' said Fortune. And she took the hair ornaments and jewels which most delighted her, and ordered Light Cloud to bring in a bowl of ready-heated wine for her to entertain the old woman.

'Please don't go to such trouble—this is only a hasty visit,' said the old woman.

But Fortune replied, 'I have very little to do with my time, and it is a great treat to have you here to sit and chat with me, old lady. If you will excuse my presumption, I should be very grateful if you would come here often.'

'It is very good of you to show affection for one who is not worthy of it,' said the old woman. 'In fact, my house is an unbearably noisy place, and it is delightful to be in such tranquil surroundings as these.'

'What trade does your son follow?' asked Fortune.

'Oh, he just looks after the jewel merchants, who are round every day cadging wine and soup and eating us out of house and home. It's I who have to scurry about making calls all over the neighbourhood. I'm not at home very much; but that's perhaps as well, for I should die of boredom if I were confined to a piece of land the size of a grave.'

'My home is close to yours,' said Fortune. 'You must come over for a chat if ever you feel bored.'

'But I should be a nuisance to you, just dropping in like that,' protested the old woman.

'Not in the least,' replied Fortune.

The two maids, meanwhile, had been making a long succession of journeys, and had set before each of them a bowl and chopsticks, two plates of dried and salted slices of meat—chicken on one and pork on the other; a plate of fresh fish, and some half a dozen more vegetable dishes and bowls of fruit.

'What a feast!' exclaimed the old woman.

'It was just what I had in,' responded Fortune. 'Please don't blame me for lack of preparation.'

Then she poured out a cup of wine, which she handed to the old woman. The latter took it and drank her health, and then they sat down facing each other and began to drink in earnest. Now in fact Fortune was not at all a poor drinker; as for the old woman herself, she was a veritable wine-jug, a wine-jar. So, drinking, very soon they were on excellent terms, and only lamented that they had not made each other's acquaintance at an earlier date.

They went on drinking until evening, by which time the rain had at last stopped. As Dame Hsüeh was expressing her thanks and preparing to leave, Fortune had a great silver goblet brought out, and urged her to empty it, more than once. She insisted on their having supper together, and afterwards she said, 'Stay on at your ease for a while, old lady, and I will let you have the half of the money that I promised you.'

'It's getting late,' said the old woman. 'Please don't worry about that tonight, lady. I'll call for it tomorrow if I may. There's this wicker basket of mine, too—I won't take it now, because the roads will be muddy and bad underfoot.'

'I shall expect you tomorrow, then,' said Fortune.

The old woman took her leave and went downstairs, picked up her tattered umbrella and left the house. Truly,

> Nothing in the world has deceived more people
> Than the tongues of these old witches.

Let us now tell rather of Ch'en Ta-lang, idling in his lodgings day after day without any news whatever. When this day of rain came along he imagined that the old woman must be at home, and so he made his way into the city to try to discover what was happening. He arrived soaked to the skin and covered with mud only to learn that she was not at home. He found a wine-shop and had a cup or two of wine and a few delicacies before presenting himself again at Dame Hsüeh's front door, but still she had not returned.

It was getting late, and he was just on the point of leaving for home when he caught sight of the old woman, her face wreathed in vinous smiles, rounding the corner of the alley and reeling her way towards him.

Ch'en Ta-lang greeted her, then asked, 'How is our little affair progressing?'

'It's early days yet,' said the old woman with a gesture of disapproval. 'We've only just sown the seed, the shoots aren't up yet. It will be another five or six years before the blossom opens and the fruit is ready for you to taste. And it's no use your coming rooting about here. I've no time to stand about gossiping.'

And indeed she was too drunk for Ch'en to do anything but take his leave.

On the next day the old woman bought a quantity of the fruits just then in season, together with some fresh chicken and fish. She had a cook prepare these things for the table and pack them in two round boxes. Then she bought a jar of a fine and potent wine and asked the lad from the wine-shop to carry this and the boxes as far as the Chiangs' gateway.

Now Fortune, impatient of Dame Hsüeh's arrival that day, had ordered Light Cloud to go into the street and look out for her, and she was just in time to meet the old woman coming along. Dame Hsüeh had the lad put the things down at the foot of the stairs and then sent him back. Meanwhile, Light Cloud announced her arrival to her mistress, who accorded the old woman the welcome due to an honoured guest by coming out to the head of the stairs to greet her.

The old woman thanked her most effusively for her kindness, then said, 'I happened to have in a drop of watery wine, so I've brought it along for your pleasure.'

'I really shouldn't allow you to go to such expense,' protested Fortune.

The old woman asked the two maids to bring the things up and set them out on a table.

'It's really too extravagant of you to make such a spread,' said Fortune.

'People of no account like myself can't offer anything worth having,' said the old woman with a deprecating smile. 'It's really nothing more than a bowl of tea.'

Light Cloud fetched bowls and chopsticks. Warm Snow blew on the charcoal in the wine-heater, and in no time at all the wine was hot.

'I am the one who wished to entertain today,' said the old woman, 'I must ask you to take the guest's seat, lady.'

'Although it is you who have gone to all this trouble,' responded Fortune, 'this is my house and I really can't allow myself to take the guest's seat.' And for several minutes they vied in politeness, until at last Dame Hsüeh was obliged to sit in the position reserved for the guest.

This was their third meeting, and they were rapidly becoming close friends. As they drank, the old woman asked, 'What can be keeping your husband so long away? I feel he is to be blamed for deserting you like this.'

'Indeed he is,' agreed Fortune. 'He said he would come back at the end of a year. I do not know what can have detained him.'

'What I want to know,' said the old woman, 'is this: what's so precious even about a fortune in gold and jade, if to acquire it means neglecting such a lovely lady as yourself?' And she continued, 'It's the same with all these merchants who roam up and down the country. They treat their lodgings as their home and their home as their lodgings. Take my fourth daughter's husband, for instance, Manager Chu Eight—now he's found himself this concubine he's happy from dawn to dusk. Never thinks about his home—goes back once every three or four years, and before he's been there more than a month or two, off he starts again. His first wife lives like a widow bringing up her orphan children, what does she know about his affairs when he's away?'

'But my husband isn't that sort of man at all,' protested Fortune.

'It was only my idle gossip,' said the old woman, 'I should never presume to make such a comparison.'

They guessed riddles and played dice-games, and separated in a fine state of intoxication. On the third day Dame Hsüeh brought along the wine-shop boy to collect her dishes. Fortune gave her the money for the jewels, half of the purchase price, and made her stay for a meal. From this time onwards the old woman was always calling, her pretext being to hear news of Chiang Hsing-ko in view of the half of the purchase money still owing to her. She was such a witty and plausible talker, and she always made such a point of acting the fool with a dubious joke or two for the maidservants, that soon she was a favourite with mistress and maid alike. If one day she chanced not to call, Fortune would feel lonely. She had her old serving-women find out Dame Hsüeh's dwelling, and sent them morning and night to invite her round. And so they grew more and more intimate.

There are four kinds of person in this world who are best left alone. Once allow them near you and you will never be rid of them. Who are the four? Wandering priests, beggars, idlers and go-betweens. The first three are not too bad, but the go-betweens make their way right into your home, and if your womenfolk are finding things a little dull you can be certain it's the go-between they'll turn to for amusement. And in this particular case, Dame Hsüeh was at bottom an evil person, but full of soft and honeyed phrases. Fortune gave her her closest friendship, and could not be without her for a minute. Truly,

A tiger's skin may be drawn, but it's hard to draw the bones;
A man's face may be known, but how can you know his heart?

Time and again did Ch'en Ta-lang ask for news of progress, but Dame Hsüeh's only reply was 'Too early yet.' By the middle of the fifth lunar month the heat was steadily increasing. Dame Hsüeh once happened to mention to Fortune the discomfort of her own home, cramped as a snail's shell, facing west and quite unsuitable for the hot weather. What a contrast with the cool spaciousness of Fortune's upper rooms!

'Wouldn't it be better for you to give up your home and spend your nights here?' suggested Fortune.

'That would be splendid,' said the old woman, 'but what if your husband returns?'

'If he does return, it won't be in the middle of the night!'

'Well, lady,' said the old woman, 'if you're sure you won't find me a nuisance, forcing my society on you like this—how would it be if I bring my bedding across and keep you company this very night?'

'We've plenty of bedding,' said Fortune, 'you've no need to bring yours. All you have to do is tell the members of your household that you've made up your mind to spend the summer here before going back home to live.'

And the old woman did in fact inform her son and daughter-in-law of this, before reappearing with just her toilet-case.

'What trouble you give yourself,' said Fortune. 'Do you think we are without combs here? Why have you brought your own?'

'I have always been reluctant to share a comb and wash-basin,' replied the old woman. 'I'm sure you must have the most exquisite toilet-things, which I wouldn't dream of borrowing;

nor should I like to use your maids' things. That is why I thought it better to bring my own. But please tell me which room I should sleep in.'

Pointing to a small rattan couch at the foot of her bed, Fortune said, 'I have already prepared a place for you where we can be nearer to each other, so that we can chat if we can't get to sleep at night.'

She then took out a green gauze bed-curtain which she asked the old woman to arrange for herself, and after drinking together for a while they retired. It had originally been the two maids who spread their bedding at the foot of Fortune's bed to keep her company, but now that she had the old woman, these two were sent to the next room for the night.

From this time on the old woman spent her days outside on business, but returned each night to sleep at the Chiang home. Often she would bring home a jar of wine and create a great deal of merriment.

The couch and the bed were arranged in the form of a letter T, so that even with the bed-curtains it was almost like sleeping together. During the night they would talk on and on until they had exhausted the salacious gossip of the entire neighbourhood. Sometimes the old woman would pretend that drinking had loosened her tongue, and then she would go into all the details of the illicit amours of her own girlhood. She would work up her friend into a fine state of excitement, until those delicately-nurtured cheeks flushed and paled, paled and flushed again. The old woman knew very well that the girl's thoughts were stirring, but that she was too embarrassed to say anything herself.

Time sped by, and there came the seventh of the seventh month, Fortune's birthday. Early in the morning the old woman made up two boxes of presents for her, and Fortune thanked her for them and wanted her to stay for a bowl of noodles. But the old woman declined: 'I shall be busy all day. But I shall come back to keep you company this evening, and we must watch the Herd-boy paying his visit to the Weaving-girl.'

With this she left. But before she was far from the house she met Ch'en Ta-lang. Not wishing to talk on the street, she followed him into a quiet alley, where Ch'en, wrinkling his brows, began to reproach her: 'What an old ditherer you are,

mother! Spring went and summer came, and now here we are
at the beginning of autumn. You'll tell me today it's "too early
yet", and tomorrow you'll still be telling me it's "too early yet".
You don't realize that for me every day is like a year. Dilly-dally a
few days longer and her husband will have returned, and then
the whole thing flies out of the window. Don't you see that it's a
living death for me? But when I reach the Court of Hades I shall
lay my death at your door!'

'Don't go on so,' said the old woman. 'I'm delighted to see
you, for I was just going to invite you to a party. The success or
failure of our venture will be settled this very night. You must do
exactly as I am going to tell you, like this . . . and this . . . and
this. . . . And mind, the whole thing must be kept absolutely
secret, or you'll have me in trouble.'

'An excellent scheme,' said Ch'en, nodding his head. 'And when
it has succeeded, I guarantee that you shall have a rich reward.'

He walked away in high spirits; truly,

> *Marshalling his troops to seize his prize,*
> *He centres every thought on love's fulfilment.*

Let us now tell how, the old woman having made her arrangements with Ch'en Ta-lang to bring the affair to a head that
evening, in the afternoon a drizzle set in which blotted out the
sky, and at night neither moon nor stars were to be seen. The
old woman led Ch'en through the darkness and concealed him
close by the house while she knocked at the door. Light Cloud
opened it, a lighted paper lantern in her hand. The old woman
was at pains to take her by the arm, with the words, 'I have lost
a handkerchief of Shantung silk. Please help me to look for it.'

In this way she tricked Light Cloud into taking her lantern out
into the street to search, while she herself seized her opening and,
beckoning Ch'en Ta-lang to follow her, slipped silently into the
house. She told Ch'en to hide in the empty space under the
staircase. Then she called out, 'I've got it! No need to look any
farther!'

'And now the lamp has gone out,' said Light Cloud. 'I'll go
and light another one for you.'

'I know the way,' said the old woman, 'there's no need for a
lantern.'

In the blackness the two of them bolted the front door and groped their way up the stairs.

'What was it you lost?' asked Fortune.

The old woman drew out a small handkerchief from her sleeve. 'It was this little sinner. It's of no value, but it was a present from a traveller from Peking, and like they say, "it isn't the value of the gift, it's the thought behind it".

'I know—it's a keepsake from an old lover of yours,' Fortune joked.

'That's about it,' replied the old woman with a smirk.

The two of them spent the evening in drinking and amusing themselves, until the old woman said, 'We have a lot of wine and dainties left—why not send some down to the kitchen and let the servants enjoy themselves, to make it a real festival?'

And Fortune accordingly set aside four dishes and two jugs of wine and told the maids to take them downstairs. There, the two old serving-women and the manservant ate and drank and then retired, and we will say no more about them.

But let us go on to tell how the old woman asked, as she and Fortune drank, 'How is it that your husband has still not returned?'

'Just think—a year and a half now!' said Fortune.

'Even the Herd-boy and the Weaving-girl come together once a year,' said the old woman. 'You have been alone now six months longer than they. It's a common saying, "if you can't be an official, a merchant's the next best thing". A travelling merchant can find romance anywhere he goes—the one who suffers is the wife he leaves behind.'

Fortune sighed and lowered her head, but did not speak.

'I've said too much,' said the old woman. 'Tonight is the wedding-night of the Herd-boy and the Weaver—we should be drinking and making merry, not wounding our feelings like this.'

She poured out another cup of wine for the lady, who by now was in the middle stages of intoxication. Then she poured more wine, this time for the maids, to whom she said, 'This is to drink the health of the Herd-boy and the Weaver, so you must drink a lot of it and then one day you will both marry devoted husbands who will never leave your side.'

So she wheedled them into forcing it down. Soon, overcome

by the wine, they reeled about the room. Fortune ordered them to fasten up the door to the staircase and then go to bed and leave Dame Hsüeh and herself to drink in peace. As the old woman drank she went chattering on : 'Lady, at what age did you marry?'

'Sixteen,' replied Fortune.

'What a shame for you, to be so old before you had a man. I was twelve when I started.'

'What an early age to be married,' exclaimed Fortune.

'Well now, married,' said the old woman, 'that was when I was seventeen. I'll tell you what happened: I used to go next-door to learn needlework, and the young master of the house started flirting with me. I found him so handsome that I agreed to try it out with him. The first time it was very painful, but after the second or third time I began to enjoy it. Was it the same with you, lady?'

But Fortune only giggled.

The old woman went on: 'It's all right as long as you don't know what it's like, but once you've tasted it you can't do without it. You're always getting the itch. It isn't too bad in the daytime, but at night it's terrible.'

'You must have had a lot of experience before you left home,' said Fortune. 'How did you manage to pass yourself off as a virgin when you were married?'

'My mother had an inkling of what had gone on, and she was terrified of the disgrace, so she gave me a recipe for restoring virginity. It involved a decoction made from pomegranate-skin and alum. Then I managed to avert suspicion by just making a lot of fuss about it hurting.'

'Still, you must have slept by yourself at night, when you were a girl?' said Fortune.

'I remember how when I was still at home my elder brother went away, and I slept with my sister-in-law. That was very nice.'

'What is there "nice" about two girls sleeping together?' asked Fortune.

The old woman crossed over and sat close beside Fortune, and said, 'You don't realize, lady. As long as you both know the ropes, it's just as enjoyable, and you can get really excited.'

'You're telling lies, it isn't true,' said Fortune, giving the old woman a playful push. Dame Hsüeh could see that her desires were stirring, and with the idea of really rousing her, she went on: 'I am fifty-one this year, but I still feel amorous many a night, and sometimes I can't put up with it. What a lucky thing that you are experienced beyond your years.'

'But if you say you can't put up with it,' said Fortune, 'why don't you find yourself another man?'

'And who would want a withered old blossom like me?' countered Dame Hsüeh. 'To tell you the truth, though, lady, I have an "emergency relief measure", a way of finding my own enjoyment.'

'You're making it up,' said Fortune. 'What sort of way could that be?'

'Just wait till we go to bed and I'll tell you all about it,' replied the old woman.

Just then a moth began to flutter round the lamp. The old woman picked up a fan and made a swipe at it, deliberately knocking the lamp over in the process. 'Aiia!' she cried, 'I'll go and get another one.'

And she opened the door to the staircase, where she found Ch'en Ta-lang. He had come upstairs on his own, in strict accordance with the old woman's previous instructions, and had been hiding by the door for what seemed ages. 'I've forgotten to get something to light your lamp with,' called out the old woman to Fortune; but turning back, she led Ch'en into the room and concealed him on her own couch. Then she went downstairs, returning after a while with the words: 'It's a pitch-black night, and all the fires are out in the kitchen. What are we to do?'

'I always go to sleep with the lamp burning,' said Fortune. 'I get frightened when it's inky black like this.'

'How would it be if I came into bed with you?' suggested the old woman.

Fortune was just wanting to ask about her 'emergency relief measure', and replied, 'That would be splendid.'

'Then get into bed, lady,' said the old woman. 'I'll join you when I have bolted the door.'

Fortune undressed and got into bed. 'Hurry up and come to bed, old lady,' she called.

'Just coming,' said Dame Hsüen; but at this point she dragged

Ch'en Ta-lang to his feet and pushed him stark naked into Fortune's bed.

Fortune touched his body with her fingers and said, 'What smooth skin you have for your age.' But the person she was addressing, in place of a reply, wriggled his way down under the bedclothes.

Now for one thing the young lady had had a cup or two of wine too many, so that her thoughts were rather hazy; and for another, her desires had been skilfully roused by Dame Hsüeh. The upshot, without going into too great detail,[9] was that she tolerated his impudence:

> She a young wife, in her seclusion longing to be loved,
> He, lady-killer, on his travels eager for romance;
> She, after lonely nights,
> A Wen-chün to his Hsiang-ju,
> He, after months of waiting,
> Like Pi-cheng finding Ch'en Nü.[10]
> Clearly, a long drought ended by a fall of welcome rain,
> A greater joy than the meeting of old friends far from home.

Ch'en Ta-lang had learnt much from his wanderings in the courts of romance. He used all the subtleties of a mating phoenix and sent the girl's soul winging from her body. It was not until after the clouds had opened and the rain scattered that she asked, 'Who are you?'

Ch'en Ta-lang gave her all the details of his glimpse of her from the street, his longing for her and his plea to Dame Hsüeh to devise a plan. 'Now that I have fulfilled the ambition of my life,' he vowed, 'I should die without regrets.'

Then Dame Hsüeh came up to the bed and said, 'It was not mere bold presumption on my part. It was rather my pity for you, lady, spending each night alone in this springtime of your youth; moreover, I was concerned to save this gentleman's life. Your union with him was predestined from a previous incarnation: it had nothing to do with me at all.'

'But now that this has happened,' said Fortune, 'what am I to do if my husband should find out?'

'Only we three know of this,' said Dame Hsüeh. 'If in addition we purchase the silence of Light Cloud and Warm Snow, who else is there to let it leak out? You may leave it to me to ensure that your nights are filled with joy without any unpleasant consequences whatever. Only, in the days to come, I trust you will not forget my services.'

Having come thus far, Fortune dismissed all further worries from her mind, and the two returned to their frenzy. The drumbeats announcing the fifth watch died away and the sky was brightening, and still they were loath to let each other go. At last the old woman urged Ch'en Ta-lang to leave the lady's bed, and saw him out of the house.

From now on they met every night, the young man coming sometimes with Dame Hsüeh, sometimes alone. The old woman coaxed the maids with sweet words and frightened them with sour, and had their mistress make them presents of clothing. Often on his visits young Ch'en also would give them a few scraps of silver to buy fruit for themselves. So successful were these efforts that they happily joined in the game. Night and morning, coming and going, it was the two maids who let him in and saw him off. Not a single obstacle presented itself. Ch'en and the lady doted on each other. They were as close as glue and lacquer, closer in fact than husband and wife. Wishing to bind her more securely to him, from time to time Ch'en bought Fortune fine clothes and costly hair-ornaments, and even paid off the remainder of her debt to Dame Hsüeh for the jewels she had purchased. Nor did he omit to reward Dame Hsüeh with one hundred ounces of silver; so that the cost to the young man of the six months and more of this transaction was near on a thousand gold pieces. Fortune, on her part, made gifts to the old woman worth over thirty ounces of silver. It was nothing but her greed for ill-gotten wealth of this kind that had made the old woman willing to direct their affair.

But let us leave all this. The ancients used to say, 'there never was a feast but the guests had to depart'.

Hardly have we passed the First Full Moon,
Already it's the third month, Feast of the Tombs.

Ch'en Ta-lang began to reflect on the trade which he had allowed to drift for so long, and on the need to return home. One night he spoke of this to Fortune. So deep had their affection

become that neither could bear the thought of separation. The
young lady wanted to pack a few things of value and run away
with him, to be his wife for ever. But Ch'en said, 'It is impossible.
Every detail of our affair is known to Dame Hsüeh. Even my
landlord, Mr Lü, must have his suspicions when he sees me
leaving for the city every night. And then, the boats we should
travel on would be crowded with passengers, none of whom we
should deceive. Nor can we take your maids with us. When your
husband returned he would work to discover what had happened,
and he certainly wouldn't let matters rest. Try to be patient for a
while, my darling. Next year at this time I will come back. I will
seek out some quiet place and let you know of it by a secret
message. There we can be together, unknown to the spirits
themselves. Isn't that the safest plan?'

'But supposing you do not return next year—what then?'
asked Fortune.

Ch'en Ta-lang thereupon made a solemn vow, and Fortune
said, 'Since you vow to be true to me, I for my part will never
reject you. When you reach your home, send a brief message to
Dame Hsüeh by anyone coming this way. Then I may set my
mind at ease.'

'You had no need to ask,' replied Ch'en, 'I had already determined on that.'

Some days later Ch'en Ta-lang hired a boat, and when it was
provisioned and made ready he came back to take his leave of the
lady. This night their devotion was redoubled. Now they talked,
now they wept, now again they disported themselves on the bed,
but never the whole night through did they close their eyes. When
they rose at the fifth watch, Fortune went to a chest from which
she took a precious object which went by the name of 'pearl-sewn
shirt'. This she gave into the hands of Ch'en Ta-lang with the
following words: 'This shirt is an heirloom of the Chiang family.
He who wears it in the hot weather feels a pleasant coolness
going down into his bones. Your journey will be made in growing
heat, it is just the time for this. I give it to you for a keepsake:
when you wear it, it will be as though I myself were close to you.'

Ch'en Ta-lang felt his heart melt inside him and was choked
with tears. With her own hands Fortune put the shirt on him.
Then she told the maids to open the door of the house, and herself

accompanied him as far as the street. There, after repeated
injunctions to him to take care of himself, she said farewell to
him. A verse reads:

Tears, long ago, as her husband said farewell,
Today she weeps as she sees her lover go.
So with many a woman, fickle as water,
Ready to exchange her drake for a wild bird passing.

Our story forks at this point. Let me now tell how Ch'en Ta-
lang, presented with the pearl-sewn shirt, wore it daily next to
his body. Even at night when he took it off he would sleep with
it under the bedclothes, so that never by a foot or an inch was it
away from him. His journey was blessed with following winds,
and within a couple of months he reached the Maple Bridge in
the prefecture of Soochow. The district was a great gathering-
place for brokers in rice and fuel, and he was sure of finding a
buyer there for his cargo. We need say no more of this. But one
day Ch'en chanced to attend a party given by a man from his own
native-place. Also among the guests was a merchant from Hsiang-
yang. This man was handsome, well-dressed—and in fact none
other than Chiang Hsing-ko himself!

What had happened was that Hsing-ko had done some trading
in Kwangtung in jewels, tortoise-shell and sapan and aloes-wood,
and then had started out in the company of others on the long
journey home. But in the course of discussion his fellow merchants had expressed their intention to do some selling in Soochow. Hsing-ko had often heard the saying, 'Above there is
paradise, here below there are Soochow and Hangchow'. Such a
city, with its great crowded wharves—he decided to go along with
them and trade there before finally returning to Hsiang-yang.

He had arrived in Soochow in the tenth month of the previous
year. He was still trading under an assumed name and was known
to all and sundry as 'Young Master Lo'. This being so, Ch'en
Ta-lang had no inkling of his true identity. The two men, so like
in age and appearance, brought together in such random fashion,
developed as they conversed a great regard for each other. At that
same party each asked where the other was staying. Subsequently,
each in turn calling on the other, they became firm friends and
spent much time together.

When Hsing-ko had completed all his dealings and was ready to leave he went to say goodbye to Ch'en Ta-lang at his lodgings. Ta-lang brought out wine in his honour, and they sat facing each other and conversing in perfect amity. It was now the end of the fifth month, the hot weather, and each man loosened his clothing as he drank.

Suddenly Hsing-ko caught sight of the pearl-sewn shirt beneath Ch'en's robe. His heart gave a bound. Yet, feeling loath to claim it as his own, he contented himself with praising its beauty. Ch'en Ta-lang by this time felt sufficiently intimate with Chiang to trust him with his secret. 'Brother Lo,' he began, 'there is a man of your home town called Chiang Hsing-ko. I don't know whether you are acquainted with him? His home is on Market Street.'

Hsing-ko made his reply with great caution and cunning. 'I have been away for so long. I know there is such a man, but I don't know him personally. Why do you ask?'

'I'll let you into a secret,' went on Ch'en. 'I've got myself rather involved with his family.' And he told him of the love between himself and Fortune. Finally he stripped off the pearl-sewn shirt and showed it to Chiang, and said, his eyes brimming with tears, 'This shirt was given to me by her. Now that you are returning to Hsiang-yang, would you do me the great kindness of taking a message for me? I will bring it to your lodgings the first thing in the morning.'

'Yes, I will do that,' replied Chiang; but in the depths of his heart he was saying, 'That such a thing could happen! Yet this is no idle boasting—the pearl-sewn shirt is the proof!' It was as though needles were thrust into his belly. Making some excuse to drink no more he hurriedly took his leave and returned to his lodging. There, he gave himself up to his thoughts. His distress grew until he longed for some magic means to abolish distance, so that he could be instantly at home.

He spent the night packing his belongings, and the next morning he boarded a boat and prepared to sail. But as the boat was on the point of leaving a man came running breathless along the bank. It was Ch'en Ta-lang. He thrust a large package into Hsing-ko's hands, and repeated several times that he must be sure to deliver it.

Hsing-ko's face turned the colour of clay with anger. He was beyond words, beyond speech, beyond living or dying. But he waited until Ch'en Ta-lang had gone and then looked at the package. On the outside was written, 'For favour of delivery to Dame Hsüeh, East Alley, off Market Street'. Hsing-ko, his gorge rising, ripped the package open. Inside was a sash some three yards in length, of crepe silk the colour of peach-blossom. There was also a long casket, paper-wrapped. Inside this was a phoenix hairpin of finest white 'mutton-fat' jade, and a note which read as follows : 'Dame Hsüeh : be so kind as to deliver these two small gifts to my darling Fortune, as a token of my love for her. Tell her that she must take good care of herself, and that we shall meet again without fail in the spring of next year.'

Hsing-ko, beside himself with rage, tore the note into fragments which he threw into the river. The jade hairpin he hurled to the deck, where it broke in two. But then a thought struck him : 'This is stupid of me. The thing to do is to keep these things as evidence.' And so he picked up the pieces of the hairpin, wrapped them up in the sash and put them away. Then he urged on the boatmen, and fumed and fretted all through the journey home.

But when at last he came in sight of his own house, despite himself he wept to recall the love they had known in the early days. 'This terrible thing has all resulted from my pursuit of a fly's-head of profit, for the sake of which I condemned her to an early widowhood. But to repent now—how can that alter what has happened?' He had made the journey home in a fever of impatience; but now that he was here, his heart filled with grief and regret.

Haltingly he walked up to the house and entered. He forced himself to restrain his anger while he went to greet his wife. He on his part remained silent; whilst Fortune herself, full of her guilt and fearful of its discovery, felt her cheeks flood with shame and was not brazen enough to make a show of loving solicitude.

When Hsing-ko had seen to his luggage he gave out that he was going to visit Fortune's parents, and went back to his boat to spend the night. In the morning he returned, and said to Fortune, 'Your parents have fallen ill, both at the same time. Their condition is so serious that I was obliged to stay yesterday to see them through the night. Their thoughts are only of you, they long to see you. I have hired a sedan-chair which is waiting below. You must go back at once—I will follow later.'

Fortune had been greatly puzzled by her husband's absence for the night. Hearing this report of her parents' illness she took it to be true, and naturally was filled with alarm. She hurriedly locked up some cases, which she handed to her husband. Then, calling to one of the serving-women to follow her, she hurried out to the sedan-chair. Hsing-ko stopped the serving-woman, and drawing out a document from his sleeve instructed her to deliver it to Mr Wang. 'When you have given it him, you may come back with the chair-bearers.'

Let us now tell how Fortune arrived at her parents' home and was startled to find the two of them in perfect health. Wang was surprised in his turn to find his daughter returning home unexpected and unannounced. He took the letter from the serving-woman, tore it open and read it. It was a bill of divorcement, and read as follows:

> Bill of divorcement instituted by Chiang Te (Hsing-ko), native of Tsao-yang in the prefecture of Hsiang-yang, betrothed in youth and married after observance of all proper preliminaries to the woman Wang. Against all expectations, this woman after entering her husband's home has been guilty of most serious misdemeanours, as defined in the recognized seven grounds for divorce.[11] Out of regard for the past affection between husband and wife, no statement is made of these misdeeds. I hereby declare my desire that she return to her own family, to marry again at her discretion. I confirm this to be a genuine bill of divorcement, and independent of any misunderstanding whatsoever. Witness my hand this —— day of the —— month, second year of the reign-period Ch'eng-hua (A.D. 1466).

With the document were enclosed a sash of peach-blossom colour and a broken phoenix hairpin of mutton-fat jade. Wang read the document in amazement, and called his daughter to give an explanation. Fortune, informed that her husband had divorced her, said not a word but began to weep. In high indignation Wang strode straight to the house of his son-in-law.

Chiang Hsing-ko hastened forward to bow him in. Wang returned his greeting, then said, 'Son-in-law: my daughter entered your home in proper manner and in all good faith. What are these misdemeanours of hers that have led you to divorce her? I demand an explanation.'

'It is not for me to say,' replied Hsing-ko. 'It is your daughter, sir, who can best explain.'

'She does nothing but weep and will not open her mouth,' said Wang. 'It breaks my heart to see her. My daughter has always been a most intelligent girl, and I cannot believe that she should have been guilty of wantonness. If it is a question of some small failing, I beg you for my sake to forgive her. You and she were betrothed at the age of six or seven, and after your marriage there was never a harsh word between you, but all was harmony. And now you have hardly been back a day from your journeyings —what is this flaw in her that has suddenly come to your notice? If you persist in this vindictiveness, your name will become a byword for cruelty and injustice.'

'Out of respect for you, sir,' Hsing-ko replied, 'I would not presume to say too much. But there is a shirt sewn with pearls, an heirloom in my family, which was in your daughter's keeping. Ask her whether it is still in her possession. If it is, then there is no further difficulty. But if it is not, then please do not blame me for what has happened.'

Mr Wang returned home and questioned his daughter: 'Your husband only wants from you something called a pearl-sewn shirt. Tell me the truth: to whom have you given it?'

At this reference to the crux of the whole affair, the girl's face flushed red for shame. She said not a word, but burst out into a loud wailing. Mr Wang was too alarmed to think what to do, but his wife began to exhort the girl: 'Don't just go on crying so, but let your mother and father know the whole truth, and then we can see if it can't all be cleared up.'

Still the girl would not speak, but went on sobbing her heart out. Mr Wang saw nothing for it but to hand over the bill of divorcement together with the sash and the hairpin to his wife, with instructions to coax the truth out of the girl; then, sorely perplexed, he went out to pass the time of day with the neighbours. Mrs Wang saw that the girl's eyes were swollen and red with weeping, and feared for her health. With a few comforting words she went off to the kitchen to heat some wine in the attempt to make her daughter feel better.

Left alone in the room, Fortune began to wonder how the secret of the pearl-sewn shirt could possibly have come to light. And where did the sash and the hairpin come from? At last, after long deliberation, she said to herself, 'I understand! The broken hairpin means "the mirror is in pieces, the pair of ornaments sundered"—it is a symbol of our broken marriage. As for the sash, it is obvious that he intends me to hang myself. Remembering the love which was ours he is unwilling to make the truth public. His whole thought is to preserve my fair name. Alas, that four years of love should be destroyed in an instant. And it is all my doing, it was I who turned my back on my husband's love! To live on in society, never knowing a day of tranquillity—no, better to hang myself and have done!'

Whereupon she wept again. Then she piled stools one on top of another, tied the sash round a beam and prepared to hang herself. But her span of years was not yet full, for she had not bolted the door of the room and her mother chose just this moment to bring in the jug of best wine that she had been heating. The sight of what her daughter was doing threw her into a panic. Without pausing to put down the wine-pot she rushed forward and dragged at the girl. In her haste she kicked over the pile of stools. Mother and daughter fell in a heap on the floor, and the wine from the jar splashed over them.

'Hanging yourself is no way out!' cried Mrs Wang as she scrambled to her feet and helped her daughter to rise also. 'A girl like you in her twenties, a blossom not yet full! What can bring you to such an act of despair? Who knows but that the day may come when your husband will change his mind? And even supposing that he has finally rejected you—with beauty such as yours, how can you think that no one else will want you? You're bound to find another good match, and then you'll be provided for in the years to come. For the moment you must try to set your mind at ease and not grieve so.'

When Mr Wang came home and discovered that his daughter had tried to kill herself he also spent some time consoling her, and ordered his wife to guard against a recurrence of the attempt.

As the days passed Fortune saw that it was impossible and gradually gave up her design. Truly,

Man and wife, like two birds in the wood;
Death, the Great Limit, sends each flying away.

I go on to tell how Chiang Hsing-ko took two lengths of rope and had Light Cloud and Warm Snow bound and questioned under torture. At first the two maids proved obstinate. But they could not put up with the beating, and in the end confessed every detail of what had happened from beginning to end. It was clearly not they who had done the mischief so much as Dame Hsüeh who had lured them into it. The next morning, Hsing-ko got together a band of men and hurried round to Dame Hsüeh's dwelling. Blows fell like snow-flakes as they tore through the place; all they left standing was the walls of her house. Dame Hsüeh was fully conscious of her own misdeeds and kept out of the way; nor did anyone dare to raise a word of protest on her behalf. Seeing how matters lay, and having vented his spleen, Hsing-ko went back home. He sought out a procuress and sold her the two maids. Then he went upstairs and collected together the valuables, sixteen trunks in all. He wrote out thirty-two strips of red paper for seals and stuck two, one across the other, on each box, leaving the boxes where they stood. What was his reason for this? Why, he and his wife had loved each other deeply. Although now they were parted, his heart was full of pain. 'Seeing an object, one thinks of its owner'—how could he bear to open the trunks and look inside?

Our story forks at this point, and I now tell of a Doctor of Letters of Nanking whose name was Wu Chieh. He had been appointed district magistrate of Ch'ao-yang, in Kwangtung province, and in the course of his journey there by river and canal had just reached Hsiang-yang. He had not brought his family with him, and was contemplating the acquisition of a good-looking concubine. None of the women he had yet seen on his journey had appealed to him. But now he discovered that the daughter of Mr Wang of Tsao-yang was celebrated throughout the whole district for her beauty. Wu Chieh brought out fifty ounces of gold as a present and engaged a go-between to negotiate the union. Fortune's father accepted with joy, but feared only an objection from his former son-in-law. He went in person to discuss the matter with Hsing-ko. Hsing-ko raised no demur; and the night before the wedding, he hired men to take the sixteen trunks, seals intact and keys attached, over to Wu Chieh's boat. They were to be given to Fortune as a wedding present. His kindness overwhelmed the girl with embarrassment. Of those who learned of this act, some praised Hsing-ko as a generous man. Others scorned him as a fool; others still despised him as a weakling—so different are the minds of men.

No more of this idle talk, but let us go on to tell how Ch'en Ta-lang returned to Hsin-an when he had sold up in Soochow. All his thoughts were of Fortune, and morning and night he gazed on the pearl-sewn shirt and sighed. His wife Madam P'ing knew very well that there was something behind all this. One night, when her husband had gone to sleep, she silently abstracted the shirt and concealed it up above the ceiling. When Ch'en awoke and was ready to put it on he failed to find it and demanded it from his wife. But she would admit to no knowledge of it, and Ch'en flew into a rage and turned every case and trunk inside out in the search for it. Nowhere could he find it, and he called his wife every name he could think of. She burst into tears and began a quarrel with him that went on for three days on end. Finally, exasperated, Ch'en threw together a pile of silver and set off with a boy on the journey back to Hsiang-yang again. But as he was approaching Tsao-yang he was surprised by a gang of robbers. They made off with every scrap of his capital and murdered his boy. Ch'en himself had the presence of mind to hide at the stern of the boat behind the rudder-post, and so managed to come through with his life. He reflected on the impossibility of returning home, and decided to go on to his old lodging and wait for a chance of meeting Fortune. From her he could borrow something to set himself up again.

Ch'en sighed, left the boat and walked on to the house of his old landlord, Lü, on the outskirts of Tsao-yang. He told him of what had happened, and continued, 'I shall now have to look up Dame Hsüeh, the jewel-vendor, and get her to borrow some capital from an acquaintance to enable me to trade.'

'Why, haven't you heard?' cried Lü. 'It seems the old woman had tricked the wife of Chiang Hsing-ko into misbehaving herself.

When Chiang came home he asked his wife for something or other called a "pearl-sewn shirt". But the trouble was that she had given it to her lover and he had gone off with it, and she had nothing to say for herself. Chiang packed her off at once, and now she has married again, to be the concubine of a Doctor Wu of Nanking. Chiang took his men round to the old woman's place and left hardly a brick standing. The old woman felt it wasn't safe for her here, so she's gone off to another district.'

When Ch'en Ta-lang heard this he felt as though a bucket of cold water had been poured over him. He was filled with alarm. That night a fever started, and he began to suffer from an illness compounded of melancholia and love-sickness, with complications brought on by shock. He lay on his bed for two months and more, tossing and turning and never at ease. He was a burden to the landlord and the servants, who grew impatient of waiting on him. Ch'en Ta-lang worried about this, and at length summoned up the strength to write a letter home. Then he discussed his position with the landlord. His idea was to find a messenger who would take the letter to his house and bring back both money for his use and a member of his family to look after him on the journey home.

This was exactly what the landlord had been waiting to hear. By a lucky chance he happened to know a government courier who was on his way to Hweichow and Ningchow with documents from his superior. He would be travelling very quickly, by land and water from one posting-house to the next. The landlord took over Ch'en's letter and gave it to this man to take with him, offering him five silver cash of his own on Ch'en's behalf.

It is a true fact that when a man travels alone he goes as fast as he likes. The government courier sped like fire and reached Hsin-an in a matter of days. He asked his way to the house of the merchant Ch'en, delivered the letter and was off again on his winged steed. And truly,

> All because of this precious letter
> Another marriage, pre-ordained, comes to fulfilment.

The story tells how Madam P'ing opened the letter, to find that it was in her husband's handwriting. It read:

Greetings from Ch'en Ta-lang to his esteemed wife Madam

P'ing. After my departure from you I met with robbers near
Hsiang-yang who stole my capital and murdered my assistant.
The shock brought on an illness and I have now been bed-
ridden for two months in my old lodging with Mr Lü. I have
not yet recovered. When you receive this, find some responsible relative to come at once to see me, bringing a plentiful
amount to cover my needs. Please excuse this hurried note.

Madam P'ing was not certain whether to accept the truth of
this. 'The last time he came home,' she said to herself, 'he had
lost his capital of a thousand gold pieces. Judging from this pearl-
sewn shirt it is evident that something underhand had been
going on. And here he comes again with a tale of a robbery, and
wants a lot of money to cover his needs. I'm afraid it's all lies.'

But then she argued with herself, 'He wants some responsible
relative to hurry to see him at once. He must be seriously ill.
Perhaps it is true—how can I be sure? Well, who is the best
person to send?' She went on thinking and worrying about it,
and discussed it with her father, old Manager P'ing.

In the end she packed up her valuables and belongings, hired
a boat and set out in person for Hsiang-yang to find her husband.
She took with her a retainer, Ch'en Wang, and his wife, and
asked her father to accompany them as well. But no sooner had
they reached the Grand Canal than old Manager P'ing contracted
a disease of the throat and had to be sent home. Madam P'ing led
her party forward on their journey, and after many days they
reached the outskirts of Tsao-yang. By making enquiries they
found their way to the house of Mr Lü.

There they discovered that ten days previously Ch'en Ta-lang
had passed away. Mr Lü had pulled out enough money to have
him placed in a rough-and-ready coffin. Madam P'ing cried out
and fell to the floor in a faint, and it was a long time before she
could be brought round. Then she hastened to don the garb of
mourning. Time and again she pleaded with Lü to allow her to
have the coffin opened, so that she could take her last sight of her
husband, and then transfer his body to a better coffin. Lü
persistently refused this request. In the end Madam P'ing had to
content herself with buying the wood for an outer coffin to
encase the first. She engaged Buddhist priests to perform the
ceremonies for the departing spirit, and burnt a great deal of

paper money for its use in the next world. Lü had already demanded twenty ounces of silver as a return for his services to Ch'en. In the face of his wrangling Madam P'ing said not a word.

When a month and more had passed Madam P'ing began to seek an auspicious date on which to set out on the journey back with the coffin. Lü felt sure that the lady was too young and attractive to remain a widow for the rest of her life. Moreover she was comfortably off. He began to think of his son, Second Lü, whose marriage was not yet arranged. Why not detain the lady for a while? Then a match could be concluded which would benefit both parties. Lü bought wine for the entertainment of Ch'en Wang, whose wife, he suggested, should be richly rewarded for putting the matter before Madam P'ing with suitable tact. But unfortunately Ch'en Wang's wife was a complete bumpkin who had never heard of the word 'tact'. With not the slightest respect for persons she came right out with it before her mistress. Madam P'ing was furious. She scolded the woman and boxed her ears, and delivered a few well-chosen words to Mr Lü and his family as well. Lü was in disgrace, but he could only fume inwardly. The truth is,

> There aren't any mutton dumplings for you,
> It's no use getting all worked up about them.

Thereupon Lü began to incite Ch'en Wang to run away. Ch'en had already come to feel that there was nothing for him in the situation. He laid plans with his wife that she should spy out the lie of the land for him. In the end the traitor within Madam P'ing's camp and the enemy outside, between them, managed to make a clean sweep of every bit of silver and jewellery that she possessed, and made off in the night with their booty. Lü of course knew very well what had happened, and yet he went grumbling to Madam P'ing: 'You should never have brought such a pair of scoundrels with you. Fortunately they've only stolen their own mistress's belongings—what a bother if they had taken anyone else's!'

He complained that the presence of the coffin was robbing him of custom and told her to make haste to remove it from his premises. Then he went on, 'It isn't right for you as a young widow to be staying here'—and he pressed her to leave. Madam

P'ing was not proof against his insistence. She was obliged to rent a house for herself and have the coffin moved there and installed within.

Her sad plight here may easily be imagined. But next door there lived a woman called Seventh Aunt Chang. She was a person of quick sympathy, who often would hear Madam P'ing crying to herself and would come round to comfort her. Madam P'ing in turn would often seek her aid in pawning articles of clothing to get money for food; and she was most grateful for Seventh Aunt's help. But before many months were out, every spare garment had been pawned. From being a girl Madam P'ing had always had great skill with the needle, and now she had the idea of entering some wealthy family to earn her keep by teaching needlework to the daughters of the house, until such time as she could make other provision. But when she discussed this scheme with Seventh Aunt Chang, the older woman said, 'It isn't for me to criticize, but a wealthy family is no place for a young woman like yourself. When it comes to dying, well, if your sands run out die you must; but if you're going to live, you've got to keep your self-respect. You have a long life before you. It wouldn't do to end your days as a sewing-mistress. Such a person has a bad name and you would be looked down on. And apart from that— what arrangements would you be able to make for your husband's burial? This is a heavy burden you must bear. And yet, to go on and on paying rent—that is no solution.'

'All these things have been worrying me,' said Madam P'ing, 'but I can see no way out.'

'I have a plan for you,' said Seventh Aunt Chang, 'but you must not be offended if I speak plainly. Here you are, a solitary widow a thousand miles from home and without a copper in your purse. You have not the slightest prospect of taking your husband's corpse back for burial. Leaving aside the difficulty of preserving independence when you lack both food and clothing— even if you do manage to hang on for a while, what good will that do? If you will take my poor advice, the best thing is to seize your chance while you are still young and pretty and find a new mate for yourself. Become his wife. But first let him give you something for a betrothal present, and use it to buy a piece of land for your deceased husband's grave. You would find support for the remainder of your days, and, I believe, "in life or in death, no regrets".'

This seemed to Madam P'ing to be very sensible, and after musing for a while she sighed and said, 'So be it, then. There is nothing deserving of ridicule in selling myself to bury my late husband.'

'If you have made up your mind to do this, lady,' said Seventh Aunt, 'I have a proposal all ready and waiting for you. It is from a very presentable gentleman of an age similar to your own, and in very comfortable circumstances.'

'If he is so well-off,' said Madam P'ing, 'I can't imagine he will want a woman who has been married before.'

But seventh Aunt replied, 'He also is marrying again, and he did in fact tell me that what he wanted was a lady of distinction, no matter whether it was her first or second marriage. Such a charming and graceful lady as yourself is certain to meet his wishes.'

What in fact had happened was that Seventh Aunt Chang had been commissioned by Chiang Hsing-ko to find him a wife. His former wife, Fortune, had been so exquisite that all he wanted now was to find someone of comparable beauty. Although Madam P'ing had not quite such a pretty face as his first wife, when it came to a quick mind and nimble fingers she was more than her match.

The next day Seventh Aunt entered the city and urged the match on Chiang Hsing-ko. He was more pleased than ever to learn that Madam P'ing was from a trading family. For her part, Madam P'ing asked not a penny in betrothal gifts, but merely stressed her need for a plot of land to provide a proper site for her deceased husband's grave. After a number of comings and goings by Seventh Aunt Chang both parties gave their assent.

We must not become long-winded, but rather tell how Madam P'ing interred her husband's corpse and wept bitterly after the ceremony had come to an end. But then in the natural course of events she set up the tablet to her husband's spirit and laid aside her widow's weeds. At the appointed time clothes for her to wear arrived from the Chiang household, and all the garments which she had pawned were redeemed for her. The wedding-night was marked by the customary blowing of pipes and banging of gongs, and by gay red candles in the bridal chamber. And in truth,

Though from past experience familiar with the rites,
Each has deeper feelings than the first marriage brought.

Chiang Hsing-ko was impressed by the dignity of Madam P'ing's demeanour, and reciprocated her deep respect for him. One day he came in from the street to find her tidying a trunk of clothes. Among the garments was a shirt sewn with pearls. Hsing-ko recognized it with a start, and asked, 'Where did you get this?'

'There is something queer about it,' replied Madam P'ing; and she told him of the fuss her former husband had made over it, and of how they had wrangled and finally quarrelled bitterly and separated. 'When I was in such difficulties a little while ago, ' she continued, 'I more than once thought of pawning it. But then I reflected that I didn't know its history, and feared that trouble might result if it were exposed to the public gaze. Even now I can't tell you where this thing came from.'

'Your former husband, "Big Fellow" Ch'en,' said Hsing-ko, '——was his personal name Shang? And was he of a fair and clear complexion, beardless, and with long fingernails on his left hand?'

'You have described him exactly,' said Madam P'ing.

Hsing-ko stuck out his tongue in wonderment, and with palms pressed together addressed Heaven: 'From this I see how clearly manifest are the workings of providence! It is a thing to tremble at!'

Madam P'ing asked what he meant, and he replied, 'This pearl-sewn shirt was an heirloom in my family. Your husband seduced my wife and was given this shirt as a love-token. I met him in Soochow, and the sight of the shirt gave me my first inkling of the affair. On my return, I put aside my wife, Madam Wang. But who could have foreseen that your husband would die on his travels? Then, when I decided to marry again, I learned only that you were the widow of a trader named Ch'en of Hweichow—how was I to know that this was none other than Ch'en Shang? Surely this is retribution piled upon retribution!'

Madam P'ing felt her flesh creep at this recital. From this time on their affection for each other was redoubled. And now you have heard the story proper of how Chiang Hsing-ko twice encountered the pearl-sewn shirt. A verse declares:

The ways of providence are clear and ineluctable:
Who reaped the advantage from the exchange of wives?
Clearly, a debt must be repaid with interest:
This love-match of three lifetimes was only withheld for a time.

It remains to tell how Chiang Hsing-ko, one year after he had acquired this lady to look after his home, made another trading expedition into Kwangtung province. Again, what was fated to happen awaited him there. One day he visited the pearl-fisheries at Ho-p'u. His offer for some pearls had been accepted by the owner, an old man, when suddenly the fellow took back the biggest jewel of the lot and secreted it in his clothing, nor would he own up when charged. Out of patience, Hsing-ko tore at the man's sleeve, where he expected to find the pearl. But he had been rougher than he knew. He had knocked the old man to the ground, where he now lay stretched out without a sound. Hsing-ko hastened to help him up, but he had breathed his last.

The old man's family and neighbours came flocking round, some weeping, some shouting. They seized hold of Hsing-ko and without waiting for explanations gave him a sound beating. Then they locked him in an empty hut, and that very night made out a writ of accusation. At daybreak when the district magistrate opened his court they brought in both prisoner and plaint together. The magistrate allowed the plaint to be filed. Being fully occupied with public business on that day, however, he gave orders for the prisoner to be kept under guard until his trial on the morrow.

Now who do you think this magistrate was? His name was Wu Chieh and he was a Doctor of Letters of Nanking—and indeed, none other than Fortune's second husband! His first appointment had been to Ch'ao-yang. There he had impressed his superiors as incorruptible, and so they had promoted him to take charge of this pearl-fishing district of Ho-p'u. That night he sat with the accusations he had accepted, closely examining them beneath a lamp. Fortune chanced to be standing by his side, and was idly glancing through the pile of documents. Her eye happened to light on a 'plaint of homicide brought by Sung

Fu against one Lo Te, merchant, of Tsao-yang . . .'; who could this be but Chiang Hsing-ko?

Memories of the love of former days brought a sudden pain to her heart. Weeping she pleaded with her husband: 'This man Lo Te is my own elder brother who was adopted by my mother's family, the Lo. Somehow on his travels he has committed this grave misdeed. I beg you, for my sake, let him keep his life and return to his home!'

'We must see what happens at the trial,' replied the magistrate. 'If homicide is established, how am I to treat him with such leniency?'

Fortune knelt, her eyes brimming with tears, and pleaded before him piteously. 'Do not distress yourself so,' said the magistrate. 'I shall find a way.'

When court opened the following morning, Fortune again clutched at the magistrate's sleeve and wailed, 'If my brother must die, I too will end my life, and you and I shall not see each other again.'

That day the magistrate took his seat and ordered that this case be brought first. The two brothers, Sung Fu and Sung Shou, came in tears to avenge their father's death. They submitted that a quarrel had arisen over some pearls, in the course of which their father had been struck in anger. He had fallen to the ground and died. Let his honour issue judgment.

The magistrate heard the evidence of all the witnesses. Some said the old man had been knocked to the ground; others said that he had stumbled after receiving a push. Chiang Hsing-ko disputed the matter: 'Their father stole a pearl from me, and I was annoyed and quarrelled with him. He was an old man and not very steady on his feet. He fell and killed himself—it had nothing to do with me.'

'What was your father's age?' the magistrate asked of Sung Fu.

'He was sixty-seven,' replied Sung Fu.

'Aged persons readily faint,' commented the magistrate. 'He may not necessarily have been struck.'

Sung Fu and Sung Shou insisted that he was knocked down and killed.

'The presence or absence of injury must be ascertained by examination,' said the magistrate. 'Since you maintain that he was knocked down and killed, let the corpse be delivered to the public cemetery, and we shall hear the result of the examination at the evening session of this court.'

Now the fact was that the Sung were a family of standing: the old man himself had in the past been local headman. His two sons were utterly unwilling to submit their father's corpse to an official post-mortem. Side by side they kotowed and pleaded, 'Our father's death was seen by all. We entreat your honour to inspect his body where it lies in our own home. We are most reluctant to submit the corpse to an official post-mortem.'

'If there is no evidence of injury to the bone,' protested the magistrate, 'how do you expect the accused to be willing to confess? If there is no post-mortem report, how am I to present this case to higher authority?'

The two brothers only renewed their pleading, until the magistrate became annoyed and said, 'How can I try this case if you will not allow a post-mortem?'

This frightened the brothers into incessant kotowing, and they said, 'We await your honour's verdict.'

'When a man is nearing seventy,' declared the magistrate, 'he must expect to die. Let us aver that his death was not the result of a blow. If we were to wrong an innocent man, this would add to the guilt of the deceased. And for you, his sons: how could your hearts be at ease in the knowledge that you had allowed your father to reach such an age, only to ruin the ending of his life by branding him a criminal? Yet, though it be false to say that he died from a blow, it is at least true that he was pushed and fell. If condign punishment be not inflicted on Lo Te, what vent is to be given to your anger? I therefore rule that Lo Te put on the hemp garments of mourning and observe the rites in the manner prescribed for a son. In addition, all expenses of burial are to be borne by him. Do you submit to this?'

'When your honour commands,' said the brothers, 'who are we to disobey?'

Hsing-ko was overjoyed to see that the magistrate had settled the whole case without prescribing any punishment for him. When plaintiffs and defendant alike had kotowed and expressed their gratitude, the magistrate concluded, 'I shall not write a report of this case. The defendant will be accompanied by an escort until such time as the ceremonies have been completed. He will then report back to me, whereupon I will cancel the writ of accusation.'

Truly,

In a court of law, retribution is easily accomplished,
Nor is it difficult there to accumulate hidden merit.
Observe, today, how his honour the magistrate Wu
Rights the wrong but releases the accused, so that both sides
*   rejoice.*

Let us now rather tell how Fortune from the moment her husband had entered court had felt as though she were sitting on a mat of needles. As soon as she heard he had retired she went to meet him to learn the news.

'I settled it like this and like this,' said the magistrate. 'Out of consideration for you I inflicted not a single stroke on him.'

Fortune expressed to the full her gratitude for this act of mercy. Then she said, 'I have been long parted from my brother and yearn to see him and to enquire after our parents. If you would do me this great kindness, please try to find a way for us to meet.'

'That is not difficult', said the magistrate.

Members of the audience: when Fortune was divorced by Chiang Hsing-ko their love was surely ended and their obligations ceased to exist? Why then do you imagine she should now show such concern for him? Well, they had loved each other at the beginning very much indeed. Hsing-ko had no alternative but to divorce Fortune because of her misconduct; but it was almost too much for him to bear. That was why he had presented her with the sixteen cases, all complete, on the night of her remarriage. For this alone it was impossible for Fortune's heart not to be softened. And now, rich and honoured as she was, she found Hsing-ko in trouble—how could she do other than go to his assistance? This is what is known as 'conscious of kindness, repaying it with kindness'.

I go on to tell how Hsing-ko carried out faithfully the magistrate's injunctions by sparing neither money nor effort in observing the rites. The Sung brothers were able to make no complaint. When the funeral ceremonies were over he was escorted back to the yamen to make his report. The magistrate had him called into his private apartments and allowed him to be seated. Then he said to him, 'I should have come near to wronging you in this suit, brother-in-law, had it not been for the reiterated pleas of your esteemed sister.'

Hsing-ko did not understand, and could make no reply. After a while, when they had taken tea, the magistrate invited him into the library in the inner apartments, and there he summoned his wife to meet the guest. Would you not agree that such an unexpected meeting was exactly like a dream? The two neither saluted nor spoke, but flew straight into a tight embrace. They wept aloud, and no more distressing sound was ever heard in the wailing for father or mother. The magistrate looking on was deeply moved, and said, 'Please do not distress yourselves so. You do not seem to me like brother and sister. Tell me the true facts at once—there may be some way I can help.'

The two dried their tears a while, but neither cared to speak. At last Fortune gave in to the magistrate's questioning, and knelt and said, 'Your wife deserves a thousand deaths for her sins. This is my former husband.'

Chiang Hsing-ko saw he could not hide the truth, and knelt in his turn. Item by item he told the magistrate of the former love between his wife and himself, of their divorce and of his remarriage. When he had finished, they clung to each other again in tears, and the magistrate Wu as well felt his tears flow unceasingly. 'How can I tear you apart,' he said, 'when you love each other so deeply? As it has happened we have been here three years and there has not yet been a child.'—And he ordered Hsing-ko to take Fortune at once in reunion.

The two of them bowed before him in gratitude as though he were a god. The magistrate hastened to order a sedan-chair and took his farewell of Fortune as she left his yamen. Next he collected some men to carry out the sixteen cases which had accompanied his bride, and which he now ordered Chiang Hsing-ko to accept. Finally, he sent one of his assistants to escort the pair to the limit of his district. Such was the goodness of the magistrate Wu. Truly,

This pearl regained at Ho-p'u gleams with added lustre,
A brighter light than that which led to the jewelled swords at Feng.[12]

Our admiration is called for the magistrate's generous conduct,
How different from those others, who lusted or coveted riches!

This man, for so long without a son, at length came to be
President of the Board of Civil Office. In Peking he took a
concubine who bore him three sons, each of whom successfully
climbed the ladder of the examinations. All agreed that this was
Wu's recompense for hidden acts of merit.

But this belongs to a later date. I go on to tell now how Chiang
Hsing-ko led Fortune back to their home, where she met Madam
P'ing. As the partner of Hsing-ko's first marriage it was Madam
Wang who took precedence; on the other hand, she had been
divorced, and he had married Madam P'ing in the prescribed
manner with a proper go-between. Furthermore, Madam P'ing
was the elder by one year; and so, Madam P'ing took the position
of first wife, and Madam Wang became his second wife. The two
called each other 'sister', and from that time onwards Chiang
Hsing-ko lived in the greatest happiness with his two wives.
There is a verse in evidence:

Two wives to comfort him, all joined in mutual love,
Now one, discredited, has returned to share with another.
Good and ill and retribution, scrupulously apportioned:
Providence is near at hand, and need not be sought afar.

Wine and Dumplings

LIKE *The Journey of the Corpse* which follows, this story is a heroic biography, the fictionalized account of the life of an authentic historical personage. The story-tellers who narrated these biographies must have come second in number and in popularity only to the love-story specialists themselves. Usually they took their material from earlier dynasties. *Wine and Dumplings* is set in the seventh century, in the T'ang period. But the story as we now have it wears many features of the prompt-book of late-Sung or Mongol times, six or seven centuries later. The voice we are hearing belongs to the story-teller of those times, who is looking back to the heroic age of T'ang.

Wine and Dumplings is the tale of the meteoric rise to fame and high office of a neglected man of worth, the poor scholar Ma Chou. It is one of the shortest of the *Stories Old and New*, but also one of the most attractive, full of humour and rather eccentric 'character'. At first glimpse, it seems very doubtful that such a person as Ma Chou ever existed, or at least that he should have had such a fairy-tale career. The story seems more likely to be a figment of the imagination of some failed examination candidate, compensating himself in this way with dreams of swift advancement.

Nevertheless Ma Chou did exist, and his career was remarkable enough to judge from the facts about him contained in the standard histories of the period. Some explanation is to be found in the circumstances of his day. In the early years of the T'ang period the administration stood in great need of able recruits, who were not yet provided in a steady flow from the examination halls. The Emperor was not so hard of access as he later became, and the times were propitious for a man of outstanding talent to make his way, given suitable personal contacts, swiftly to the top.

The whole essence of the story of Ma Chou is contained in the *Old* and *New T'ang Histories*. The following extracts offer material for comparison with our story:

Ma Chou, styled Pin-wang, of Chuang-p'ing, Ch'ing-ho.

He was orphaned early in life, and was poor. He was fond of study and particularly well-versed in the *Book of Songs* and the commentaries (to the *Spring and Autumn Annals*). But he was a failure and was shown no respect by the people of the district. During the reign-period Wu-te (618–627) he took a post as assistant teacher in Pochou. But he drank himself drunk every day and paid no attention to his teaching, and was frequently reprimanded by his superior, Ta Hsi-shu.

The story, as might be expected, gives a vivid description of Ma Chou's inadequacies as a teacher.

One subsequent incident in particular is seized upon by the story-teller as a golden opportunity for elaboration. Here is the incident as recorded in the standard history:

> Once, when Ma Chou was spending the night in an inn at Hsin-feng, the innkeeper was devoting himself to the needs of some travelling merchants, and paid no heed to Ma Chou's request for service. Ma thereupon ordered eighteen pints of wine, which he proceeded quietly to drink by himself, to the astonishment of the innkeeper.

There is exact correspondence of detail in the story's version of this, except on the point of the quantity of wine: here, the story exaggerates, to allow Ma Chou the eccentric performance of washing his feet in wine.

The official biographies go on to relate how Ma Chou was brought to the notice of the Emperor through the recommendation of General Ch'ang Ho, and how he was very quickly given high office:

> On arrival at Ch'ang-an (the capital) Ma Chou stayed at the home of General Ch'ang Ho. In the year 631 the Emperor ordered all officials to submit comments on his successes and failures. Ch'ang Ho was a military man and had no learning, but Ma Chou set out some twenty or more items of urgent contemporary concern. Surprised, the Emperor T'ai-tsung questioned Ch'ang Ho about this. Ch'ang Ho replied, 'This is not something that I could have done. It was written by a guest in my house, the teacher Ma Chou, a loyal and filial man.'
>
> The Emperor ordered Ma Chou to attend audience that very day, and officers were dispatched four times to press him to

come, before he eventually presented himself. The Emperor
was greatly pleased with Ma Chou's words during the audience,
and ordered his appointment as *men-hsia-hsing* (a kind of
personal secretary to the Emperor). In the sixth year (632) he
received appointment as a Supervising Censor, in accordance
with the Imperial command. Ch'ang Ho received a gift of 300
rolls of silk from the Emperor for his service in recommending
Ma Chou.

There are two slight discrepancies in the story: Ch'ang Ho there
receives only 100 rolls of silk; and Ma Chou's appointment as
Supervising Censor is made, more dramatically, during his first
audience instead of in the following year as in the histories. Ma
Chou's reluctance to attend for audience is explained in the story,
although from what has been revealed of his habits the reason
would not have been difficult to guess:

> Ma Chou had been drinking early in the day, and was snoring,
> nor did he wake when they called him. Again the Imperial
> command was sent forth, and in all he was sent for three times,
> before at last Ch'ang Ho himself came. . . . Ch'ang Ho went
> himself into the study and made the servants hold Ma Chou up
> while cold water was spurted over his face. Only then did he
> wake. When he was informed of the Emperor's command, he
> mounted hurriedly on horseback, and at length was led by
> Ch'ang Ho into the Imperial presence.

In addition to what is narrated in the official biographies, the
story introduces a romance between Ma Chou and a dumpling-
seller, 'Dame Wang'. She is the niece of the Hsin-feng innkeeper who was so impressed by Ma Chou's behaviour, and she
is being wooed by Ch'ang Ho. (She has the attraction of being
destined to become a lady of the highest rank, according to a
trusted physiognomist.) She is thus the link, which is missing
from the official biographies, between Ma Chou and Ch'ang Ho.
But she is not likely to be an authentic personage. Someone may
indeed have existed whose great achievement it was to introduce
Ma Chou to Ch'ang Ho and thus assist his phenomenal rise to
success. But there is too much unlikelihood about the figure of
Dame Wang. Whatever her physiognomy, it is most improbable
that first the General and then the Censor should have courted

the humble niece of an innkeeper, a woman who was both a dumpling-seller and the widow of a dumpling-seller. She is moreover the subject of the only unrealistic element in the story, when the night before Ma Chou's arrival at her house she dreams of being carried to the skies by a white horse (the meaning of the surname Ma is 'horse', and Ma Chou arrives dressed in white clothes).

Otherwise, the story of Ma Chou is perfectly authentic. He was no doubt something of a legend in his own day. Ch'en Wen-pen, a favourite of the Emperor, is recorded in the story as being responsible for a painting depicting Ma Chou washing his feet in wine at the inn. Since Ch'en was an authentic historical person and an acquaintance of Ma Chou, there is no reason to doubt that the picture really existed, and consequently that the incident of the feet-washing did in fact take place.

WINE AND DUMPLINGS

Difficult to envisage, your future, wrapped in darkness;
Moon in autumn, flowers in spring, everything has its season.
Calm yourself, and follow the word of the Lord of Heaven:
This frantic twilight bustle—to what end, for what reason?

IT IS told that the Emperor T'ai-tsung of the great T'ang dynasty, who ascended the dragon throne in the year 627, was a good and enlightened ruler who chose men of worth as his ministers. In perfect and brilliant array they stood, the Eighteen Scholars of the civil administration [1] with the Eighteen Military Governors. There was no man of talent and wisdom in the whole land but was summoned to office and enabled to fulfil his ambition, so that the empire was at peace and the people happy and secure.

But of all I will show you now one man only, Ma Chou, styled Pin-wang, of Ch'i-p'ing in the district of Pochou. This man was an orphan, with no more possessions than were on his back. He had passed the age of thirty without taking a wife and was alone in the world. Having acquired from his earliest years a remarkable understanding of the classics and histories, he was a man of wide learning and in his grasp of military strategy surpassed all his fellows. But being poor and friendless, he had found no one to advance him in life. Clearly, a mighty dragon trapped in the mud, unable to take flight. One after another he watched them, men without a thousandth part of his own learning and ability, taking their place and making their name, enjoying rank and office, whilst he alone must cherish his great gifts in obscurity. Daily he grew more melancholy, sighing, 'It is the times, it is my luck, it is my fate.'

Through the years he had cultivated a marvellous capacity for wine, to which he turned in his distress, stopping only when helplessly drunk. He seldom worried whether he had or had not food to eat; but he could not do without something to fill his cup. If he had no money of his own to buy wine, but discovered that a neighbour had some in, he would go along and guzzle that up.

Unfortunately his behaviour was very extravagant and he was far from discreet, and when he was drunk he would rant and rail at the whole assembly. The neighbours one and all grew tired of his ravings and began to detest him, calling him 'pauper' and 'tosspot' behind his back. Ma Chou came to know of this, but took no notice: truly,

> Before the meeting of dragon and tiger [2]
> Ignore the bleating of sheep and goat.

Now let us tell of the Prefect of Pochou, Ta Hsi. This man had heard frequent reports of Ma Chou's classical learning, and invited him to a post as assistant teacher in the prefectural city. But on the day Ma Chou arrived to take up his duties the assembled graduates pledged his health in wine: and Ma Chou inadvertently drank himself into a stupor. The next morning the Prefect himself visited the college to request instruction. Ma Chou was too befuddled to stand on his feet, and the Prefect left in a rage. When Ma Chou recovered and was informed of the Prefect's visit he went straight to the yamen to apologize. The Prefect remonstrated with him loud and long, and Ma Chou agreed with every word; but he was unable to change his ways. Every time a student came to ask about some point of difficulty in his classical studies, Ma Chou would have him stay for a drink. All the fees he received were paid into the wineshop, and if these were not enough he would visit his students, as formerly he had visited his neighbours, and soak himself in their wine.

One day he had got drunk and was being assisted by two students, supporting him one on either side, the three of them singing all the way, when they chanced to come face to face with the Prefect. The latter shouted at them to get out of his way, but Ma Chou was in no mood to give place. His eyes glaring, he began to curse all and sundry. The Prefect gave him a good dressing-down right there in the street. Ma Chou was drunk at the time and knew nothing about it, but when he woke the next morning his students came to urge him to go to the Prefect and apologize. Ma Chou said with a sigh, 'It was only because I was orphaned and poor, with no one to help me, and yet wished to take a step forward in my career, that I curbed my ambitions and submitted to the dictates of others. After all these scoldings from the Prefect for getting drunk, I should be ashamed to go to him again to make my bows and ask for his sympathy. The ancients did not bend their backs for five pecks of rice,[3] and this post of assistant teacher is not something that will keep me all my life.' So he handed over his official gown to a student with instructions to return it to the Prefect, and raising his eyes to the sky and giving a great laugh he went out of the door and away. Indeed,

His tongue sustains him when he leaves,
Still without a penny to call his own.

It has always been said that a man is like water, which only sparkles when you stir it up. All because he couldn't face a scolding from the Prefect for getting drunk, Ma Chou spoke his mind and left, and went to a certain place and met a certain man who helped him along, until he rose to the position of President of the Board of Civil Office.

But all this is yet to come. Let us now tell how Ma Chou wondered where he should go. He felt sure there was no great opportunity to be met with in the provinces. The thing was to find among the noblemen and heads of government in the imperial capital someone like those figures of the past: Hsiao Ho,[4] who excelled in bringing men forward, or Wei Wu-chih,[5] who could recognize talent and worth. Only thus could he find an opening and fulfil the aspirations of a lifetime. Therefore he set his face towards the west, and before very long arrived in Hsin-feng.

Hsin-feng or 'new' Feng has a curious history. The city was founded by the Han Emperor Kao-tsu. He was born in old Feng. He led a successful rising, executed the Ch'in Emperor and destroyed his rival Hsiang Yü; and when he had become First Emperor of the great Han dynasty, he honoured his father with the title of Father of the Empire. Now, the Father of the Empire, as he stood in the streets of Ch'ang-an, pined for the scenes of his native place. So Kao-tsu assembled cunning craftsmen and ordered them to construct a city on the model of old Feng, and transferred the population of the old city to the new. All the streets and market-places and houses were on exactly the same lines as in Feng. They got the Changs' hens and the Lis' dogs and let them loose on the streets, and they all recognized the doorways of the houses they belonged to and went home by themselves. The Father of the Empire was so delighted that he bestowed the name of Hsin-feng, 'New Feng', on the city.

And now that Ch'ang-an was once again the capital, under the new dynasty of T'ang, Hsin-feng, so closely-situated in the north-west, was filled again with a bustle of activity in its streets and markets. And indeed the number of inns which provided for travelling merchants was beyond compute. It was already late in the day when Ma Chou reached Hsin-feng. He chose a large inn and was just about to enter when along came a busy throng of people with horses and carriages. They were travelling merchants, loaded with their wares, and they crowded into the inn to rest. The inn-keeper came out to receive them and gave a flurry of orders to the servants to find space for all their luggage, while the whole crowd found seats for themselves in their various groups. The waiters ran back and forward ceaselessly with their orders for food and wine, as busy as the running horses on a lantern.[6] Ma Chou sat quietly by himself at one side, and no one took the slightest notice of him. Pretending annoyance, he banged on the table and roared, 'Innkeeper, you're a fraud! Am I no guest of yours that you don't bother to look after me? What's the meaning of this?'

Hearing this commotion the innkeeper left off what he was doing and said, 'Please do not be angry, sir. There are so many of them, we have to get them settled first. You are by yourself, sir, it will be easy to see to you. Just tell me what food or wine you want, and that will be all right.'

'I've been travelling all this way,' said Ma Chou, 'without washing my feet. So bring me some clean hot water.'

'We have no pans free,' replied the innkeeper, 'you'll have to wait a while for hot water.'

'In that case,' said Ma Chou, 'let me have some wine first.'

'How much wine would you like?' asked the innkeeper.

Ma Chou indicated a company of travellers seated across from him, and said to the innkeeper, 'Bring me as much as they are having between them.'

'There are five gentlemen there,' said Wang, 'and each of them is having ten pints of best wine.'

'To tell the truth,' said Ma Chou, 'that would not get me half-way towards being drunk. But I am drinking sparingly while travelling, so just fifty pints will do. And bring anything you have that is good to eat.'

Wang gave the order to the waiter, who heated up fifty pints of wine and set it on the table, together with a great porcelain bowl and several bowls of meat and vegetables. Ma Chou, all by himself, raised the bowl and drank as though there were no one else about. When he had drunk some thirty-odd pints he asked for a basin to wash his feet in, and poured into it what remained of the wine. Then he kicked off his boots and stretched out his feet and washed them. When the other customers saw him do this they all stared in astonishment. Wang silently marvelled at him, realizing that this was no ordinary man.

An artist of the day, Ch'en Wen-pen, painted a 'Portrait of Ma Chou Bathing his Feet', which bears an encomium composed by 'the Angler in the Waves of Mist'. His words read as follows:

> *Most men esteem the mouth;*
> *I honour my feet alone.*
> *The mouth stirs up the waves of dispute,*
> *The feet stay close to solid ground.*
>
> *Lowly-placed, yet ever loyal,*
> *Willing to carry me a thousand miles;*
> *Heavy their task, slight their reward,*
> *Never a word of complaint escapes them.*
>
> *With wine I repay you*
> *For all your trouble;*
> *Better that you should forget your cares*
> *Than that my belly should swill.*
>
> *—— O admirable Ma Chou,*
> *How rare such vision as this!*

There is nothing to record of that night, when Ma Chou took his rest. The next morning Wang rose early to collect his dues and see off the departing patrons. Ma Chou was without money, but reflecting that the weather was steadily growing warmer he took off his fox-fur coat and offered it to Wang in payment for the wine. But Wang, perceiving him to be such an open-handed gentleman and the coat of greater value than was required, persistently refused to take it. Ma Chou thereupon asked for a brush and wrote up the following verses on the wall:

> *In gratitude for a bowl of rice*
> *The ancients gave freely a bar of gold.*
> *They rewarded not what went in the dish*
> *But the comradeship which inspired it.*

> *At Hsin-feng I drank wine*
> *And was not allowed to give my coat:*
> *A man of worth, mine host,*
> *Of spirit above his station!*

He added his signature, 'Ma Chou of Ch'i-p'ing'. Wang was filled with admiration for the excellence both of his composition and of his calligraphy. He asked where he was making for. 'I am bound for Ch'ang-an, where I shall make my name', replied Ma Chou.

'Have you a lodging there to go to?' asked Wang. Ma Chou replied that he had none, and Wang continued: 'I see that you possess great gifts, sir, and this journey will surely bring you wealth and honour. But Ch'ang-an is a place where 'rice is the price of pearls and firewood the price of cinnamon'. How are you going to live there, sir, with an empty purse? However, I have a niece there, married to a dumpling-seller by the name of Chao San-lang, who lives in Long Life Street. I will write them a letter and you can lodge there, which will save you a little trouble. And if it is not too little to offer, I have an ounce of silver here which may be useful to you on the road.'

Ma Chou accepted the silver, full of gratitude for the innkeeper's kindness. When Wang had written his letter he placed it in the hands of Ma Chou, who said, 'Should the day come when my fortunes improve, I shall never forget this.'

Ma Chou took his leave, with many thanks, and proceeded to Ch'ang-an. He found indeed a place where 'the skies were painted and the earth brocaded', a very different city from Hsin-feng. He went straight to the house of the dumpling-seller Chao San-lang in Long Life Street, where he presented his letter from Wang the innkeeper.

Now in fact several generations of the Chao family had made a living from selling pastries. Chao San-lang had died the previous year, and his widow lived on in the shop and kept the business going: this, then, was the niece of the innkeeper Wang of Hsinfeng. Though past thirty she was a remarkably attractive woman. The people of the capital knew her simply as 'the dumpling woman'.[7] Once, during Madam Wang's early days in the shop, the gifted physiognomist Yüan T'ien-kang had been startled by his first sight of her. With a sigh, he said, 'This woman has cheeks like the full moon, lips like red lotus-petals, a voice of marvellous clarity and a regular line of the neck. Hers is a physiognomy of the highest promise and one day she will undoubtedly become a lady of the first rank. How does she come to be living in a place like this?'

He chanced to speak of this in the presence of the Lieutenant-General Ch'ang Ho. The latter, having perfect faith in the utterances of Yüan T'ien-kang, commissioned an old serving-man to visit the shop daily, under the pretext of buying dumplings, but in reality to persuade Madam Wang to join the General as his concubine. But Madam Wang merely gave a contemptuous laugh and made no reply. Indeed,

An affinity is predestined from a previous existence;
If there is no affinity, don't try to force the issue.

Let us rather tell how Madam Wang in the night preceding Ma Chou's arrival had a curious dream, of a white horse which came from the east, entered her shop and ate up all her dumplings non-stop. She, in her dream, had seized hold of a whip and was going after the horse, when she found herself on its back, and the horse transformed into a fiery dragon which soared up into the sky. She awoke feeling hot all over, and was sure that her dream had some strange significance. And then, that very day, there came into her hands the letter from her uncle, the innkeeper Wang, introducing this stranger with the surname Ma, which means 'horse'; moreover, Ma Chou was dressed in white clothes. Her heart full of wonderment, she invited him to make her shop his lodging-place.

She fed him three good meals a day and attended to his every want. Ma Chou had no hesitation in accepting her services, and seemed to regard it all as a matter of course, whilst Madam Wang for her part never wearied in her ministrations.

But the trouble was that the neighbourhood housed a gang of young idlers who had taken a great interest in the pretty widow, and used to find nothing better to do with their time than loll in the doorway of her shop and try to rouse her with their wild talk and insolent remarks. As Madam Wang refused to be provoked by them they came to admit that she was an honourable woman; but now that they found her entertaining in her home a solitary traveller from far away, naturally enough they began to manufacture all kinds of rumours and speculations. Madam Wang, being a person of sensitivity, was well aware of all this, and spoke to Ma Chou about it.

'I myself am very anxious for you to stay here,' she said, 'but what am I to do? This kind of talk is very unpleasant for a widow. You, sir, have a great future before you: you should select a more fitting resting-place from which to plot your advancement. It is a pitiful waste to see talents like yours lying buried here.'

'I am only too willing to be taken into someone's service,' replied Ma Chou, 'but where am I to turn?'

Just as they were talking the old servant from General Ch'ang's mansion turned up again to buy some dumplings. Madam Wang reflected that since Ch'ang Ho was a high officer of the military administration he was bound to require the services of a man of learning. And so she put a question to the servant: 'I have here a relative of mine, the graduate Ma, who is an accomplished scholar. He is seeking employment—would his services be of any use to your master?'

'Very good,' replied the old man.

Now it so happened that a great drought was raging at this time, and the Emperor T'ai-tsung had ordered all officers of the fifth rank and above to submit for his consideration their careful and detailed criticisms of his administration. Ch'ang Ho's own rank obliged him to submit such a memorial, and he was just on the look-out for an accomplished scholar who could wield the brush on his behalf. And here was Madam Wang bringing forward this graduate Ma—clearly it was rice to the starving, drink to the thirsty, it 'scratched him precisely where he itched'. Delighted by the old servant's news, Ch'ang Ho at once had his men saddle a horse to bring Ma Chou to him.

Ma Chou took his leave of Madam Wang and entered the mansion of Ch'ang Ho, who was impressed by his distinguished appearance and treated him with high esteem. That same day he set out wine to feast him, and had his study swept out to provide quarters for him. The next morning he brought in person twenty taels of silver and ten lengths of dyed silk cloth, which he presented to Ma Chou in the study as an initial fee for the services he required. This done, he discussed with him the matter of the Emperor's command. Ma Chou asked for brush and ink-slab and spread a scroll of white paper on his desk, and then, his brush never ceasing in its flow, he rushed off his Twenty Desiderata to the accompaniment of repeated sighs of admiration from Ch'ang Ho.

The latter copied them out in his own hand overnight, and at the morning audience on the next day submitted them for the Emperor's approval. As the Emperor T'ai-tsung read them through he bestowed praise on each successive paragraph. Then, turning to Ch'ang Ho, he asked, 'The wisdom and logic of these are beyond your capacities. How did you come by them?'

Ch'ang Ho prostrated himself and acknowledged that he deserved to die. 'It is indeed true that I am too stupid to be capable of such work. These Twenty Desiderata were drawn up by one Ma Chou, a member of my household.'

'Where is this Ma Chou?' asked the Emperor. 'Let him be brought at once to audience.'

On receipt of the Imperial command the eunuchs went straight to General Ch'ang's mansion to summon Ma Chou. But Ma Chou had been doing his morning's drinking and was snoring, nor did he wake when they called him. Again the Imperial command was issued, until on the third mission Ch'ang Ho himself was sent. From this we can see the extent of the regard in which the Emperor T'ai-tsung held men of talent. There is a verse by a court historiographer which runs:

On three successive journeys the summons came to call him,
So great the Imperial love for men of worth and talent.
If only every court were so to regard its servants
Where should we find a hero languishing in the wilderness?

Ch'ang Ho went in person into the study and made the servants hold up Ma Chou while cold water was spurted over his face, whereupon he at last woke up. Informed of the Emperor's command, he mounted hurriedly on horse back, and at length was led by Ch'ang Ho into the Imperial presence.

When Ma Chou had finished his prostrations, the august Imperial voice asked, 'What is your place of origin? Have you yet held office?'

'Your servant is from Ch'i-p'ing,' responded Ma Chou. 'I was at one time an assistant teacher in Pochou, but finding no scope there for my ambition I relinquished the post and came to the capital. The glimpse of the divine countenance which I am now granted is the great honour of my life.'

The speech delighted the Emperor, who forthwith appointed him a Supervising Censor and personally bestowed on him the robe, tablet and girdle of office. Equipped with these Ma Chou expressed his debt to the Imperial bounty and retired, returning to the mansion of Ch'ang Ho to thank him with obeisances for the favour of his recommendation. Ch'ang Ho gave a second banquet and pledged him in wine, and it was night-time before the feast was over. Ch'ang Ho felt it would be an insult to Ma Chou to have him stay on in the study, and expressed his intention 'to order a sedan-chair to take you back to the home of your relative, Madam Wang'.

But Ma Chou replied, 'Madam Wang is no relative of mine. I am merely lodging in her house.'

Astonished, Ch'ang Ho asked, 'Then has the Censor in fact no family?'

'I am ashamed to say that poverty has prevented me from marrying,' answered Ma Chou.

Then Ch'ang Ho said, 'The physiognomist Yüan T'ien-kang once predicted that Madam Wang was destined to become a lady of the first rank. Believing her to be your relative, I feared only that there might be something standing in her way; but it is the design of Providence that you have been thrown together like this. If you are not averse to the match, I am willing to act as your go-between.'

Ma Chou, impressed by Madam Wang's conscientiousness

had the same plan in mind, and said, 'I should be most deeply grateful, sir, if you could bring about this happy union.'

Ma Chou stayed on that night in Ch'ang Ho's mansion, and the next morning the two of them attended audience. It was a time of risings by the Turks and Tartars, and the Emperor T'ai-tsung had just appointed four commanders to lead expeditions to suppress them. He ordered Ma Chou to present a plan for the pacification of the barbarians. Ma Chou before the throne spoke with the greatest fluency, and the Emperor gave agreement to every word he said. He promoted him to the rank of Counsellor, and Ch'ang Ho's service in bringing forward this man of worth was rewarded with a hundred bolts of silk.

Having expressed his gratitude and retired, Ch'ang Ho ordered his men to take him straight to the dumpling-seller's shop, where he asked to speak with Madam Wang. But Madam Wang was convinced that General Ch'ang had come to carry her off by force, and she hid, panic-stricken, and wouldn't come out at any price. Thereupon Ch'ang Ho took a seat in the shop and ordered his servant to go off and find some old woman of the neighbourhood.

This woman spoke on his behalf: 'General Ch'ang has come today for no other reason than to ask your hand in marriage for the Counsellor Ma.'

On enquiry Madam Wang was told that this 'Counsellor Ma' was none other than Ma Chou: her former dream of the white horse changing into a dragon had today been realized! This was a marriage affinity ordained by heaven, and not to be gainsaid. When Ch'ang Ho discovered that Madam Wang assented to the match he presented her on Ma Chou's behalf with his own Imperial gift of silk, rented a house for Ma Chou's use and selected an auspicious day for the wedding. This, when the day came, was attended by a great crowd of officials who offered their felicitations. Indeed,

> See the poor scholar of beggarly appearance
> Transformed overnight into an honoured guest of the court.

When Madam Wang became the wife of Ma Chou she transferred all her possessions from her house to his, and won the admiration of the entire neighbourhood. We will say no more of this, but rather tell how Ma Chou, from the time of his first meeting with the Emperor, spoke no word but was carefully considered and gave no advice but was followed. Within three years he had risen to be President of the Board of Civil Office, and Madam Wang was ennobled as a lady of the first rank.

The old innkeeper Wang of Hsin-feng learned of Ma Chou's rise to eminence and decided to pay a visit to the capital expressly to see him. On the way he thought he would look up his niece; but on arrival in Long Life Street he found no sign of the dumpling shop, and suspected that she must have moved house. Only after making enquiries of the neighbours did he discover that his niece had been widowed and had married again, her second husband being none other than the President Ma himself. Old Wang's joy knew no bounds. He enquired his way to the President's mansion and gained the presence of Ma Chou and his wife, and the three of them talked over old times together.

Old Wang stayed for over a month, and when he was leaving Ma Chou made him a present of a thousand pieces of gold. He flatly refused to accept the gift, but Ma Chou said, 'My poem must still be there on your wall. How am I to forget the generosity of your gift of food, which was worth a thousand gold pieces to me?'

Only then was Wang induced to accept the gold. He gave thanks and left to return to Hsin-feng, where he now became a member of the wealthy gentry. This was a case of 'offering a melon and receiving a jade', and also of 'rewarding kindness with kindness'.

We will say no more of this, but tell further how the Prefect Ta Hsi had retired to his native place to mourn his parents, proceeding when the three years had elapsed to the capital. But there he heard that Ma Chou had become President of the Board of Civil Office. Conscious of having incurred Ma's disfavour he was too scared to present himself for appointment. But when Ma Chou came to know of this matter he insisted on seeing him. Ta Hsi prostrated himself on the floor, muttering, ' "Though I had eyes I did not recognize Mount T'ai"—I beg you to forgive me.'

Ma Chou hastened to raise him to his feet, and said, 'It was necessary for you to admonish, in order to ensure the dignified behaviour of your charges. The wine-bibbing and wild ranting were my own shortcomings, not yours.'

And forthwith Ma Chou recommended the appointment of Ta Hsi as Metropolitan Prefect; and there was no official in the capital but revered Ma Chou for his magnanimity.

Ma Chou enjoyed wealth and honour for the remainder of his days, and grew old in the company of Madam Wang. A poet of a later age wrote the following in admiration:

The statesman of the age was found among the topers;
Outstanding, also, the dumpling-woman Wang.
But for the rare vision of the men then in power
These bright jewels would have stayed hidden in common dust.

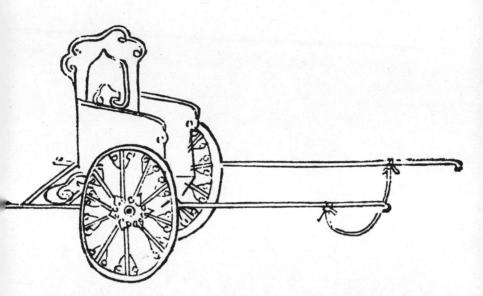

The Journey of the Corpse

THIS story is another 'heroic biography'. It was written probably during the late Ming period in colloquial language and in imitation of the prompt-book manner. Its material throughout was taken from a much earlier story, *The Story of Wu Pao-an*, which is a fair example of the T'ang classical-style short story. The writer of this was a man named Niu Su, active about the year 804. I have translated both these pieces because I believe that the comparison of them illustrates some of the developments which had taken place by late Ming times in the art of fiction.

Both stories follow faithfully the factual version of Wu Pao-an's life contained in the standard history of the T'ang period. The authenticity of the main facts is beyond question. But, interestingly enough, in four matters the fictional versions make identical innovations on the standard biography: obviously, the author of *The Journey of the Corpse* had *The Story of Wu Pao-an* firmly in mind as he wrote. In both stories, Wu Pao-an writes a letter to Kuo Chung-hsiang instead of going in person to see him; and the nailing of Kuo's feet, the marking of Wu Pao-an's bones on their disinterment, and Kuo's attempt to present Yang An-chü with ten barbarian girls are all elements which are not to be found in the standard biography.

The language of *The Journey of the Corpse* presents a mixture of archaic and modern. Archaisms, often in the form of phrases and whole sentences lifted verbatim from the T'ang story, give a 'period' effect to documents and dialogue. In the T'ang story, letters provide the author with an opportunity for stylistic virtuosity. The same does not apply to *The Journey of the Corpse*; but the writer of this, no doubt under the influence of his T'ang predecessor, does indulge towards the end in a lengthy and quite unnecessary memorial to the throne, full of high-sounding phrases.

The late Ming story shows several advances in the art of story-telling. When occasion offers there is vivid and realistic descriptive narrative, especially in the battle scenes. The construction is much improved: Wu Pao-an is introduced at a more fitting point, as is also the account of Kuo Chung-hsiang's sufferings in captivity. Finally, more attention is paid to the delineation of character, and to the assessment of the effects of the action on the minor personages concerned. This is particularly the case with Wu Pao-an's wife and son.

The Story of Wu Pao-an

by Niu Su of the T'ang dynasty

WU PAO-AN was styled Yung-ku. He was from Hopei, and held office as Captain of the *fang-yi* Guard at Suichou. A man from the same district as himself, Kuo Chung-hsiang, was the nephew of the Prime Minister Kuo Yüan-chen. Chung-hsiang was a man of talent and learning, and Yüan-chen was seeking to instal him in an official position of suitable eminence. It was a time of insurrections by the barbarians of the south, and Li Meng was appointed Military Governor at Yaochou and put at the head of an army to suppress them. On the eve of his departure, Meng went to take leave of Yüan-chen, who, catching sight of his nephew, spoke of him to Meng: 'This youth,' he said, 'is the orphan son of my younger brother, and he has not yet been given a position of eminence. You are leaving us for a while. Since you are now to prove your worth by crushing the rebels, and play your part in the affairs of the state, perhaps you would take him under your wing, so that he may receive some trifling salary.' Meng gave his assent to this. Chung-hsiang was a capable man, and so Meng made him his aide and entrusted him with military matters.

When they reached Shu (modern Szechuan), Chung-hsiang received a letter from Wu Pao-an which ran as follows: 'To my great good fortune, we share the same native place, and your renown for wise counsel is well known to me. Although, through gross neglect, I have omitted to prostrate myself before you, my heart has always been filled with admiration and respect. You are the nephew of the Prime Minister, and have made use of your outstanding talents in his service. In consequence of this, your high ability has been rewarded with a commission. General Li is highly-qualified both as a civil and as a military official, and has been put in full command of the expedition. In his hands he unites mighty forces, and he cannot fail to bring these petty brigands to order. By the alliance of the General's heroic valour and your own talent and ability, your armies' task of subjugation will be but the work of a day. I, in my youth, devoted myself to study. Reaching manhood, I paid close attention to the classics. But in talent I do not compare with other men, and so far I have held office only as an officer of the guard. I languish in this out-of-the-way corner beyond the Chien,[1] close to the haunts of the barbarians. My native place is thousands of miles away, and many passes and rivers lie between. What is more, my term of office here is completed, and I cannot tell when I shall receive my next appointment. So lacking in talent, I fear I am but poorly fitted to be selected for an official post ; far less can I entertain the hope of some meagre salary. I can only retire, when old age comes, to some quiet rustic retreat, and "turn aside to die in a ditch". I have heard by devious ways of your readiness to help those in distress. If you will not overlook a man from your native place, be quick to bestow your special favour on me, so that I may render you service "as a humble groom". Grant me some small salary, and a share however slight in your deeds of merit. If by your boundless favour I could take part in this triumphal progress, even as a member of the rearmost company, the day would live engraved on my memory. I do not dare to hope, but my longings lead me to such imaginings. I beg you to take notice only of the sincerity of my thoughts and to forgive their disorder. I spur on my jaded horse in anticipation of arriving in your presence.'

Chung-hsiang was deeply moved by the letter. He mentioned the matter at once to General Li, who summoned Wu Pao-an to join him as a secretary. But before Wu's arrival, the rebel barbarians launched fresh attacks. Reaching Yaochou, General Li fought a battle with the barbarian forces and crushed them. Following up the victory, he drove deep into enemy territory, but the rebels turned and defeated him. Li himself died and his armies were lost, and Chung-hsiang was taken prisoner.

The barbarians had found a way to profit from the wealth of the Chinese : those who fell into their hands sent messages to their families to ransom them. The ransom for each man was thirty rolls of cloth.

Wu Pao-an, having reached Yaochou just as the news came through of the loss of the armies, had lingered on there for a

while instead of going back, and Chung-hsiang, in distress in the
midst of the barbarians, sent the following letter to Pao-an: 'I
trust that you are in good health, Yung-ku. I was filled with shame
that I had not replied to your letter, and now the great legions
have been led forth, they have penetrated deep into the home of
the rebels, and in the end have suffered utter rout. General Li
died in battle, and I am a prisoner. Here, at the border of the
sky and in the earth's most distant corner, I borrow a moment's
breath and steal a second's life. I grieve that this life is over for
me, I pine for my far-off home. My talents pale beside those of
Chung Yi,[2] and thus I remain in fetters. My name is not Chi
Tzu,[3] and so each new day sees me still a slave. My position is
that of Su Wu,[4] tending sheep by the seashore; but I long to be
like Li Ling,[5] shooting wild geese at the palace. Since I fell into
the barbarians' trap, I have suffered hardship and misery. My
flesh has been scraped from my bones, full pools are made of my
blood and tears. Of the greatest hardships that could befall a man,
my body has suffered all. Scion of a family honoured in China
through generations, I am become a poor captive at the ends of
the earth. "O sun, O moon, waxing and waning, summer
declines and winter comes on." As I brood on bygone days with
my kinsmen in the old places, as I strain my gaze towards the
pines and catalpas about the graves of my forefathers, a sudden
madness assails me, I fail to restrain my grief, and without
knowing it I weep over my impotence. If you were to come across
me in the street, how you should be moved to pity! Although you
and I have never entertained one another, you are an elder of my
own village, we are men of like ways, and the longing to see your
face never leaves my dreams. The other day you made a request
of me, which I fear was of no avail. After receiving your letter, I
found the opportunity to put in a word for you. General Li had
long been aware of your reputation as a man of talent, and so he
invited you to join him as a secretary. But the great armies
advanced too fast for you to reach us in time. It was not that I
left you to languish in your rustic retreat, but that you were
prevented from reaching your post until the battle had been
fought. But great joy fills your house to overflowing, as the good
deeds of a lifetime bring down on you the blessing of Heaven.
Although you were unable to enter on your duties, both rank and

fame are yours in full perfection. If you had already been serving at that time under our banner, joining with me in the work of the staff, by now you too would have been an exile in a land apart, in a plight no different from my own. I find myself now in sore distress, my strength crushed and my resources exhausted. But the practice of the barbarians is to allow those who fall into their hands to be ransomed by their relatives. Because I am the nephew of the Prime Minister and so unlike the common run of men, although at first they demanded a ransom of ten rolls of silk,[6] when the news of my status became more widely known the amount was increased a hundredfold. I must beg you to forward this to my uncle, with an explanatory note of your own, so that in course of time I may be ransomed and return. For the return of my spirit to my body, for these dead bones to put on flesh again, my hopes are centred on you alone. I beg you, do not decline the heavy burden I impose on you today. Should my uncle have left the Court, it may be difficult to pass the news to him. In that case, let me ask you to imitate the men of Sung and, escaping from Father Shih, untie Yi Wu's horse and ride to the ransom of Hua Yüan.[7] The way of salvation was hard even for the ancients. But you have always cherished a high sense of the right and honourable, your moral integrity is clearly manifest, and so I make this request of you with a confident heart. If you should fail to extend your sympathy to me, but curl like a hedge-hog in the face of danger, as would the common sort of man, then living I shall be a captive slave, and dead a ghost to haunt the barbarians. What other hope have I? Noble Wu Pao-an, do not disdain to help me!'

The letter pierced Pao-an to the heart. Kuo Yüan-chen was already dead, and Pao-an made a vow to ransom Chung-hsiang in recompense for the favours he had enjoyed. By selling up his home he obtained two hundred rolls of silk. He left for Ning-yüan, where he stayed for two years without returning home. Trading in goods, he amassed altogether seven hundred rolls of silk, but he was still short of the full ransom. Pao-an had long been living in want. His wife was still in Suichou, for Pao-an, in his eagerness to ransom Chung-hsiang, had cut himself off from his family. Every time he made profit from a transaction, though it was only a foot of cloth or a pint of grain, he would add it to his slowly-accumulated savings. In the end his wife, suffering from hunger and cold, could no longer support herself. Taking with her their little child, she set out on a donkey for Lu-nan to look for the place where Wu Pao-an was living. Food gave out while they were on the road, still hundreds of miles from Yaochou. Wu's wife was at the end of her resources, and wept by the side of the highway, stirring pity in the hearts of passers-by.

It happened at this time that the new Military Governor at Yaochou, Yang An-chü, was on the way to the prefectural city to take up his appointment. Riding by on his post-horse, he saw Wu's wife weeping there, and, wondering, stopped to ask her the reason. 'My husband,' said the woman, 'is Wu Pao-an, Captain of the *fang-yi* Guard at Suichou. His friend was taken prisoner by the barbarians, and begged my husband to ransom him back. So my husband went to live in Yaochou and cast us aside, wife and child. We have had no word from him for ten years. I was in bitter poverty, and set out in search of Pao-an. But food is scarce and the road is long, and so I weep in my misery.'

Filled with amazement by her words, An-chü said to her, 'I will go on to the posting-house, and wait for you there, so that I can help you with the things you need.'

When Wu Pao-an's wife reached the posting house, An-chü gave her several thousand cash, and provided her with a carriage to continue her journey. He himself rode on to the prefectural city, where first of all he found out the whereabouts of Wu Pao-an and summoned him for interview. He took Pao-an by the hand and led him to the hall of audience, where he said to him, 'I have often read the works of the ancients and observed how they conducted their affairs, but I did not expect to see in these days, with my own eyes, such things as you have done. How deep your sense of duty, that you should go to such lengths, setting so little store by wife and child, and giving up your home to seek to ransom a friend. Since I met your wife, my thoughts have been all of your high honour, and my heart full of eager longing to see your face. Having only now arrived here, I have nothing with which to help you, but I will borrow four hundred rolls of government silk from the treasury to relieve your need. After your friend has come back, I shall be able to return it a little at a time.'

Pao-an, overjoyed, took the silk and sent off one of those who acted as messengers to the barbarians, on this special mission. After two hundred days, Chung-hsiang reached Yaochou. His appearance was haggard and hardly that of a man. This was his first meeting with Pao-an, and their tears fell as they talked. Yang An-chü had formerly been in the service of the Minister Kuo, and so, when he had arranged a bath for Chung-hsiang and given him clothes to wear, he feasted and entertained him, sitting by his side. An-chü held Wu Pao-an in high esteem for the way he had acted, and showed him many favours. In due course, he arranged for Chung-hsiang to take office as a junior officer of the guard. Chung-hsiang, who had spent long years amongst the barbarians, was well acquainted with their ways of entertaining themselves. So he sent men to their hideouts to buy ten beautiful girls. When they had arrived, Chung-hsiang presented them to Yang An-chü before taking leave of him to return to the north. An-chü declined them with the words, 'I am not a tradesman, that I should expect a return for what I do! Out of respect for Wu's strong sense of duty, I did no more than make it possible for him to achieve his object. Moreover, you have still kinsmen in the north whom it is your duty to provide with good things.'

'My return,' said Chung-hsiang, wishing to express his gratitude, 'is due to your bounty, my continued existence is a gift from you. Even in death I shall not dare to forget your noble deed. It was for you that I had these barbarian girls brought here, and I would rather die than have you refuse them now.'

An-chü found it hard to resist such pleading, and chancing to see his small daughter just then, he said, 'Since you speak with such insistence, I dare not decline this kindness. This daughter of mine is very young, and I dote on her. So I will accept just one of your girls for her.' And he declined the other nine. Pao-an received substantial gifts from Yang, and went away loaded with goods.

When Chung-hsiang arrived home, he had been away from his family for fully fifteen years. He left again for the capital, where his merit was rewarded with the post of Staff Officer in the Records Department at Weichou. Rejoined by his family, he proceeded to his post. Two years later, he was transferred to Taichou as Staff Officer in the Revenue Department. At the end of his term of office there, his wife died. After the funeral, he observed the mourning rites by the side of her grave. This done, he said to himself, 'It was through Wu Pao-an that I was ransomed, and thus enabled to hold office and support my family. Now that my parents and my wife are dead and my duties are over, I can fulfil my desire.' Thereupon he set out to look for Wu Pao-an.

From his post with the *fang-yi* Guard, Wu Pao-an had been selected for the position of assistant magistrate at P'eng-shan, Meichou, and so Chung-hsiang travelled to Shu to enquire after him. Pao-an, his term of office completed, had been unable to return home. Both he and his wife had died where they were, and had received temporary burial in a monastery. When Chung-hsiang heard this news, he wept in bitter grief. He put on the sackcloth of mourning, and with a girdle of white hemp about his waist and a staff in his hand, he set out barefoot from the provincial city of Shu, weeping incessantly as he went along. When he came to P'eng-shan, he made sacrifice and poured out a libation. Then he disinterred the bones of Wu Pao-an, marking each with ink, and wrapped them in a bag of coarse cloth. He disinterred the bones of Wu's wife also, marking them in the same way. He placed the bags in a basket of bamboo, which he took up on his own back, and then, barefoot, he walked the distance of many hundreds of miles to Wei-chün.

Pao-an left an only son, whom Chung-hsiang cared for like a brother. Then Chung-hsiang spent his whole fortune, two hundred thousand taels, in giving Wu Pao-an a magnificent burial, and had a stone engraved in his honour. He built a hut by the grave-side, where he lived for a three-years' mourning. At the end of this period, he was made Records Officer at Lanchou and given the honorary rank of *ch'ao-san tai-fu*. When he went to take up his duties he took Pao-an's son with him. He found a wife for the boy and continued to treat him with the utmost kindness. There was no end to Chung-hsiang's efforts to pay off his debt of gratitude to Wu Pao-an. In the twelfth year of the T'ien-pao reign-period (753), he went into retirement and relinquished his red sash and his official position to Pao-an's son, again by way of recompense. He stood high in the regard of his contemporaries for these things.

When he was captured by the barbarians, Chung-hsiang had at first been given to their chief as a slave. His master grew fond of him, and gave him the same things to eat and drink as he had himself. But with the passing years, Chung-hsiang grew homesick for the north, and attempted to escape and return there. He was pursued and recaptured, and re-sold to a cave further south. The chief of this was cruel and vicious. When he obtained Chung-hsiang he gave him the hardest of tasks to perform, and floggings with whip or bamboo were frequent. Again Chung-hsiang ran away, and again he was hunted down. He was sold once more, this time to one of the hideouts in the south whose inhabitants are known as P'u-sa Man. He spent years there, until hardship and distress forced him to make yet another escape. Again the barbarians pursued him, and again he was recaptured. He was sold to yet another hideout. The chief, when Chung-hsiang was brought to him, said angrily, 'So this is a slave who is fond of running away, and hard to keep in captivity?' Then he took two boards, each several feet in length, and ordered Chung-hsiang to stand on them. He drove nails through the top of his feet and into the wood. Every time Chung-hsiang had a task to perform he had to move about with the two boards nailed beneath his feet. At night he was forced into a barred underground cell, and fetters were put on his body. It was only after many years had passed that the sores on his feet healed up. The boards and the fetters and the underground cell he endured for seven years, and at the beginning the agony was almost more than he could bear. When Wu Pao-an sent messengers with his ransom, they went first to Chung-hsiang's original overlord. From there they were sent to the other places in turn, until they found him, and thus Chung-hsiang was able to return.

THE JOURNEY OF THE CORPSE

Friendship, for the ancients, was a contract between hearts;
For the men of today, the contract is between faces.
With hearts united, men will live and die together;
Friends of the surface will not share each other's poverty.
The highways every day are thronged with riders,
Time sets no end to the pursuing and detaining, the escorting and
visiting.
The liberal host brings out his family for the guest to see,
While the wine goes round, the friends salute as brothers.
But whisper 'profit', and friendship turns to loathing:
How then will they behave in the hour of peril?
Now consider Yang and Tso,[8] friends until death of former days,
Even yet they hold a high place in our annals.

THE name of this poem is 'The Conduct of Friendship'. It laments the meanness of men's hearts in these latter days, and the difficulty of forming a true friendship. In normal times, when the wine-cups are passing, we are as brother to brother. But when the slightest matter arises where profit and loss have to be taken into account, then you and I behave as strangers. True it is that though a thousand brothers flock to our table when it is loaded with meat and wine, in adversity we have not one to turn to; or again, there are those who in the morning are as brothers and by evening have become enemies. Putting down their wine-cups, they go out and face each other with drawn bows. For this reason, T'ao Yüan-ming [9] desired seclusion from the world; Chi Shu-yeh [10] wished to sever his friendships; Liu Hsiao-piao wrote his essay 'On Cutting off All Acquaintance'. These men deplored the behaviour of society, and expressed themselves in angry words.

The two friends I am now going to tell you about had never once seen each other. But because of their loyalty of spirit, when great distress came upon them they went to each other's help in

129

life and in death. Only such a friendship as theirs can be called a
friendship of true hearts. Truly it was

> *As when Kung Yü flipped the dust from his cap* [11]
> *Or when Ching K'o's courage failed.*[12]

It is said that at one time during the K'ai-yüan reign-period
(713–742) of the great T'ang dynasty, the office of Prime Minister
was held by Kuo Chen, who was styled Yüan-chen and held the
title of Duke Tai-kuo. He was a man of Wu-yang in Hopei. His
nephew, Kuo Chung-hsiang, was a man gifted in both civil and
military matters. But he had always been high-spirited and
independent, refusing to be bound by convention, and so no one
had seen fit to recommend him for office. His father, seeing him
grown to manhood without having achieved anything, sent him
with a letter of introduction to pay his respects to his uncle in
the capital, and enlist his uncle's help in entering on a career.

Yüan-chen spoke to him as follows : 'The man of worth is not
content to have high rank thrust upon him. To reach the top,
to set your feet above the stars, you must do as Pan Ch'ao and
Fu Chieh-tzu [13] did : establish your merit in a distant place, to
attain wealth and renown. Rely merely on your position in
society as a stepping-stone, and how far do you think you will
get?'

Chung-hsiang expressed his agreement. Now just at this time,
reports from the frontier were reaching the capital, bringing
news of insurrections by the cave-barbarians of the south. What
had happened was that when the Empress Wu Tse-t'ien [14]
assumed power, her policy was to bribe her subjects into submission. These barbarians of the 'Nine Creeks and Eighteen
Caves' were given a small bounty each year, and every third year
a larger one. When the Emperor Hsüan-tsung (713–756) ascended
the throne he put a stop to this system, and it was in consequence
of this that the barbarian hordes at once rebelled, invading and
pillaging wide areas. The Emperor appointed Li Meng Military
Governor at Yaochou, and moved troops there to suppress them.

After receiving the Imperial decree, and on the eve of his
departure, Li Meng paid a special visit of leave-taking to the
mansion of the Prime Minister, and requested instructions. Kuo
Yüan-chen said, 'When the noble Chu-ko Liang, of former days,

seven times seized Meng Huo,[15] he did it by using his brains, not the strength of his arm. If you, General, exercise due care in carrying out this commission, victory must be yours. My nephew, Kuo Chung-hsiang, is a man of some ability. I am sending him with you on this expedition, so that when in due course you have proved your worth by crushing the rebels, he may advance himself with your aid, "like a fly on the tail of a horse".'

Then he called for Chung-hsiang and presented him to Li Meng. Li noted the youth's distinguished appearance; moreover, he was the nephew of the Prime Minister, from whose own lips the command had come; he did not therefore dare to decline. And so Chung-hsiang was at once commissioned as aide on active service. He took leave of his uncle, and set out in the train of Li Meng. They reached the region south of the Chien.

In this region there was a man from the same district as Kuo Chung-hsiang. This man's surname was Wu, his personal name Pao-an, and his courtesy-name Yung-ku. He held office as Captain of the *fang-yi* Guard at Suichou in the East River district.[16] Though he had never met Kuo Chung-hsiang, he had long known of him as a man of high integrity, one ready to assist and advance his fellows. So he composed a letter and despatched it by special courier to Chung-hsiang. Chung-hsiang opened the letter and read the contents: 'I, Wu Pao-an, am unworthy to address you. But to my great good fortune I was born in the same district as your noble self. Although I have omitted to come to prostrate myself before you, I have long regarded you with admiration and respect. Now that you, with your great talents, are helping General Li to bring these petty brigands to order, your task will be but the work of a day. I have spent many years in arduous study, but hold office only as a Captain of the Guard. I languish in this out-of-the-way corner beyond the Chien, my native place as far off as a dream. What is more, my term of office here is completed, and I cannot tell when I shall receive my next appointment. I fear I am but poorly fitted to be selected for an official post. I have heard of your readiness to share the burden of distress and to help those in trouble, in the manner of the ancients. Now, when the great armies are advancing to the suppression of the rebels, is the time when men are needed. Only remember this man from your own native place, grant me some small salary, and let me render you service "as a humble groom", or fill some lowly office in your camp; and I shall never forget your boundless favour.'

Kuo Chung-hsiang pondered over the import of Wu's letter, then said with a sigh, 'Never in my life have I heard of this man, and yet he turns to me at once for help in his emergency: surely he is one who understands me. The man of worth who meets with such a friend and is not ready to exert himself on his account has ample cause for shame.' And so Chung-hsiang extolled Wu's abilities before Li Meng, and begged that he be summoned for duty in their army. The Military Governor agreed, and had orders made out and sent to Suichou, summoning the Captain of the *fang-yi* Guard Wu Pao-an to join him as a secretary.

But no sooner had the messenger been despatched than spies brought in reports that the barbarians in a fresh outburst of violence were attacking the interior. The Military Governor ordered a forced march by night. They reached Yaochou, where they found the barbarian forces engaged in looting and plunder. The barbarians were not bothering about precautions and were taken completely by surprise. They fled in all directions, in no sort of formation. Large numbers were killed, and the rout was complete. General Li's confidence knew no bounds. He rallied his troops, and following up his success pursued the enemy for fully twenty miles. Then, as night drew on, they pitched camp.

Kuo Chung-hsiang began to remonstrate with General Li. 'For cunning and deceit,' he said, 'no one can compare with the barbarians. Now that their forces have been defeated and routed, your prestige is secure. Our best plan is to withdraw to our base, and send men out to make known your might and your virtue. We should send envoys into enemy territory, but not venture too far ourselves, for fear of being trapped by some cunning ruse.'

But Li Meng shouted back, 'The barbarian hordes have lost heart. If we don't seize our chance now and clear them from these creeks and caves, when shall we be able to do so? Say no more; just watch how I shall crush these rebels.'

The following day they struck camp and started out again. After a march of several days they reached the region of the Black Barbarians. Range upon range of mountains folded in upon them, dense woods and undergrowth covered all, and no one could tell where the road lay. Grave anxieties began to spring up in Li Meng's mind, and he ordered a temporary retreat to the plain. There they could pitch camp, and meanwhile find natives of the place to give them directions.

Then suddenly, all round them, gongs and drums began to clamour amid the mountains and the valleys. The wild country was full of barbarian warriors, they swarmed down every mountain-side. Their chief, Meng Hsi-nu-lo, held in his hands a bow of wood and poisoned arrows, and of a hundred that he loosed a hundred hit the mark. He urged on the headmen from every cave, through the forests and over the ranges. They came on like birds in flight or like wild beasts in motion, seemingly without effort. The troops of T'ang were caught in their ambush. In unknown country, and with their strength at an end, they could offer no resistance. The Military Governor was a valiant man, but even a hero is lost without room to use his weapons. Observing that there were few left alive of the men under him, he said with a sigh, 'I did wrong to ignore the words of the aide, Kuo Chung-hsiang, and so to suffer disgrace from such dogs and sheep as these.' Then Li Meng drew from his boot a short dagger, and piercing his throat with it took his own life. The greater part of the army perished at the hands of the barbarians. In later days this poem was composed, describing the event:

Bearing Ma Yüan's post of brass [17] to be a landmark for all ages,
Flying the banner of Chu-ko Liang they set out for the Nine
    Creeks.
What was it caused the forces of T'ang to perish in defeat?
The ill fortune of the man named Li, their General.

Another poem censures the Military Governor Li for ignoring the words of Kuo Chung-hsiang, and so bringing defeat upon himself:

It was not that the General was ill-fated:
The army hesitated to advance, but rashly he ignored the danger.
Had he but listened then to the plan of retreat,
Who of the barbarian hordes would have dared to show himself?

As for Kuo Chung-hsiang, he was taken prisoner. Hsi-nu-lo,

observing how his refined appearance differed from that of ordinary men, questioned him about himself. When he discovered that Kuo Chung-hsiang was the nephew of Kuo Yüan-chen, he gave him into the charge of Wu Lo, the headman of his own cave. For in reality the southern barbarians had never entertained any very high ambitions, but were simply covetous of the wealth of China. When they took Chinese prisoners, the headmen of the various caves shared them out, those whose achievements had been the greatest taking a proportionately larger share of prisoners. When they were apportioning the prisoners, they did not distinguish the men of worth from the stupid and ignorant, but treated all alike as slaves, to run errands for them, chop wood and cut grass, feed the horses and tend the sheep. If there were a good number of these slaves, they would be traded between one master and another. Of the Chinese taken by the barbarians, nine out of ten had no wish to live, but wanted only to die. But the barbarians kept watch over them, so that even if they wanted to die they could not. They suffered hardships of every possible kind. A large number of Chinese were taken prisoner after this *débâcle*, and many of them were men of rank. The barbarians interrogated them one by one, and allowed them to send messages back to China requesting their relatives to send ransoms for them. By this means the barbarians could make a fat profit. And how many of the prisoners do you think there were who did not long to go back home? When they heard the barbarians' offer they all, whether of rich family or poor, sent off letters to their homes. If a man was without kith or kin, there was nothing he could do, and that was an end of it. But if he had relatives to turn to, what family was not prepared to borrow money, a little here and a little there, to make up the ransom? These barbarians were both covetous and hard-hearted. Let a man be as poor as you like, and alone in this world, they would still demand thirty rolls of good cloth before they would let him go back. For a man of higher station they would demand a good deal more.

When Wu Lo heard that Kuo Chung-hsiang was the nephew of the Prime Minister of the day, he raised the price of his ransom to one thousand rolls of silk. Chung-hsiang thought to himself, 'If it is a thousand rolls of silk that they want, there is only my uncle who could raise such an amount. But he is far away beyond the mountains. How can I get a message to him?' Then suddenly the thought occurred to him, 'There is Wu Pao-an, a true friend who understands me. I had never met him face to face, but on the strength of a few lines he wrote me, I commended him strongly to the Military Governor, Li Meng, who summoned him to his side as a secretary. He cannot fail to take account of my efforts on his behalf. Fortunately he set out too late to be involved in this disaster. By now he must have reached Yaochou. Surely it would be no trouble to send a message for me to Ch'ang-an.'

So he composed a letter to Pao-an, in which he described all the hardships he was suffering, and gave details of the price Wu Lo was demanding for his ransom. If Yung-ku would not turn aside from him, but would pass on the message to his uncle, then he might soon be ransomed and return even yet to the land of the living. Otherwise, living he would be a captive slave, and dead a ghost to haunt the barbarians. And could Yung-ku, he asked, suffer this to happen? (Yung-ku was the courtesy name of Wu Pao-an.) Chung-hsiang concluded the letter with this poem:

> *Like Chi Tzu I am a slave, but in a strange land,*
> *Like Su Wu I suffer hardship, but in my early youth.*
> *I know that you are a righteous man, and will grieve for me.*
> *I long to put away my saddle and study the ancient sages.*

When Chung-hsiang had finished the letter, it so happened that one of the officials in charge of the issue of grain at Yaochou had just been ransomed and released, and Chung-hsiang took the opportunity to send the letter by him. With anxious eyes he watched the man go. As he grieved that he himself could not spread his wings and fly off, a thousand arrows seemed to pierce his heart, and without his realizing it his tears fell like rain. Indeed,

> *He watched with his eyes another bird soar away,*
> *But he was locked in a cage—how could he escape?*

We will say no more for a while of Kuo Chung-hsiang in the hands of the barbarians, but go on to describe how Wu Pao-an, when he received the summons from the Military Governor, Li Meng, realized that he had been recommended by Kuo. He left in Suichou his wife, Madam Chang, and their newly-born child, not yet a year old. With just one servant he set out in great haste, and hurried to Yaochou to take up his duties. When he heard the news of Li Meng's death in battle, he was startled. He had no means of knowing whether Chung-hsiang were alive or dead, and could only stay on where he was to await news. It was at this point that the grain official was released from the land of the barbarians, bringing back with him the letter from Chung-hsiang. Grief overcame Wu Pao-an as he opened and read the letter. He wrote a letter in reply, promising to secure Chung-hsiang's ransom, and left it with the grain official, asking him to despatch it to the barbarians when the occasion arose, so that Chung-hsiang might have some consolation. Then he hurriedly packed his baggage and set out for Ch'ang-an. From Yaochou to Ch'ang-an is more than a thousand miles, but the East River provides a good route. Pao-an did not call at his home but went straight to the capital, where he sought an interview with the Prime Minister Kuo Yüan-chen. But who would have thought that a month previously Yüan-chen had passed away? The members of his family had all left to escort the coffin back to his native place.

Wu Pao-an fell into despair. He had no money left to meet the expenses of the road, and was compelled to sell his servant and his horse to bring in something for his needs. He turned round and went back to Suichou. When he came to his wife, he wept aloud. She asked him the reason, and in reply he told her of Kuo Chung-hsiang's captivity in the south. 'I myself,' he said, 'must now go there and ransom him. I know I have not the means to do it, but if I were to leave him there in such distressful surroundings, anxiously hoping for release, what peace of mind could I find?'

When he had finished speaking he began again to weep, and his wife urged him to dry his tears: 'They say "even the cleverest wife can't cook without rice". You haven't the means to do what your heart desires. There is nothing for it but to turn to someone else.'

Pao-an shook his head: 'Simply because of a letter I sent him, the noble Kuo at once did me the great kindness of recommending me for a high post. And now he is on the borderline between life and death, and has put his life into my hands. How could I bear to turn my back on him? If I cannot secure Kuo's return, I swear I shall not live on alone.'

And thereupon Wu Pao-an sold up his home and everything in it. But when all was reckoned up, it had brought no more than two hundred rolls of silk. So he left his wife and took to the road as a merchant. In case some message should shortly come from the barbarians, he stayed close by Yaochou carrying on his business. He travelled about from dawn to dusk, hurrying and scurrying in every direction. He dressed in rags and ate the coarsest food. He took care not to waste a single cash or a grain of corn, but scraped and saved all he could to buy silk. When he had got one roll he set his eyes on ten, and when he had got ten he set his eyes on a hundred. Then when he had a full hundred rolls he deposited them in the treasury at Yaochou. In his sleep and in his dreams his thoughts were full of the one name Kuo Chung-hsiang. Even his wife was forgotten. In all he spent ten years away from home, and in this time he amassed seven hundred rolls of silk, still short of the thousand rolls required. Indeed,

A thousand miles from home, adding coin to coin,
So strong his sense of duty to a comrade.
Ten years, and still the barbarians wait to be paid—
How long before his friend can find release?

Our story forks at this point, and we go on to describe how Wu Pao-an's wife, Madam Chang, lived on lonely and sad in Suichou together with their little child. At first there were still some who, out of regard for Wu's position as Captain of the Guard, would help them with small presents. But as the years passed without any news of Wu Pao-an people ceased to pay any attention to them. And since there were no family savings to draw on, after ten years and more their clothes wore thin and food was short, a thousand gathering hardships assailed them. The only thing Madam Chang could do was sell off one after another her old bits of furniture to provide funds for the journey, and then, leading her ten-year-old child and asking the way as she went, make for Yaochou to seek out her husband Wu Pao-an. She rested at night and took the road again at dawn, covering only ten or a dozen miles in a day. By the time she reached the neighbourhood of Jungchou, her funds were exhausted and she was at her wits' end. She thought of begging her way onwards, but was ashamed of such an unfamiliar course. She began to think that death would be preferable to such a misfortune as hers; but gazing on the child of ten she felt she could not leave him. She cast back and forth in her mind. Gradually evening drew on, and she sat down at the foot of the mountain Wu-meng and burst into tears.

The sound of her weeping startled an official who happened to be passing. This official's name was Yang An-chü, and he was the new Military Governor at Yaochou, filling the post which had once been Li Meng's. He was on his way by post-stage from Ch'ang-an to his new place of office, when passing the foot of the mountain Wu-meng he heard this sound of bitter weeping. Seeing moreover that it was a lady, he halted his carriage and called her across to question her. Madam Chang, her hands supporting her ten-year-old son, came forward and told her sad story: 'I, sir, am the wife of Wu Pao-an, Captain of the *fang-yi* Guard at Suichou. This child is my son. My husband is trying to amass a thousand rolls of silk so that he may ransom his friend, Kuo Chung-hsiang, who was taken prisoner by the barbarians. He cast us aside, wife and child, and has long been living in Yaochou. We have had no word from him for ten years. I was in bitter poverty and helpless, and set out myself in search of him. But food is at an end and the road is long, and so I weep in my misery.'

An-chü said to himself, marvelling at this story, 'There is a real man of honour. How I regret that I was not predestined to be his friend!' Then he said to Madam Chang, 'Lady, do not distress yourself. Though unworthy I have been appointed Military Governor at Yaochou. When I reach there I will send men out to look for your husband. I will myself provide for your expenses on your journey. Please continue to the next posting-house, where I will arrange lodging for you.'

Madam Chang restrained her tears and respectfully expressed her gratitude. But even so her heart was still full of misgivings. The carriage of the Military Governor Yang went off as if winged. Madam Chang and her son, each helping the other along, made their way step by step to the posting-house. Yang had already ordered the officer in command to care for them, and this man, when he had questioned them, showed them to a vacant room where a meal awaited them. At the fifth watch on the following day the Military Governor had his carriage made ready and started off before them. The officer of the posting-house, acting on Yang's instructions, gave them ten thousand cash as travelling expenses, prepared a carriage for them and detailed some of his men to escort them to Yaochou, where they were installed in the P'u-p'eng posting-house. There was no end to the gratitude in Madam Chang's heart. Indeed.

The good will meet with help from the good,
The wicked will suffer oppression from the wicked.

To continue, as soon as Yang An-chü arrived in Yaochou he sent men out in every direction to seek out the whereabouts of Wu Pao-an, and before three or four days had elapsed they had found him. An-chü invited him to his official residence. He descended the steps to receive him, took his hand in his own and led him up to the hall of audience with kind expressions of consolation. Then he spoke to Pao-an as follows: 'I have often heard how the friendships of the ancients endured through life and death; now at last, in you, I see for myself a man capable of such a friendship. Your noble wife and son have come a great distance to seek you, and are lodging now in the posting-house. You must go to them, sir, and exchange accounts of your ten-year separation. I will take care of the rolls of silk that you still need.'

'The efforts I am making,' replied Pao-an, 'are surely no more than my duty to my friend dictates. How then, noble sir, should I presume to involve you in them?'

'I respect your integrity and merely wish to help you fulfil your ambition,' said An-chü.

At this Pao-an kotowed and said, 'Since, noble sir, you shower your high favours upon me, I dare not persist in declining. I still lack one-third of my total. If I could get the whole sum at once, I could go myself to the barbarians and ransom my friend, and it would not be too late to visit my wife and child afterwards.'

Yang An-chü was newly arrived at his post, and so he was obliged to borrow four hundred rolls of government silk from the treasury. These he presented to Wu Pao-an, together with a horse, saddled and harnessed. In great joy, Pao-an collected the four hundred rolls, which together with the seven hundred he had already stored in the treasury made a total of one thousand one hundred rolls, and rode out into the territory of the southern barbarians. There he found a friendly barbarian to take a message for him to the enemy, and to this man he gave the whole of the one hundred rolls of silk he had over, for his use. If only he could bring about the return of Chung-hsiang, his heart and mind would be filled with contentment. Indeed,

> *To see his face on his timely return—*
> *Far better than all the gold of Yüeh-yang.*

We will now tell how Kuo Chung-hsiang lived under the dominion of Wu Lo. At first Wu Lo, expecting a high price for his ransom, treated him very well, and he lacked nothing to eat or drink. But when a year and more had passed without any messenger from China coming to discuss the matter, Wu Lo was displeased. He cut down Kuo's food to one meal a day, and set him to tending the elephants used in warfare. Chung-hsiang could not endure this life, and ardent thoughts of home possessed him. One day when Wu Lo was out hunting, he seized his opportunity and escaped, making towards the north. The only roads in the land of the barbarians were precipitous mountain paths, and after Chung-hsiang had walked for a day and a night the soles of his feet were torn to shreds. He was pursued by a company of barbarians, elephant-herdsmen, who sped along as if winged, and caught him and took him back. Wu Lo, greatly angered, resold him to Hsin Ting, the chief of a cave seventy miles to the south, as a slave. This Hsin Ting was a very cruel man. If Chung-hsiang's work displeased him in the slightest, he was flogged a hundred strokes with leather thongs until his back was all black and swollen; and this happened more than once. Chung-hsiang could not bear this misery, and seizing his chance when his guards were absent made a fresh attempt to escape. But he did not know the way, and merely wandered in circles in the hollows of the hills. Again he was pursued and recaptured, this time by the barbarians of that region, who took him back to Hsin Ting. Hsin Ting would not keep him any longer, and resold him to a cave still further south. With every move Chung-hsiang was being taken further from his countrymen.

The chief of this new cave was one of the P'u-sa Man. He was worse than ever. When he found out that Chung-hsiang had made repeated attempts to escape, he took two boards, each five or six feet in length and three or four inches thick, and made Chung-hsiang stand with one foot on each board. He drove iron nails through the top of his feet right into the boards. Every day he moved about with the boards nailed beneath his feet. At night he was thrust into a pit in the ground which was then closed up with a door of thick boards. The barbarians of the cave guarded him by sleeping on top of the boards. He could not make the slightest move to get away. From time to time the places on his feet where the nails had entered suppurated with blood and pus. Clearly, it was like the tortures of hell, and there is a poem in evidence:

> Sold to the barbarians of the south, farther and farther south he goes,
> Loaded with chains and wooden boards, caged in a pit, in agony,
> For ten long years no message comes from the Central Plain,
> He yearns for some sign from his trusted friend but dare not open his mouth.

We go on to describe how the friendly barbarian, following the instructions of Wu Pao-an, came into the presence of Wu Lo and informed him of the attempt to ransom Kuo Chung-hsiang. When Wu Lo discovered that the full thousand rolls of silk were ready, his delight knew no bounds. He sent messengers to the cave in the south to buy back Chung-hsiang. The chief of this cave, who was Hsin Ting, directed them on to the cave of the P'u-sa Man. They handed over the amount asked for him, and with pincers pulled out the nails which fastened Kuo Chung-hsiang's feet to the boards. These nails had been in Kuo's flesh for a long time, and after the pus had dried up it was almost as though they had grown there naturally. So that now, when they were pulled out again, the pain was even harder to bear than when first the nails had been driven in. Blood flowed everywhere. Chung-hsiang at once fainted away, and it was a long time before he recovered consciousness. He could scarcely move an inch, and all they could do was wrap him in a leather sack and let two of the barbarians carry it slung from a pole between them. In this manner they brought him to the tent of Wu Lo. The latter took the rolls of silk in payment and then, caring little whether he were alive or dead, handed over Chung-hsiang to the friendly barbarian, who escorted him back to Wu Pao-an.

Pao-an received him as though he were of his own flesh and blood. The two friends now came face to face for the first time. Before he could find anything to say, each gazed at the other with eyes wide open, and then they embraced and wept, convinced that this was a meeting in a dream. The depth of Chung-hsiang's gratitude to Wu Pao-an does not need to be described. Pao-an was filled wjth grief to see how haggard was Chung-hsiang's appearance: he seemed half man, half ghost, and his feet had lost the power to move. Pao-an gave up his horse for Kuo to ride, and, himself following on foot, together they entered the gate of Yaochou and reported to the Military Governor Yang.

Now as it happened, Yang An-chü had in the past worked as a private secretary in the yamen of Kuo Yüan-chen, so that although he had never actually met Chung-hsiang, he had some connection with the family. Moreover, he was an upright man and a gentleman, and not one whose regard for others ceases with their death. As soon as he set eyes on Chung-hsiang his delight knew no bounds. He arranged a bath for him and gave him a change of clothes. Then he ordered the army medical officer to attend to the wounds in his feet. He gave him good things to eat and drink, caring for him and letting him rest. In less than a month Chung-hsiang had recovered his former health.

We go on to tell how Wu Pao-an did not visit the P'u-p'eng posting-house to see his wife and child until after his return from the land of the barbarians. When first he had left them, the child was still in swaddling-clothes, and now he had reached the age of eleven. Time had passed swiftly, and Pao-an could not prevent feelings of distress. Yang An-chü was full of esteem for Pao-an's noble conduct, and frequently sang his praises before others. He also wrote letters to men of authority and influence in Ch'ang-an, describing how Wu had neglected his family to ransom a friend. Then he made Pao-an substantial presents and saw him off to the capital, where office awaited him. All the officials in the district of Yaochou, seeing the Military Governor bestow such favours, themselves gave presents in their turn. As for Kuo Chung-hsiang, he remained with the Military Governor as aide. Pao-an gave him for his use a half-share of the presents everyone had made him. Again and again Chung-hsiang declined, but how was Pao-an to be refused? They simply had to be accepted. Wu Pao-an, having expressed his gratitude to the Military Governor, left with his family for Ch'ang-an. Chung-hsiang escorted him beyond the bounds of Yaochou, and there they parted with tears of sorrow. Pao-an left his family behind in Suichou and went on alone to the capital. There he was promoted to the post of assistant-magistrate at P'eng-shan, Meichou. Meichou was a district in western Shu, and the appointment conveniently allowed him to rejoin his family.

We will not speak of Pao-an as he goes happily off to take up his new duties, but go on to speak of Kuo Chung-hsiang, who having passed such a great length of time among the barbarians was well acquainted with their ways of entertaining themselves. The women of the barbarians were very beautiful, yet they were sold at a lower price than the men. During Chung-hsiang's three years of office, he was continually sending men to the barbarians' caves to buy young and beautiful girls. Altogether he bought ten girls, whom he himself taught to sing and dance to perfection. Then, dressed in new robes and adorned with beautiful ornaments, they were specially presented to Yang An-chü to wait on him, in recompense for his goodness to Chung-hsiang. But An-chü said with a smile, 'I value human life and prize integrity, and therefore simply took pleasure in bringing a good deed to completion. But to speak of repayment—you must not treat me as a tradesman.'

Chung-hsiang replied, 'Noble sir, I owe the restoration of this poor body to your goodness and mercy. I bought these barbarian women on purpose to offer to you as a trifling token of gratitude. If, noble sir, you were to decline them, then in death I should be unable to close my eyes.'

Before such earnest entreaties, An-chü could only say, 'I have a small daughter on whom I dote. If you insist, I will accept one of these girls as a personal slave for her. For the rest, I dare not accept them as you wish.'

So Chung-hsiang distributed the other nine beautiful girls as presents among nine of Yang's most trusted senior officers, in order to make manifest the virtues of their noble commander.

About this time, the Emperor, reflecting on the military achievements of the late Kuo Yüan-chen, Duke Tai-kuo, decided to instal his sons and nephews in the government service. In a memorial to the throne, Yang An-chü spoke of Chung-hsiang, the nephew of the former Prime Minister. He described how Chung-hsiang had foreseen the outcome of Li Meng's campaign against the barbarians, and had warned Li beforehand. Throughout his captivity in the barbarian caves, his virtue had remained untarnished. Only after ten years had passed was he able to return home. Now for three years he had devoted his talents to Yang's service. Since what had been hidden could now be told, it was fitting to reward such merit. As a consequence of this, Kuo Chung-hsiang was appointed Staff Officer in the Records Department at Weichou. Altogether, it was now fifteen years since he had first left his home. There, his father and his wife had learnt of his capture by the barbarians, and hearing no more news of him for so many years had presumed him long-since dead. Then suddenly they received a letter in his own hand; and when he came to join them and take them to his new place of office at Weichou, the whole family was filled with joy. For two years Chung-hsiang held office at Weichou, and great was his fame there. He was then promoted Staff Officer in the Revenue Department and transferred to Taichou, where he spent a further three years. His father then fell ill and soon after died, upon which he escorted the coffin back to Hopei.

One day, when the funeral ceremonies were completed, Chung-hsiang gave a sudden sigh, and said, 'It was through Wu Pao-an that I was ransomed and received an extra span of life. While my father was with me, I worked to support him, and I have had until now no opportunity to make any return to Pao-an for his great kindness. Now that my father is dead and my duties are over, how can I leave my benefactor out of my plans?' On enquiry he learned that Pao-an had not returned from his place of office, and so he went himself to P'eng-shan, Meichou, to visit him. There he heard the unexpected news that Wu Pao-an, his term of office completed, had been too poor to proceed to the capital for re-appointment. He had lived on as best he could at P'eng-shan, but six years previously he had contracted a disease

and died, and his wife with him. They had received crude burial
in waste ground behind the Yellow Dragon Monastery. Their
son, Wu T'ien-yu, had been educated from his earliest years by
his mother, and could read and write. He was earning a living by
teaching beginners in the neighbourhood.

When he heard all this, Chung-hsiang wept endless tears of
remorse. He put on the sackcloth of mourning, and with a girdle
of white hemp about his waist and a staff in his hand, entered the
grounds of the monastery and wailed and mourned before the
grave. With full ceremony he offered sacrifice and poured out a
libation. This done, he sought out Wu T'ien-yu. He took off his
own robes and put them on him, addressing him as his younger
brother, and spoke to him of taking the bodies back to their
native place for burial. He then composed a document announcing this to the spirit of Wu Pao-an. When the mound was opened,
all that remained was two dried skeletons. Chung-hsiang cried
bitterly without ceasing, and of those who stood looking on there
was not one whose eyes remained dry. Chung-hsiang had made
ready two bags of coarse cloth to contain the bones of Pao-an and
his wife. Fearing that the bones might be disarranged, making it
difficult to prepare the remains for reburial, he marked each with
ink. He wrapped them in the bags, placed these in a basket of
bamboo, and set out on foot with the basket on his own back.
Wu T'ien-yu declared that as they were the bones of his own
father and mother it was for him to carry them, and he tried to
take over the basket himself. But Chung-hsiang refused to
relinquish it, saying as his tears fell, 'Yung-ku hastened about
for ten years on my account. Now that I can carry for a while his
bones on my back, it is some slight effort I can make for him.'

Throughout the journey he wept as he walked. Each time they
came to an inn, he would place the basket in the seat of honour
and set out wine and food before it, before he and T'ien-yu ate
their meal. In the same way, at night he would see that the basket
was suitably settled before he himself dared take his rest. From
Meichou to Weichün is many hundreds of miles, and he travelled
the whole distance on foot. Although his feet had recovered from
being nailed to the boards years previously, in fact the veins and
arteries had been damaged, so that when he had walked for
several days together purple swellings arose on his feet, and

within the swellings the pain was intense. He feared he would soon be able to walk no longer; but he was determined not to let the other undertake the task for him, and so he forced himself to bear with the pain and go on. There is a poem in evidence:

Hastening to the burial, his only way of recompense,
With the bones on his back he hurries day and night.
He gazes towards P'ing-yang, hundreds of miles away;
How long before he comes to the native place?

Chung-hsiang, thinking how long was the road before him, pondered what was best to do. As evening fell they found an inn where they could spend the night. Chung-hsiang set food and wine before the basket and then, with tears in his eyes, made repeated prostrations, earnestly and devoutly pleading that Wu Yung-ku and his wife display their divine efficacy, so that with their aid the pain in his feet might be wiped away. Thus he might walk with ease and soon reach Wu-yang to perform the burial. By his side Wu T'ien-yu also prostrated himself again and again in prayer. On the next day they set out again, and at once Chung-hsiang felt his feet to be light and strong; he went all the way to Wu-yang without feeling any more pain. This was a case of divine Heaven protecting a good man, and was not due merely to the efficacy of Wu Pao-an's spirit.

To continue, when Kuo Chung-hsiang reached his home he insisted that Wu T'ien-yu should live in his house. He swept clean the great hall and there set up the spirit-tablets of Wu Pao-an and his wife. He bought burial garments and inner and outer coffins, and performed the re-burial. He put mourner's clothes upon himself, and mourned and watched by the grave in company with Wu T'ien-yu. He engaged masons to build a tomb. Everything he did for this burial was exactly as he had done when previously he buried his father. Then in addition he erected a stone tablet, commemorating in detail Pao-an's deed in neglecting his family to ransom a friend. In this way, every passer-by who read the tablet learned the full extent of Pao-an's goodness. For three years Chung-hsiang lived with Wu T'ien-yu in a hut by the grave-side. Throughout this period he instructed T'ien-yu in the classics, until he was well-versed in questions of scholarship and ready to enter on an official career. When the three years had passed, Chung-hsiang decided to go to Ch'ang-an to seek office. Reflecting that Wu T'ien-yu had no family and had not yet taken a wife, he selected a woman of worth and virtue from among the nieces of his own clan. He sent betrothal presents on T'ien-yu's behalf, and divided off a court-yard in the eastern part of his house, where T'ien-yu could live with his bride. So that they might live comfortably, Chung-hsiang divided his possessions and gave them half of all he had. Indeed,

Years before, a man set aside his wife to save his friend;
Today, it is the turn of his orphan son to receive favours.
Truly, ' give but a melon and you will get something in return.'
A good man never turns his back on a man of goodwill.

Chung-hsiang left off mourning and went to the capital, where he was appointed Records Officer at Lanchou and given the honorary rank of *ch'ao-san tai-fu*. Thoughts of Pao-an never left him, and eventually he sent in a memorial to the throne, the gist of which was as follows:
'Your servant has heard that where there is good it should be encouraged, and the whole nation holds this as a canon; where there is kindness it should be repaid, and even the lowest observe this. Some years ago your servant went in the service of the late Military Governor at Yaochou, Li Meng, on an expedition to put down the barbarians of the south. In the first encounter, victory was ours. Your servant said that we should do wrong to penetrate too deep into enemy territory, but that we should consolidate our position. Our commander paid no heed to this, and in consequence out entire army was lost. Scion of a family honoured in China through generations, I became a poor captive at the ends of the earth. The barbarian rebels were greedy for gain, and demanded silk in exchange for the return of prisoners. They said that, since your servant was the nephew of the Prime Minister, they would require a thousand rolls. But I was cut off from my home by thousands of miles and no message could get through. For ten years I suffered hardship and grief. My flesh was scraped from my bones, and there was not a moment when my tears did not flow. I forced myself to follow like Su Wu the life of the shepherd, I never desired to shoot wild geese in the manner of Li Ling. But the Captain of the *fang-yi* Guard at Suichou, Wu Pao-an,

happened at that time to arrive in Yaochou. Although he was of
the same native place as your servant, we had never met. But
merely because we respected each other as men of honour, Pao-an
resolved to ransom me. He planned and worked in a hundred ways,
and cut himself off from his family for many years, until his own
appearance was haggard and worn and his wife suffered from cold
and hunger. He plucked me back from the brink of death and
set my feet on the road to life. Before I had made recompense for
this great deed of mercy, of a sudden my benefactor died. And
now your servant has been honoured with the red sash of rank,
whilst Wu T'ien-yu, the son of Pao-an, lives by "snaring and
eating coarse food". Thinking of this I feel a secret shame.
Moreover, T'ien-yu has reached manhood and his learning is
profound, so that he is fully fitted for office. I submit that the
post at present filled by your servant be granted to Wu T'ien-yu,
that the state may benefit by the encouragement of the good and
your servant have the opportunity properly to repay the kindness
done to him. In this way, two ends may be achieved by one
action. Your servant would gladly go into retirement, and in his
declining years would have no regrets. Though with respect, I
speak without reserve, risking death in order to make known my
request.'

It was then the twelfth year of the reign-period T'ien-pao
(753). When the memorial was sent in it was passed to the Board
of Rites for detailed discussion. The story created a great stir
among all the officials of the court, and although it was Pao-an
who had performed the initial act of kindness there was high
praise for the integrity of Kuo Chung-hsiang, who indeed needed
to feel no shame before his dead friend. The Board of Rites therefore transmitted the memorial to the throne with a note praising
in glowing terms the conduct of Kuo Chung-hsiang and recommending that the regulations be waived and his wish granted, as
an example to the degenerate commonalty. Thus, Wu T'ien-yu
was to be given, on probation, the post of Captain of the Guard at
Lan-ku *hsien*, whilst Chung-hsiang was to retain his original post.
This Lan-ku *hsien* was close to Lanchou, and so the two men
could meet morning and evening to comfort each other. In this
way did the officials of the Board of Rites express their goodwill.
The Emperor complied with the requests, and Chung-hsiang,

having received the notification of appointment for Wu T'ien-yu, expressed his gratitude for the Imperial favour and left the capital.

He returned to Wu-yang *hsien*, where he handed over the document of notification to Wu T'ien-yu. Then they prepared sacrifices and libations and performed ceremonies of worship, prior to their departure, before the graves of both families. Selecting a day of happy omen, the two men with their families took the road for the Western Capital to take up their duties.

The people of the time held this for a tale of wonder. It spread far and wide, and all declared that the affection between Wu and Kuo was not equalled even by Kuan and Pao or Yang and Tso.[18] Subsequently, both Kuo Chung-hsiang in Lanchou and Wu T'ien-yu in Lan-ku *hsien* attained success in the administration and were promoted to posts elsewhere. The people of Lanchou, to perpetuate their esteem, erected a temple, the Temple of Twin Loyalties, where sacrifices were made to Wu Pao-an and Kuo Chung-hsiang. All in the town who had contracts to make or oaths to swear would accompany these by prayer in the temple, and to this day there has been no break in the burning of incense. There is a poem in evidence:

> *They had barely clasped each other's hands, and were not as yet related,*
> *But in time of stress they found that their loyalty was true.*
> *If we consider the integrity of these men,*
> *How different we find them from the mass of so-called 'friends'!*

The Canary Murders

IN contrast with the preceding story, which was a late-Ming 'imitation prompt-book', *The Canary Murders* provides us beyond question with a genuine specimen of the work of the twelfth-century story-tellers. Eighty years before Feng Menglung selected it for his *Stories Old and New* the story was listed, under a different title, in the catalogue of a library called the Pao-wen-t'ang; already by that time it must have been an old and well-known tale. Feng, when he republished the story, cannot have altered it much. There are no obvious signs of any 'touching-up'. There is no prologue, nor does the piece end, as many do, with the comment that the tale has been passed down the generations to the present day, or that such-and-such a relic of one of the personages concerned is 'still to be seen'. The moral, which is no more than 'eschew evil', is carried exclusively by short verses which punctuate the prose, rather than being pointed by long homilies of the sort which interrupt the action in many later pieces. On the other hand, the age of the story is evidenced by the stylized opening phrases and by the complement of 'story-teller phrases' and popular saws, the most comprehensive to be found in any of the *Stories Old and New*. The language throughout both narrative and dialogue is Sung colloquial, quite free from any admixture of consciously 'literary' expressions.

The story commemorates a series of incidents alleged to have taken place in the vicinity of Lin-an in the year 1121, six years before the city was made the capital of the Southern Sung court. Although there is no means of establishing the authenticity of the events recorded or the personages concerned, there is equally no reason to doubt that the story was based on an actual crime of local and contemporary notoriety, and written down while the public memory was fresh. A more modern instance of such a process would be the notorious nine-fold murder perpetrated in Canton about 1725. A fictionalized account of the murder written not long after it took place served as basis for a nineteenth-century novel, Wu Wo-yao's *Strange Tale of Nine Deaths*.

Our story is a forerunner of the detective story which had its greatest vogue in the nineteenth century. Perhaps 'detective' is a misnomer : more properly, these are stories of clever magistrates. Unfortunately in *The Canary Murders* the magistrate makes only a brief and undistinguished appearance. In many stories he is the central figure. The reason is that as the highest civil authority in the district, the magistrate shouldered all the manifold responsibilities for the maintenance of law and order. It was his duty in a criminal case to bring the offender to book, to conduct the trial and to pronounce sentence. Since he alone was responsible for ascertaining the true facts of the case, it followed that where there was any element of mystery he must function as his own detective. He could rely on his runners to make enquiries, detain witnesses and arrest suspects, contenting himself with making deductions from the statements he heard or extracted in court ; or, as often happens in stories, he could leave his court incognito to conduct his own investigations.

Material from the case-histories of a succession of brilliant magistrates was worked up by the application of all the techniques evolved by the story-tellers. Already by the year 1600 the detective story was an established genre. Readers found in such works a type of interest on the intellectual level of the crossword-puzzle. By Chinese convention the criminal is introduced at the beginning of the story, so that there is no possibility of the kind of suspense essential to our modern whodunit. Yet, the Chinese 'lawsuit story' succeeds well enough in holding the reader's attention as the magistrate surmounts all obstacles in his inexorable progress towards the *exposé*.

As a model of realist fiction *The Canary Murders* is incomparable. I am particularly impressed by a number of little extra touches. To give just one instance : when the two friends of Li Chi are seeking the true facts of the crime for which he was wrongfully executed, they are given directions to find two coopers, one of whom they suspect to be the murderer. Here the story-teller adds verisimilitude, and increases the tension, by sending them first to the wrong man, and only secondly to the man they are looking for.

THE CANARY MURDERS

A bird it was at the root of the trouble:
Seven lives lost—what a lamentable case!
Note, all of you, this tragic lesson:
Do not let your sons and daughters neglect their home.

IT IS told how in the year 1121, the third year of the period
Hsüan-ho in the reign of the Emperor Hui-tsung of the great
Sung dynasty, a master-weaver named Shen Yü had his home in
the prefecture of Hai-ning, near Hangchow. He lived below the
New North Bridge, outside the Wu-lin Gate. This Shen Yü,
styled Pi-hsien, was in a prosperous way of business, and he and
his wife, Madam Yen, were devoted to each other. They had an
only son, Shen Hsiu, who had reached the age of sixteen but had
not yet married. The father made his living solely from weaving
silk cloth, but to everyone's surprise Shen Hsiu took no heed of
his duty to earn his keep. He devoted himself to pleasure and
amusement and spent all his time breeding canaries,[1] and his
parents doted on their only child and had no control over him.
The neighbours gave him the nickname 'Birdie' Shen. Every
day at dawn he would take up one of his canaries and hurry off to
match it against others in the park of willows inside the city.

This went on day after day, until it came to the end of spring,
when the weather is neither too hot nor too cold, when the
flowers bloom red and the willows are green. One morning at this
time Shen Hsiu got up at the crack of dawn, washed and dressed
and ate his breakfast, and made ready a cage, into which he put
one matchless canary. This creature was the sort that is found
only in heaven and not here below. He took it all over the place to
fight, and it had never been defeated. It had won him over a
hundred strings of cash, and he doted on it and held it dearer than
life itself. He had made a cage for it of gold lacquer, with a brass
hook, a green gauze cover, and seed-pot and water-pot of Ko-yao
porcelain.[2] This particular morning Shen Hsiu took up the cage
and proudly hurried off through the city-gate to match his bird

in the willow park. And who would have thought that Shen Hsiu, off on this jaunt of his, was going to his death? Just like

> *A pig or a lamb to the slaughter,*
> *Seeking with every step the road to death.*

Shen Hsiu took his bird into the willow park, but he was later than he had thought and the bird-fanciers had dispersed. The place was silent and gloomy, with not a soul about. Shen Hsiu, finding himself alone, hung the bird in its cage on a willow-branch, where it sang for a while. Then, disappointed, he took the cage down again and was just about to go back, when suddenly a bout of pain came surging up from his belly and forced him to his knees.

The fact was that Shen Hsiu was a sufferer from what is known as 'dumplings on the heart', or hernia. Every attack sent him into a dead faint. It must have been that he had risen earlier than usual that morning, and then, arriving late to find no one there, he felt disappointed and miserable, so that this time the attack was particularly severe. He collapsed on the ground at the foot of a willow-tree, where he lay unconscious for four whole hours.

Now, wouldn't you agree that 'there is such a thing as co-incidence'? This very day a cooper called Chang came walking through the park, his pack on his back, on the way to a job at the Ch'u household. He saw from a distance that there was someone lying at the foot of this tree, and so he came bounding up to the spot, set down his load and had a look. Shen Hsiu's face was a waxy yellow, and he was still in a coma. There was nothing of any value on him, but at one side was the canary in its cage; and the canary chose just this moment to sing away more beautifully than ever. It was a case of 'the sight of the treasure provides the motive', and 'the plan is born when the man is poorest'. Chang thought, 'I might work all day for a couple of silver cents. What good would that do me?'

Shen Hsiu must have been doomed to die, for at the sight of Chang the canary began to sing harder than ever. Chang said to himself, 'The rest doesn't matter, but this canary alone is worth two or three silver taels at least.' So he picked up the cage and was just making off, when to his surprise Shen Hsiu came round. Shen opened his eyes to see Chang picking up the cage. He tried to get up but couldn't. All he could do was cry out, 'Where are you off to with my canary, you old blackguard?'

'This little fool has too quick a tongue,' Chang thought to himself. 'Suppose I take it, and he manages to get up and comes after me—he'll make trouble for me. There's only one thing for it, one way or the other I'm in a mess.' So he went to the barrel he had been carrying and took out a curved paring-knife, then turned to Shen Hsiu and struck at him. The knife was sharp and he used all his strength, and Shen Hsiu's head rolled away to one side.

Chang cast panic-stricken glances to left and right, fearful lest someone should have seen him. Then, looking up, he saw that to one side stood a hollow tree. Hurriedly he picked up the head and dropped it into the hollow trunk, returned the knife to the barrel, and hung the bird-cage from his pack. He did not go on to the job at the Ch'u house, but went off like a puff of smoke, through the streets and alleys of the town, looking for somewhere to hide.

Now, how many lives do you think were lost on account of this one live bird? Indeed,

> Private words among men,
> Heard in Heaven like thunder;
> A misdeed in a dark room,
> But the gods have eyes like lightning.

As Chang walked along the thought came to him, 'There is a travelling merchant who stays in an inn at Huchou-shu, and I have often seen him buying pets. Why not go there and sell the bird to him?' And he made straight for the suburb past the Wu-lin Gate.

The evil fate in store must have been determined from a previous existence, for there he saw three merchants with two youths at their heels, five persons all told. They had just packed up their goods to go back, and he met them coming in through the gate. The merchants were all men of the Eastern Capital, Pien-liang (Kaifeng). One of them was called Li Chi, a trader in herbs. He had always had a fancy for canaries, and seeing this lovely bird on the cooper's back he called to Chang to let him see it. Chang set down his pack. The merchant examined the

canary's plumage and eyes, and saw that it was a fine bird. It had
a lovely singing-voice, too, and he was delighted with it. 'Would
you like to sell him?' he asked Chang.

By this time Chang's only concern was to be rid of the evidence.
So he said, 'How much will you give me, sir?'

The longer Li Chi looked at the bird the more he liked it. 'I'll
give you a tael of silver,' he said.

Chang realized the deal was on. 'I don't want to haggle,' he
said. 'It's just that this bird's very precious to me. But give me a
little more and you can have him.'

Li Chi took out three pieces of silver and weighed them: there
was one tael and a fifth. 'That's the lot,' he said, handing it to
Chang.

Chang took the silver, examined it and put it in his wallet. He
gave the canary to the merchant and took his leave. 'That's a
good deed done, getting rid of the evidence,' he told himself.
He did not go back to his work, but hurried straight home. But
still he felt certain misgivings at heart. Indeed,

> The evil-doer fears the wrath of Heaven and earth,
> The swindler dreads discovery by gods and demons.

Chang's home was in fact against the city-wall by the Yung-
chin Gate. There was only himself and his wife, they had no
children. When his wife saw him coming back, she said, 'You
haven't used a single splint. Why have you come home so early?
What's the trouble?'

Chang said not a word until he had entered the house, taken
off his pack and turned back to bolt the door. Then he said,
'Come here, wife, I've something to tell you. Today I've been to
such-and-such and done such-and-such, and I've come by this
ounce and a fifth of silver. I'm giving it to you so that you can
enjoy yourself for a while.' And the two of them gloated over the
money.

But this does not concern us. Let us rather go on to tell how
there was no one about in the willow park until late morning,
when two peasants carrying loads of manure happened to pass
through. The headless corpse blocking their path gave them a
fright, and they began to kick up a fuss, quickly rousing the ward-
headman and all the citizens of the neighbourhood. The ward

submitted the matter to the *hsien*, and the *hsien* to the prefecture, and the next day a coroner and other officers were sent to the willow park to investigate. They found no mark on the body: the only thing wrong was that the head was missing; nor had anyone come forward as plaintiff. The officers made their report to the authorities at the prefecture, who despatched runners to arrest the criminal. Within the city and out in the suburbs, all was thrown into an uproar.

Let us now rather tell how Shen Hsiu's parents, when evening came and he still had not returned, sent people out in every direction to search for him, but without success. When again at dawn searchers were sent into the city, in the vicinity of the inn at Hu-chou-shu they heard a commotion about the headless corpse of a murdered man being found in the willow park. When Shen Hsiu's mother heard of this she thought, 'My boy went into the city yesterday to show his canary, and there's still no sign of him. Can it be him?' And at once she cried to her husband, 'You must go into the city yourself and make enquiries.'

Shen Yü gave a jump when he heard this, and filled with alarm he hurried off to the willow park. There he saw the headless corpse, which, after a careful look at the clothing, he recognized as his own son. He began to wail in a loud voice. 'Here is the plaintiff,' said the ward headman. 'Now all that is missing is the criminal.'

Shen Yü went at once to make accusation before the Prefect of Lin-an. 'It is my son', he said. 'Early yesterday morning he went into the city to show his canary, and he has been murdered, no one knows how or why. Your Highness, I demand justice!'

Runners and detectives were sent from the prefecture throughout the area, with orders to arrest the criminal within ten days. Shen Yü was ordered to prepare a coffin in the willow park to contain the corpse. He went straight home and said to his wife, 'It's our son, he's been murdered. But no one knows where the head has been taken. I have made accusation at the prefecture, and they have sent runners out everywhere to arrest the criminal. I've been told to buy a coffin for him. What is best for us to do about it all?'

At this news, Madam Yen began to wail aloud and collapsed

to the floor. 'If you don't know how she felt inside, first see how she lies there motionless.' Indeed,

> *Body like the waning moon at cock-crow, half-hidden behind the hills;*
> *Spirit like a dying lamp at the third watch, the oil already gone.*

They proceeded to revive her by forcing hot soup down her throat, and when she came to she said, through her tears, 'My boy would never listen to good advice, and now he is dead and we cannot bury him.[3] O my son, so young, and dead in such a grievous manner. Who could have told that in my old age I should be left without support?' All the time she was speaking her tears flowed ceaselessly. She would take neither food nor drink, although her husband used every effort to console her. Somehow or other they got through the next fortnight, without any news. Then Shen Yü and his wife began to discuss the matter. 'Our boy would never heed our words, and now this terrible thing has happened and he has been murdered. Nor can the murderer be found. There is nothing we can do about it. But at least it would be something if his corpse could be made whole. Our best plan is to write out a notice and inform people everywhere that if they find the head, so that the corpse can be made whole, they will be rewarded for it.'

When the two had come to this decision they promptly wrote out copies of a notice and went out to paste them up all over the city. The notice ran:

'To all citizens: One thousand strings of cash reward to anyone discovering the whereabouts of the head of Shen Hsiu. Two thousand strings of cash reward to anyone apprehending the murderer.'

They informed the prefecture of this, and the authorities issued fresh orders to the runners to arrest the criminal within so many days, and put out an official notice, as follows:

'Official reward of five hundred strings of cash to anyone discovering the whereabouts of the head of Shen Hsiu. One thousand strings of cash reward to anyone apprehending the murderer.'

We will leave the town in its ferment of excitement over the notices, and go on to tell how at the foot of the Southern Peak there lived an old pauper whose name was Huang and who was known by the nickname 'Old Dog'. He was an ignorant man who had spent his life as a chair-coolie. With old age he had lost his sight, and he depended entirely on the support of his two sons, Big Pao and Little Pao. The three of them, father and sons, had neither enough clothes to wear nor enough food to eat. They lived from hand to mouth and their bellies were never full. One day Old Dog Huang called Big Pao and Little Pao to him and said, 'I hear talk of some rich man or other called Shen Hsiu, who's been murdered, and his head is missing. And now they're offering a reward, and they say if anyone finds this head, the family will give them a thousand strings of cash and the authorities will give them another five hundred. I've called you together now just to say this: I'm an old man now anyway, and I'm no use, I can't see and I've no money. So I've decided to give you two a chance to make something and enjoy yourselves. Tonight you must cut off my head. Hide it in the water at the edge of the Western Lake, and in a few days it will be unrecognizable. Then you must take it to the prefecture and claim the reward, and altogether you'll get one thousand five hundred strings of cash. It's better than staying on here in misery. It's a very clever scheme, and you mustn't waste any time, because if somebody else gets in first I'll have lost my life for nothing.'

This 'Old Dog' made this speech because he had given up in despair; moreover, his two sons were very stupid men and understood nothing of the law. Indeed,

> *The mouth is the gateway of disaster,*
> *The tongue is an executioner's knife.*
> *Keep your mouth shut and your tongue well-hidden,*
> *And you will live at peace and secure.*

The two went outside to discuss the matter. 'This is a brilliant idea of our father's,' said Little Pao. 'Not even a Commander-in-Chief or a Field-Marshal could have thought up a plan like this. It's a very good one, although it's a pity we have to lose Dad.'

Big Pao was by nature both cruel and stupid. He said, 'He's got to die sooner or later anyway. Why shouldn't we seize this opportunity and do him in? We can dig a pit at the foot of the mountain and bury him, and there'll be no trace, so how can we be found out? This is what they call "doing it while the water's hot", and "leaving no trace". Men's hearts are governed by Heaven: it wasn't ourselves who forced him to it, he told us to do this of his own accord.'

'All right then,' said Little Pao, 'only we'll not set to work until he's fast asleep.'

Having laid their plans, the brothers went bustling off and bought two bottles of wine on credit. They came back to their father, and the three of them got good and drunk and sprawled about all over the place. The two brothers slept right through to the early hours of the morning, when they crept out of bed to watch the old man lying there, snoring. Then Big Pao took a kitchen-knife from in front of the stove, and with one powerful stroke at his father's neck cut his head clean off. Hurriedly they wrapped it in an old garment and hid it in the bed. Then they went off to the foot of the mountain and dug a deep pit. They carried the body there and buried it, and before it was daylight they had hidden the head in the shallow water at the edge of the lake, near the Lotus House at the foot of the Nan-p'ing hills.

A fortnight later they went into the city and looked at the notice. First of all they went to Shen Yü's house to make their report: 'The two of us were shrimping yesterday when we saw a human head by the edge of the lake near the Lotus House. We thought it must be your son's head.'

'If it really is,' said Shen Yü at this, 'there is a reward of a thousand strings of cash for you, not a copper short.' Then he prepared food and wine for them, and presently they took him straight to the point by the Lotus House at the foot of the Nan-p'ing hills. There they found the head, lightly buried in the mud. When they picked it up and examined it, they found it had been under water so long that the features were bloated and past recognition. But Shen Yü thought, 'It must be my son's head. If it isn't how does another head come to be here?'

Shen Yü wrapped the head in a kerchief, and accompanied the two of them straight to the prefecture, where they reported the discovery of Shen Hsiu's head. The Prefect repeatedly questioned the two brothers, who replied, 'We saw it when we were shrimping. We don't know anything else about it.' Their word was accepted, and they were given the five hundred strings of cash. Then, taking the head with them, they accompanied Shen Yü to the willow park. They opened the coffin, set the head on the shoulders of the corpse, and nailed the coffin up again. Then Shen Yü took the brothers back to his home. When Madam Yen heard that her son's head had been found she was much happier, and at once set out food and wine to feast the brothers. They received the thousand strings of cash as their reward, and took their leave and returned home. There, they built a house, and bought farming implements and household goods. 'We are not going to work as chair-coolies any longer,' they said to each other. 'We'll work hard at our farming, and we can make a bit extra by gathering firewood from the hillside and selling that.'

But this does not concern us. Indeed, 'time flew like an arrow' and 'days and months passed like a weaver's shuttle'. Several months passed unnoticed, and the authorities grew lax and concerned themselves less every day with the affair.

We will say no more of all this, but go on to tell how the time came for Shen Yü, who was a master-weaver for the Eastern Capital, to make a journey there to deliver a consignment of cloth. When all his weavers had completed their quotas he went to the prefecture for the delivery permit, returned home to order his affairs there, and then started out. This journey, just because Shen Yü chanced to see a bird which had belonged to his own family, resulted in the forfeiture of another life. Indeed,

> Take no illegal goods,
> Commit no illegal acts.
> Here above the law will catch you,
> Down below the demons pursue you.

Let us now tell how Shen Yü, on his journey, ate when hungry and drank when thirsty, rested each night and set out again each morning, and after more than one day like this arrived in the Eastern Capital. He delivered each and every bolt of cloth, and collected his permit to return. Then he thought, 'I have heard that the sights of the Eastern Capital are unique. Why shouldn't I stroll about for a while? This is an opportunity which doesn't come often.' He visited all the historic sites and beauty-spots, the monasteries both Taoist and Buddhist, and all the

other celebrated sights. Then he chanced to pass by the gate of
the Imperial Aviary. Now, Shen Yü was very fond of pets, and he
felt he would like to have a look inside. On distributing a dozen
or so cash at the gate he was allowed in to have a look round. All
at once he heard a canary singing beautifully. Taking a careful
look at it, he realized it was his son's canary which had disappeared. When the canary saw Shen Yü's familiar face it sang
louder than ever, and hopped about its cage jerking its head
towards him. The sight of the bird reminded Shen Yü of his son.
Tears streamed down his face and his heart filled with sorrow.
Without reflecting where he was he began to cry out and make
an uproar, shouting, 'Could such a thing come to pass?'

The guard who was keeper of the Aviary shouted, 'Here's a
fool who doesn't know the regulations. Where do you think you
are, making such a fuss?'

Shen Yü, unable to contain his grief, began to yell louder still,
and the guard, fearful of bringing trouble on his own head, found
nothing for it but to arrest Shen Yü and have him brought before
the Grand Court. The officer of the Grand Court shouted, 'Where
do you come from, that you dare to enter a part of the palace
itself and make a disturbance like this? If you have some griev-
ance, come straight out with it like an honest fellow, and you'll
be let off.'

So Shen Yü told how his son had gone off to match his canary
and had been murdered, the whole story from beginning to end.
The officer of the Grand Court was dumbfounded by the story.
Then he reflected that the bird had been presented as tribute by
a man of the capital, Li Chi; but whoever had dreamt there could
be all this business behind it? He sent off runners to arrest Li Chi
and bring him to court on the instant. The questioning com-
menced: 'What was your reason for murdering this man's son
in Hai-ning, and bringing his canary here as tribute? Make a full
and open statement, or you will be punished.'

'I went to Hangchow on business,' said Li Chi, 'and as I was
going through the Wu-lin Gate I chanced to see a cooper who
had this canary in a cage hanging from his pack. When I heard
it singing and saw that it was a fine bird I bought it, for an ounce
and a fifth of silver. I brought it back with me; but I did not dare
to keep it for myself, because it was such a fine specimen, and

so I presented it as tribute for the Emperor's use. I know nothing about any murder.'

'Who are you trying to implicate?' said his interrogator. 'This canary is concrete evidence. Tell the truth!'

Li Chi pleaded again and again: 'It is the truth that I bought it from an old cooper. I know nothing about a murder. How would I dare to make a false statement?'

'This old man you bought it from,' went on the interrogating officer, 'what was his name and where did he come from? Give me the true facts and I will have him brought in. Then we shall get at the truth, and you will be released.'

'I simply bought it from him when I ran into him on the street,' said Li Chi. 'I really don't know what his name is or where he lives.'

The interrogating officer began to abuse him: 'You're only trying to confuse the issue. Are you hoping to make someone else pay for this man's life? We must go by the concrete evidence, this canary. This rascal won't confess until he's beaten.'

Li Chi was flogged over and over until the flesh was ripped open. He could not bear the pain, and had no alternative but to make up a story that when he saw what a fine bird this canary was he had killed Shen Hsiu and cast his head away. Thereupon Li Chi was committed to the main jail, while the officer of the Grand Court prepared his report for submission to the Emperor. The Imperial rescript ran: 'Li Chi was beyond doubt the murderer of Shen Hsiu, the canary being evidence of this. The law requires that he shall be executed.' The canary was returned to Shen Yü, who was also given a permit and allowed to return to his home; whilst Li Chi was sent under escort to the execution-ground, and there beheaded. Indeed,

> *When the old turtle won't turn tender*
> *You shift the blame on to the firewood.*

At this time, the two merchants who had accompanied Li Chi to Hai-ning on business could hardly keep still for indignation. 'How could such an injustice be done,' they complained, 'when it was plain for all to see that he had bought the canary. We would have pleaded for him, but what could we do? Although we would recognize the man who sold Li Chi the canary, we don't know his name any more than Li did. Moreover he is in Hangchow. We should not have been able to clear Li Chi, and we should have implicated ourselves. How can the truth be brought to light? A man has been executed when he was obviously innocent, and all because of one single bird. The only thing is for us to go to Hangchow, and when we get there, to wring the truth out of this fellow.'

Let us say no more of this, but rather tell how Shen Yü packed his baggage, picked up his canary and hurried home, travelling day and night. He reported to his wife: 'When I was in the Eastern Capital I succeeded in avenging our son.'

'How did that come about?' asked Madam Yen. Shen Yü told her the whole story right through, beginning with his seeing the canary in the Imperial Aviary. When Madam Yen saw the canary she burst out weeping, for the sight of things brings back sad memories; but we will say no more of this. The next day Shen Yü took up the canary again and went to the prefecture to have his permit cancelled, and there he reported all that had happened. 'What a lucky coincidence,' cried the delighted Prefect. Indeed,

> *Do nothing of which you need feel ashamed:*
> *Who, throughout time, has been allowed to escape?*

And murder, needless to say, is the concern of Heaven, not to be taken lightly. The Prefect dismissed Shen Yü with the words, 'Since the criminal has been caught and executed, you may have the coffin cremated.' Shen Yü had the coffin cremated and the remains scattered, and we will say no more of this, but go on to tell how of the two merchants who had accompanied Li Chi to Hangchow on that former occasion to sell herbs, one was called Ho and the other Chu. These two got some more herbs together and went straight to Hangchow, to stay in the inn at Hu-chou-shu. They quickly sold up their herbs, then, their hearts filled with a sense of injustice, they went into the city to look for the cooper. They searched all day without finding a trace of him, and returned, weary and dispirited, to the inn to sleep. The next morning they returned to the city, and as luck would have it they chanced to see a man with a cooper's pack. 'Tell us, brother,' they said, calling to him to stay, 'is there another cooper here, an old man who looks like this?' And they described him. 'We don't know his name, but perhaps you know him?'

'Gentlemen,' said the cooper, 'there are only two old men here in the cooper's trade. One is called Li, and lives in Pomegranate Garden Street; the other is called Chang, and he lives by the city-wall on the west side. I don't know which one it is that you want.'

The two merchants thanked him and carried their search straight to Pomegranate Garden Street. As it happened, the man named Li was sitting there cutting splints. The two took a look at him, but he was not their man. Then they found the house by the western wall, and coming up to the door they asked if Chang was at home. 'No, he isn't,' replied Chang's wife. 'He's gone out to a job.'

The two men turned away again without more ado. It was now early afternoon. They had gone no more than a few hundred yards when they saw in the distance a man carrying a cooper's pack. And this man's fate it was to pay for the life of Shen Hsiu and to clear the name of Li Chi. Indeed, 'let mercy and right-eousness everywhere prevail, and you will meet with them at every turn of your life; never make an enemy, for when you meet him in a narrow path it is not easy to turn back'. Chang was walking south towards his home, and the two men were walking towards the north, so that they met face to face. Chang did not recognize the pair, but they recognized him. They stopped him and asked his name. 'My name is Chang', he replied.

'It must be you who live by the western wall,' they continued. 'That is so,' replied Chang. 'What do you want of me?'

'We have some things at the inn that need repairing,' said the merchants, 'and we are looking for an experienced man to do the job. That's why we wanted you. Where are you going now?'

'I'm on my way home,' said Chang. The three of them talked as they went along, until they came to Chang's door. 'Please sit down and have some tea,' said Chang.

But the others replied, 'It is getting late. We'll come again tomorrow.'

'Then I won't go out tomorrow, but will wait for you here,' said Chang.

The two men took their leave of him, but they did not return to the inn: they went straight to the prefecture to inform on him. The court had just begun its evening session, and the two men went straight in and knelt down. They told the whole story of Shen Yü's recognition of the canary and Li Chi's execution, and of Li's earlier meeting with Chang when he bought the canary. 'We two are filled with a sense of injustice, and with the desire to avenge Li Chi. We entreat your honour to question Chang throughly and to find out how he came by the canary.'

'The Shen Hsiu case has been wound up,' said the Prefect. 'The criminal has been executed—what more remains to be done?'

So the two merchants made accusation: 'The officer of the Grand Court was misled. He took the canary as evidence, but did not look carefully into the details of the case. It is plain for all to see that Li Chi was wrongfully executed. We have "found injustice in our path", and are determined to avenge Li Chi. If we were not speaking the truth, how would we dare to make a nuisance of ourselves with this accusation? We beg your honour in your mercy to intervene in this matter.'

Observing how earnestly they pleaded, the Prefect at once sent out runners to arrest Chang that very night. It was just like

Vultures chasing a purple swallow,
Fierce tigers slavering over a lamb.

That night the men from the court hurried to the western wall. They tied Chang's arms behind his back and delivered him up to the prefecture, where he was committed to the main jail. When court opened the next day, Chang was brought from the jail and forced to his knees. The Prefect said, 'What was your reason for murdering Shen Hsiu and making Li Chi pay for it with his life? Today the facts have come to light, and the right must prevail.' The Prefect shouted to his men to flog the prisoner, and Chang received thirty strokes to begin with, till his flesh was ripped open and the blood came soaking out. Over and over again he was flogged, but he would not confess.

The merchants and the two youths who had been with them shouted at him: 'Although Li Chi is dead, we four are still here, and we were with him when he bought your canary for an ounce and a fifth of silver. Who are you going to put the blame on now?

If you say it wasn't you who did it, then tell us where the canary came from. Tell the truth: you can't lie your way out of this, and it's no use trying to make excuses.'

But Chang continued to defy them, and at last the Prefect roared at him, 'The canary is genuine evidence of the theft, and these four are eye-witnesses. If you still refuse to confess, we'll have the finger-press out and torture you.' Terrified, Chang had no choice but to confess everything, how he had stolen the canary and cut off Shen Hsiu's head.

'When you had killed him, where did you put the head?' asked the Prefect.

'I was seized by panic,' Chang answered, 'and seeing a hollow tree nearby I dropped the head into the hole. Then I picked up the bird and went straight to the Wu-lin Gate. There I happened to come across three merchants, with two youths. They wanted to buy the canary, and I got an ounce and a fifth of silver for it. I took the money home and spent it, and this is the truth.'

The Prefect ordered Chang to make his mark on his deposition, and sent men to summon Shen Yü. Then they all proceeded, with Chang under escort, to the willow park to search for the head. Hundreds of people on the streets, all agog, gathered round and followed them to the willow park to look for it. They found that there was indeed a hollow tree, and when they had sawn it down they gave a shout of excitement, for there inside the trunk was a human head. When they examined it they saw it to be completely unaffected by the passage of time.[4] When Shen Yü saw the head he took a close look and recognized it as that of his son. He cried out in a loud voice and fainted to the ground, remaining unconscious for a long time. Then they wrapped the head in a cloth and returned to the prefecture, with Chang still under escort.

'Now that the head has been found,' said the Prefect, 'the facts are clear and the guilt established.' They put a large wooden cangue round Chang's neck, fettered his hands and feet and dragged him off to the condemned cells, where he was put under close guard. The Prefect then put a question to Shen Yü: 'Those two Huang brothers, Big Pao and Little Pao: where did they get that human head, when they came to claim the reward? There is some mystery here. Your son's head has been found now: whose head was that?'

Runners were immediately ordered to bring in the Huang brothers for interrogation. Shen Yü led the runners to the Huangs' house in the southern hills. The two brothers were arrested and brought to court, where they were forced to kneel. 'The murderer of Shen Hsiu has been arrested,' the Prefect told them, 'and Shen Hsiu's head has been recovered. Who was it that you two conspired together to murder, so that you could claim the reward for his head? Confess or you will be tortured!' Big Pao and Little Pao were dumbfounded and bewildered and could make no reply. The Prefect, enraged, ordered them to be strung up and flogged, but for a long time they refused to confess. But then they were branded with red-hot irons. This was more than they could bear, and they fainted away. When water was spurted over them and they revived, they saw there was nothing for it but to blurt out the truth. 'Seeing that our father was old and sick and miserable,' they said, 'on an evil impulse we got him drunk and cut off his head. We hid it at the edge of the Western Lake near the Lotus House, and then made up a story to claim the reward.'

'Where did you bury your father's body?' asked the Prefect. 'At the foot of the Southern Peak,' they replied. When the brothers were taken there under escort and the ground was dug, there did indeed prove to be a headless corpse buried at the spot. The two men were taken back to the prefecture and the guards reported: 'There is indeed a headless corpse, in a shallow grave in the southern hills.'

'That such a thing should happen!' said the Prefect. 'It is a most abominable crime. If there really are such evil men in this world, I want neither to speak nor hear nor write of them. Let them be flogged to death here and now, and we shall be rid of them; how can this evil deed ever be expiated?' He shouted to his men to flog them without keeping count of the strokes. The two brothers were flogged unconscious and revived again many times, then large cangues were placed on them and they were taken off to the condemned cells to be closely guarded.

Shen Yü and the original plaintiffs returned to their homes to await events, while a report on the wrongful execution of Li Chi was at once submitted in the form of a memorial. The Imperial rescript ordered the Board of Punishments and the Censorate to investigate the conduct of the officer of the Grand Court who had originally questioned Li Chi, and to reduce him to the status of commoner and banish him to Ling-nan (in the southernmost province of Kwangtung). Li Chi was declared to have been innocent and wrongfully convicted. The Imperial sympathy was expressed, and his family was granted one thousand strings of cash in compensation and his descendants exempted from compulsory service. Chang, for premeditated murder for gain and for wronging an innocent man, was to be executed in accordance with the law. In view of the seriousness of the crime, the execution was to be performed by the slow process, with two hundred and forty cuts, and his corpse dismembered. The Huang brothers, convicted of patricide for gain, were both without distinction to be executed by the slow process, with two hundred and forty cuts, their corpses dismembered and their heads publicly exposed as a warning. Indeed,

> Heaven, clear and profound, is not to be deceived,
> Before the design appears to you it is already known.
> Do nothing of which you need feel ashamed:
> Who, throughout time, has been allowed to escape?

When the rescript reached the prefecture, officers and executioners and the rest mounted the three criminals on 'wooden mules', and it was broadcast throughout the city that in three days' time they were to be executed by the slow process, their corpses dismembered and their heads publicly exposed as a warning.

When Chang's wife heard that her husband was to be sliced to death she went to the execution-ground in the hope of catching a glimpse of him. Who would have thought it possible?—when the executioners were given the signal to start, they all began to slice their victims, and it was indeed a frightful sight: Chang's wife was frightened out of her wits, and she turned to go, her body bent with grief. But by accident she tripped and fell heavily, injuring her whole body, and when she reached home she died. Indeed,

> Store up good deeds and you will meet with good,
> Store up evil and you will meet with evil.
> If you think about it carefully,
> Things usually turn out right.

The Fairy's Rescue

ABOUT a third of the *Stories Old and New* traffic in the supernatural. They are either rebirth stories or fairy stories—if 'fairy' can be taken so loosely to cover gods, spirits, immortals and what have you. The difference is that the material of the rebirth story is the adventures of human beings in the next world after death or in successive incarnations, whereas the fairy stories centre round either human beings who have attained immortality or supernatural beings who have never been human at all. Thus, although the supernatural element is strong in all these pieces, it is possible to distinguish different degrees of realism. The rebirth stories attempt to interpret the affairs of the world in theological terms; the fairy stories, in contrast, have almost nothing to do with the affairs of the world, and to this extent are more in the nature of straightforward entertainments.

The Fairy's Rescue is about the nearest one could come in Chinese writing to the Western concept of a fairy-tale. It is a very old Taoist story. The events it purports to narrate took place during the sixth century. They were first recorded in a collection of marvels called *Hsü Hsüan kuai lu*, by a writer of the T'ang dynasty named Li Fu-yen. The story as we have it here is again a product of the Sung story-tellers, and like *The Canary Murders* was recorded in the Pao-wen-t'ang catalogue well before its republication in the *Stories Old and New*.

Li Fu-yen's account is typical of its time in its brusque, matter-of-fact presentation of the 'facts'. It was left to the storyteller of the market-place to mould them into a piece of fiction, a fully-developed fairy story. This he achieved partly by contriving a satisfactory ending to the series of events by deifying the young hero Wei I-fang. In the earlier account this personage is left, as the Chinese critics would say, 'without an exit from the stage'. Partly, also, the story-teller achieved his goal by emphasizing the element of causality, which is the essence of plot. As E. M. Forster says, ' "The king died and then the queen died" is a story; "the king died and then the queen died of grief" is a plot.' In fiction, it is not enough to record events: the relations between them must be so organized that a significant pattern is made.

The story-teller, therefore, is engaged in creating fiction when he makes the introduction of the old wizard Chang to the Wei family a matter of predestination (via a runaway horse) rather than of mere accident; when he explains the reason for the girl's acceptance of Chang as a husband; and above all, when at the end of the story he interprets the whole adventure in terms of the salvation of a fairy girl from mortal snares.

As a natural result of this process of 'fictionization', the shadowy personages of the ninth-century T'ang account become quite real in the prompt-book story. Old Chang's awkwardness and his stubborn refusal to accept his mortal role are well brought out in his discussion with the Wei family on the subject of marriage; when after meeting their daughter he contracts love-sickness one is moved to laughing pity for the old man. Wei I-fang, an insignificant message-bearer in Li Fu-yen's account, becomes recognizably a man, a brother thirsting for vengeance on the monster who has, as he construes it, degraded his sister.

Lastly, the story-teller adds to the attractiveness of his product by introducing from time to time an element of humour quite absent from the T'ang account. In addition to exploiting potentially comic situations to the full, he frequently sounds a mocking note in the verses which punctuate his narrative, and exhibits generally a more sophisticated attitude towards his marvels.

THE FAIRY'S RESCUE

A thousand miles of sky, the clouds layered red,
Slowly a welcome glow suffuses the pavilion.
Not yet the season for the willow-floss to wander,
First one thinks of plum-blossom breaking from the bud.
The curtains, at its touch, give out a gentle rustle,
Outside, no sound, as its fine rain fills the air.
Night long it has gathered on the heads of ancient pines,
Undisturbed at dawn though the north wind blows.

THE subject of this verse is snow. The falling of snow recalls three things: salt, willow-floss, pear-blossom. How can I show that snow is like salt? There was a line spoken by Hsieh Ling-yün [1] in praise of snow:

> *Is it salt scattered in the air?—One can't be certain.*

And there is a *tz'u* by Su Tung-p'o [2] to the metre of 'The River Spirit':

> *Falling still at dusk, like finest rain:*
> *At dawn I looked out—*
> *The sheet of jade touched the eaves.*
> *The river has broadened, the sky come near,*
> *No wine-shop flag is visible now.*
> *Composing in solitude, no one to respond—*
> *To stroke my thin beard*
> *First I must blow on my fingers.*
>
> *If only you should call—how drunk we should get!*
> *These crystals of salt—*
> *Who is to taste them?* [3]
> *In my fingers a sprig of plum*
> *I look to the east and think of T'ao Ch'ien.* [4]
> *Snow recalls the old poet, and he the snow:*
> *However delightful*
> *Some will find fault.*

How can I show that snow is like willow-floss? There was a line spoken by Hsieh Tao-yün in praise of snow [5]:

> *More like the willow-floss swirling in the wind. . .*

177

And there is a *tz'u* by Huang Lu-chih to the metre of 'Treading the Rushes':

> *Magic petals heaped high,*
> *Willow-floss spread on the ground,*
> *By dawn all paths were hidden from the traveller.*
> *Still the red clouds show no sign of a break,*
> *On and on goes the swirling in every gust of wind.*
>
> *Cup to my lips I watch the scene,*
> *Forming my verse in face of the wind.*
> *I turn away and smile—no words come yet.*
> *How is it they have eluded me all day?*
> *—Over in the hills there is still a patch of green.*

And how can I show that snow is like pear-blossom? There is a line from the poetess Li I-an:

> *The traveller shakes his sleeves to brush off the 'pear-*
> *blossom'.*

And there is a *tz'u* by Chao Shu-yung to the metre of 'The Fairy by the River':

> *Red clouds close-packed for a thousand miles,*
> *A crimson glow spreading across the sky.*
> *A drifting-down like willow-floss, down to the mud.*
> *On the road to the village*
> *They shake the 'pear-blossom' from their sleeves.*
>
> *What scene can I find now that will match my brush?*
> *River and lake, the boats, the fishermen's huts.*
> *I pour out more of my wine to toast the season's glory,*
> *Seize my cloak in my urge to be away*
> *And, rainhat on my head, am off to the creek.*

Thus, snow can be likened to three things; and it is in the charge of three fairies. These three fairies are the Fairy of Ku-she,[6] Chou Ch'iung-i and Tung Shuang-ch'eng. Chou Ch'iung-i is in charge of 'Hibiscus Village' or Fairyland, and Tung Shuang-ch'eng looks after the crystal snow-vase. This vase contains a number of snowflakes. Whenever the clouds are close-packed and red, it is the task of the Fairy of Ku-she to pick out, with gold chopsticks, one of these snowflakes, whereupon there will fall a foot of seasonable snow. There was indeed one occasion when the Fairy of the Purple Palace gave a banquet to which he invited the Fairy of Ku-she and Tung Shuang-ch'eng. They both got drunk and decided to sing, beating time with the gold chopsticks on the vase. Unfortunately the vase broke and out came the snow, and what a mighty fall of snow they had that year! The incident is celebrated in a song called 'Memories of the Fairy Maid':

The Fairy of Ku-she
Feasting with Shuang-ch'eng in the Purple Palace broke the
*   precious vase,*
And white and pearly flakes
Settled like pollen on the fairy folk.
Shaken off into space
They filled the night of earth and heaven with brilliance,
Catching the radiance of moon and sea.
The jade-trees,[7] with the dawn, were silver-coated
And from each branch there hung a gleaming whiplash.

In hollows of the thorny hills,[8]
On loops of the green river—
Birds, benighted,
Flew through the cold, but found no trace of nest.
Hairpins, chopsticks of ice hang from the eaves, a lovely sight—
Don't let the children take sticks to knock them down!
We must model ourselves on Yüan An of old,[9] or like Miss
*   Hsieh [10]*
Skilfully rhyme our praise.

The Fairy of Ku-she is in charge of the snow; but then there is the spirit of the snow who is a white mule. When he loses a hair, there is a ten-foot fall of snow. But he is looked after by a fairy gentleman called Hung Yai, who keeps him in a gourd. On one occasion, drunk after a party with the other fairies in the Purple Palace, he omitted to put the stopper in tight enough and the white mule escaped. It lost some hair among the western tribes, and an enormous fall of snow was the consequence of Hung Yai's carelessness.

And now let us tell of another man, an official, who also lost a white horse in the snow, and thereby became involved in an

amazing fairy adventure until finally his whole family ascended
to heaven in broad daylight. To this day their story is still told.

It was in the winter of the year 525, the sixth year of the reign-
period P'u-t'ung of the Liang Emperor Wu-ti, in the twelfth
month. A certain Imperial Counsellor by the name of Wei Shu
had given offence by disapproving of the Emperor Wu-ti's
addiction to the Buddhist religion, and had been reduced to the
post of Inspector of the Imperial Stud. This was an official

> *Of upright mind, of strength of character,*
> *Ready to gainsay the Emperor himself,*
> *Longing to rid the world of the false and the base.*

And so Wei was appointed to the Imperial Stud, which was in
the district of Liu-ho near Chenchou. Now, the Emperor Wu-ti
possessed a white horse which was known as the Jade Lion,
Glory of the Palace :

> *Hooves carved as from jade, body inlaid as with jasper,*
> *Broad breast banded with purest white,*
> *Tail a flashing of silver threads.*
> *Galloped or laden—able to cover a thousand miles;*
> *Easily breathing—flying over a triple hazard.*
> *As though the Lionhorse* [11] *were born on earth,*
> *As if Whitemarsh* [12] *were come among men.*

Ever since the Emperor Wu-ti had engaged in the pursuit of
Bodhidharma [13] he had been absent from the hunting-field, and
this white horse was therefore condemned to enter the Imperial
Stud. Now one night there was a heavy snowfall, and when the
staff got up in the morning what should they hear but a groom
reporting to the Counsellor Wei Shu, 'A terrible thing has
happened. Last night when I went to the stall of the Jade Lion
Glory of the Palace, he had gone!'

In alarm Wei Shu hurriedly got together every man of his
staff, but what was to be done? Then one of the grooms came
forward and said, 'It won't be difficult to find this horse. If we
just follow his tracks in the snow we shall soon know where he's
got to.'

'You are right,' said Wei Shu ; and he sent this groom off at
once at the head of a party of men to look for the hoofmarks.

They strayed on for several miles across the fields, until they came to a garden in the snow. And this is what they saw:

> Summer-house with painted walls,
> Pavilion, door-bolts of jasper.
> Flanking these, balustrades of jade slant down
> To a trim level path, a silvery ribbon.
> Intricate T'ai-hu rocks [14]—
> One would think a crouching tiger carved from salt [15];
> Branches of fir and cypress
> Like a jade dragon rearing high.
> The grass by the path is withered, its colour disguised,
> The plum-trees send their fragrance, a promise to bloom.

It was in fact a smallholding. The groom turned to his men and said, 'The horse is in here.'

They went straight to the door of the gardener's cottage and knocked, and an old fellow came out. The groom saluted him and said, 'It's just an enquiry. Last night in the snow we lost a white horse from the Imperial Stud. This horse is called the Jade Lion, Glory of the Palace, and is the mount of the Emperor of Liang himself. Judging from the hoof-marks he has jumped the fence into your holding. If you've still got him here, we will tell our Counsellor and he will reward you with wine and money.'

'Splendid,' said the old man to this. 'Sit down for a while, all of you, and I will bring you something I want you to eat.'

When they were all seated the old man went down into his garden, and there they saw him plunge his hands into the snow and pull up a melon, and when they saw the melon, truly,

> Tender in leaf and in root,
> Yellow flower at the tip,
> Out of the dung, what fragrance,
> Out of the muck, what sweetness!

The melon was complete with root, tendril, stalk and leaf. Each man said to himself, 'Surely the old man can't have just gathered it?'—and yet, it was a lovely fresh colour. The old man took out his knife and peeled and sliced the melon, whereupon a rare fragrance filled their nostrils. He invited them to share it between them, and then went back into the snow and picked three more, saying, 'I want you to pass on my message to your Counsellor. Tell him that Mr Chang sends these melons for him.'

The men having accepted the melons, the old gardener brought out the white horse from the rear of his garden and handed it over to the groom. The groom took hold of its bridle and thanked the old man, and then they all returned to the Imperial Stud and reported to the Counsellor Wei.

'This is an amazing thing,' said Wei Shu. 'How can he have grown these melons in the snow?' He called at once to his wife and his seventeen-year-old-daughter, and they cut open the melons and shared them.

'Really, we are in this old man's debt,' said Wei Shu's wife, 'not only for keeping the horse for us but for sending these melons as well. How shall we ever be able to thank him?'

Two months went by 'in the crooking of a finger', the year had turned and it was the clear sunshine of spring. 'It's fine and pleasant out today,' said Wei Shu's wife. 'We must go and see that Mr Chang who sent the melons, and thank him for keeping our horse for us.'

And so the Counsellor gave orders for jars of wine and picnic dishes to be made ready, hot soup and fritters and various delicacies. He sent for his seventeen-year-old daughter and said, 'Today I am visiting Mr Chang to thank him for his kindness, and your mother and yourself may come along with me and enjoy the trip.'[16]

The Counsellor on horseback, his wife and daughter following in two sedan-chairs, they arrived before Mr Chang's gate and sent in word to him. The old man hurried out to greet them, and Wei Shu's wife said, 'A little while ago we gave you the trouble of looking after our horse for us, and today the Counsellor has brought wine on purpose to thank you for your kindness.'

They entered the rough cottage and set out the wine-jars and bowls and plates, and invited Mr Chang to sit down with them. The old man again and again declined the honour, but finally drew out a stool and sat down at one side. When they had reached their third bowl of wine, Wei's wife asked, 'What is your age, sir?'

'I am over eighty,' replied the old man.

She asked after his family, and the old man said, 'I am alone in the world.'

'Really you ought to have a wife to look after you,' said Wei's wife.

'Oh,' replied the old man, 'I haven't the wit to get one.'

'What I mean is someone of seventy or so,' said the lady.

'That's too old,' said the old gardener. 'After all,

A hundred years are like the crooking of a finger,
But how many live to be much past seventy?'

'Well, what about sixty or so?' asked the lady.

'Too old,' said the old man—

'In the later part of the month, the moon's light dims;
When people pass middle age, they're not much use.'

'What about fifty or so?' asked the lady.

'Too old,' said the old man—

'Unknown at thirty,
Still poor at forty,
By fifty you've one foot in the grave.'

Wei Shu's wife was beginning to lose patience, and said to herself, 'All right, I'll have some fun with him.' To Mr Chang, she said, 'Well sir, what about a thirty-year-old?'

'Too old,' replied the old man.

'Very well then, sir, what age would you say?' asked the lady.

The old man rose to his feet and pointed to the young lady of seventeen: 'I should be satisfied with her for my bride.'

When the Counsellor Wei heard this, 'anger rose from his heart, hatred was born in his belly'. Without waiting for explanations he ordered his attendants to beat the old man. But his wife intervened: 'You can't do that. We came on purpose to thank him, how can you have him beaten? He is an old man and says foolish things. Take no notice of him, but let us pack our things and go home.'

But now the story tells how Mr Chang for three days never opened his door until Third Wang and Fourth Chao, two flower-sellers of Liu-ho, came along with their big wicker baskets to ask Mr Chang for some blooms. Seeing his gate shut they knocked and called to him. He came out to them, mumbling to himself and coughing the while, exactly as though he were wasting away from a love-sickness. His breathing was laboured: and how can

I show you all this? There is a *tz'u* to the metre of 'A Night Stroll in the Palace':

> *Of four hundred and four diseases a man may catch*
> *Love-sickness is the worst to bear.*
> *No pain, no ache in the heart,*
> *But the body is consumed by magic.*
>
> *Moonlight and flowers bring sorrow,*
> *The time to be feared is the dusk.*
> *Then, the heart begins its itching,*
> *Then, you hear him cough and cough again.*

Now here was this old man, wheezing his way along to them. 'It's good of you to call,' he said. 'I haven't been myself these last two days. If you want some flowers just go and pick them. I don't want any money from you, but there is something you can do for me. I want you to find me two go-betweens. If you can bring them here, there will be two hundred cash for you to buy some wine with.'

The two men picked their blooms and went off, and in a little while they reappeared with a couple of go-betweens. Now these go-betweens,

> *One word from them and the match is made;*
> *They speak, and conjugal bliss is sure.*
> *They care for all unmated turtle-doves,*[17]
> *They show concern for all who sleep alone.*
> *No triple gate but they break down,*
> *No twelve-storied tower is proof against them,*
> *Rousing desire in the dullest of men,*
> *Stirring the dreams of the purest of maids.*
> *At their request, the Jade Maiden* [18]
> *By her arts grasps you firmly by the hand;*
> *They offer incense to the Golden Boy*
> *Who grapples you with words and brings you down.*
> *They snare the rake who snatches at Wu-shan's joys,*[19]
> *And bring love-sickness to the Weaving-girl herself.*[20]

These two go-betweens were brought along and exchanged greetings with the old man, who then said, 'I want you to arrange a match for me if you will. Now this match . . . I have already seen the girl, and it is not going to be easy for you. Here are three taels of silver for each of you. If you bring me a reply each of you will receive a further five taels. And if you are successful, there will be a small fortune in it for you.'

And so Dame Chang and Dame Li asked him, 'Whose family does the young lady belong to, sir?'

'She is the daughter,' replied Mr Chang, 'of the Counsellor Wei Shu of the Imperial Stud, and she is seventeen years old. I want you to go there and ask for her, please.'

Laughing to themselves, the two go-betweens took the silver and left him. But when they had gone a few hundred yards they sat down on a bank and Dame Chang said to Dame Li, 'How are we to speak for him in Counsellor Wei's house?'

'Easy,' said Dame Li. 'First we buy a jar of wine and drink it so that our cheeks become flushed. Then we go and walk up and down for a while in front of Counsellor Wei's gate. Then we come back and report to Mr. Chang. We'll say we've spoken for him, but there isn't any answer yet.'

While they were still discussing this they heard a shout, 'Wait a minute!', and turning round they saw Mr Chang hurrying up to them. 'I suspected that the two of you planned to buy a jar of wine to make your cheeks flushed,' he said, 'and then go and walk up and down in front of Counsellor Wei's gate, and tell me there wasn't any answer yet. That's what you're up to, isn't it? Now if you know what's good for you you'll go straight off at once, and I must have a reply.'

After what Mr Chang had said the two go-betweens had no alternative but to go to the Imperial Stud and find someone to report their arrival to the Counsellor Wei Shu. 'Have them brought in,' said Wei Shu, and when Dame Chang and Dame Li had made their greetings he began, 'I suppose you must have come with an offer of marriage?'

The go-betweens were afraid to open their mouths, but simply stood there giggling. 'I have a grown-up son,' said Wei Shu, 'twenty-one years of age. He is not at home now, he is with Wang Seng-pien on an expedition to the north.[21] Then I have a daughter of seventeen; but an honest official remains poor, and I have no money to offer as a dowry.'

The two go-betweens made obeisances at the foot of the steps, still not daring to speak. 'There is no need for all these obeisances,' said Wei Shu. 'If you have something to say, out with it.'

Dame Chang began to speak: 'We have a matter to discuss, although we would rather not mention it; on the other hand, we should rather like to mention it on account of the six taels of silver he gave us. We fear you may be angry, but then it is really rather comical.'

Wei Shu asked what it was, and Dame Chang went on, 'The old man who grows melons, old Chang, has suddenly taken it into his head to send for my partner here and myself and get us to ask for your daughter, sir, in marriage. We were given six taels of silver—see!'—and taking out the silver from her bodice she showed it to the Counsellor, and continued: 'If you secure it for us we get this silver, and if you don't we have to give it back to him.'

'The old man must be crazy,' said Wei Shu. 'My daughter is only seventeen and I have no intention of arranging her marriage yet. How can I possibly secure these six taels for you?'

'What he said,' replied Dame Chang, 'was only that we had to take him your answer. For that we should get the silver.'

At this Wei Shu rose and pointed his finger at the go-between, and said, 'Give him this message from me: if this naïve old fool wants to marry my daughter he must deliver tomorrow a betrothal present of one hundred thousand strings, each of one thousand cash, and what is more they must all be copper coins of the same kind, I want no gold coins making up the amount.'

Wei Shu had wine brought in for the go-betweens, and urged them to have a drink before he dismissed them. The two respectfully took their leave and went back to Mr Chang's cottage. The latter gentleman was soon in view, neck outstretched like a roosting goose watching for its gander. As soon as they stood before him he said, 'Do sit down, I'm afraid I have caused you a great deal of trouble.' Then, drawing out ten taels of silver, which he put on the table, he said, 'Thanks to your efforts, this matter of my marriage is perfectly settled.'

'What do you mean?' asked Dame Chang.

'My future father-in-law,' replied the old man, 'wants a betrothal present from me of a hundred thousand strings, each of a thousand cash, and what is more they must all be copper coins of the same kind, and he must have all this before we can be married.'

'You've guessed it exactly,' said the go-betweens, 'that's just what the Counsellor said. How are you going to manage it, sir?'

The old man opened a jar of wine, which he placed on the table. When they had finished their fourth bowl, he led them out to look at the trough of the roof, behind the low eaves. 'Look,' he said, pointing. The omnivorous omnipresent left and right pupils of the go-betweens' eyes fixed themselves on the trough of the roof, and there, piled high, they saw precisely one hundred thousand strings, each of one thousand copper cash.

'You see?' said the old man. 'It's all ready for him.' And he assured them that it would be sent over that very day, if they would first go back again to the Counsellor to report this. The go-betweens went off, and meanwhile Mr Chang prepared the means of transport. From inside his house he summoned a procession of men wearing purple tunics and silver headcloths patterned in red. Before them they pushed carts of the flat, four-wheeled type:

> Like thunder roaring down the river, a stormtide sweeping across
>   the plain,
> An earthquake, one would think, or the heavens reeling,
> It seems the very sun and stars are falling.
> A scene, at first glimpse, to recall
> The devils fleeing to the hills when Ch'in-shih-huang blocked the
>   sea;
> Bringing to mind, in its grandeur,
> The mighty Ao, prodigious, driving his boat across dry land.[22]
> The length of the river, the wild geese call,
> A line of pheasants answer.

Banners above the carts bore the legend, 'Gift of Mr Chang to the family of the Counsellor Wei Shu'. At length the men had wheeled their carts up to the gate of the Counsellor's residence, where they gave three shouts of salutation, and after lining up the carts in two ranks sent in one of their number to report their arrival. Wei Shu, confronted with the carts as he came out, was left speechless and gaping with astonishment. He sent in word for

his wife, of whom he demanded what they were going to do about
it?

'You had no right ever to demand the hundred thousand
strings of cash from him,' said his wife. 'Heaven knows how the
old man has managed to scrape them together like this. And now
if we decline the match, it means that our word is worthless; yet
if we accept it, whoever heard of a young lady of good family
marrying a gardener?'

Since no solution offered itself, they called for their seventeen-
year-old daughter to be brought before them,[23] and asked her
what should be done. By way of reply the girl brought out from
her bosom a purse of brocade. Now the fact was that this girl
had reached the age of six before she was able to speak. Then
suddenly one day she gave voice to the following lines:

> *How can we know the will of Heaven?*
> *My mate will be found in southern Ch'u.*
> *Grey embers shall prove fiery hot,*
> *The withered willow shoot afresh.*

From this time forward she was able to compose, and they
changed her name to 'Lady of Letters'. She made a purse of
brocade to hold the poem, and had now kept it by her for eleven
years.

Now, showing the poem to her father, she said, 'Although Mr
Chang is of such a great age, I believe this to be the will of
Heaven—although one cannot know.'

Wei Shu's wife reflected that if her daughter was willing, and
if Mr Chang really had brought the hundred thousand strings of
cash, then clearly he was a man of singular destiny and there was
nothing for it but to accept the match. They chose an auspicious
day and the wedding was duly performed, to the great delight
of Mr Chang—truly,

> *Rain after drought, the lotus grows fresh roots,*
> *In spring the withered tree puts out new shoots.*

The wedding over, the guests dispersed, and Mr Chang took
his young bride back to his home. The Counsellor Wei Shu
prohibited all members of his household from visiting Chang's
cottage.

In the summer of the year 526, in the sixth month, the
Counsellor's son, Wei I-fang, a man accomplished in both the
polite and the military arts, returned home to Liu-ho from service
on the northern expedition led by Wang Seng-pien. It was a hot
day—and how can I show this?—

> *No cloud in the sky for the six dragons* [24] *to ride,*
> *Mile upon mile of forest, but no bird rises.*
> *Soil burns, stone cracks, river and lake bubble,*
> *And still no breath of wind comes from the south.*

Just before he reached his home, Wei I-fang caught sight of a
woman selling melons by the roadside, before the gate of a smallholding. Her hair was matted and unkempt, she wore a plain blue
skirt, and common sandals were on her feet. But the melons she
was selling—

> *From the fragrant dew of their bed in the west garden*
> *They come to ease the southern heat of the summer-house.*
> *No need to wonder that there seem to be no flies—*
> *Winter itself is not so cold as the ice in this jade globe.*
> *The golden melon flowers, floating against the green.*
> *Waking from a dream at noon*
> *We miss the old poet, still tending his fruit—*
> *Where else could they be grown, unless by the Green Gate of old?* [25]

Thirsty from his journey, Wei I-fang decided to buy a melon,
but on coming face to face with the woman he gave a wild cry:
'Lady of Letters! What are you doing here?'

'Oh, my brother,' replied Lady of Letters, 'our father married
me off into this house.'

'I heard some story on my way here,' said Wei I-fang, 'about
father selling you to a melon-grower called Chang for one hundred
thousand strings of cash. What is the meaning of it all?'

In answer Lady of Letters told her brother the whole story
right from the beginning. 'How would it be if I have a word with
him now?' asked Wei I-fang when she had finished.

'If you want to see Mr Chang,' said Lady of Letters, 'just wait
while I speak to him first, and then you can go in.'

And Lady of Letters turned away and hurried into the house,
where she spoke to Mr Chang. On her return, she said, 'Mr
Chang says that you are of a fiery nature and that your present

purpose serves only to fan the flames; therefore he would rather not meet you. If you insist on seeing him now, you may—but you must rid your mind of any evil intent.'

With this Lady of Letters conducted I-fang into the house, where the old man at once came out, rubbing his side, to receive them. At sight of him, Wei I-fang began: 'For a man like you to produce a hundred thousand strings of cash and marry my sister—it is unthinkable. For certain, you can only be an evil demon.'

In a flash he drew his precious sword T'ai-o [26] and came at Mr Chang aiming to strike off his head. But suddenly, there was the hilt of the sword still stuck in his hand, while the blade shivered into fragments.

'Pity!' said Mr Chang. 'That's another fairy lost to the world!'

Lady of Letters hustled her brother out of the house, scolding him: 'I told you to rid yourself of any evil intent—why did you draw your sword against him?'

Wei I-fang completed his homeward journey, and when he had greeted his parents he asked them why they had married Lady of Letters to Mr Chang.

'The old man is a monster,' replied the Counsellor Wei Shu.

'That is just what I thought,' said I-fang, 'and then when I drew my sword on him I found I could not touch him, but he ruined my sword for me.'

The next morning, Wei I-fang rose and washed and rinsed his mouth, and prepared himself for a journey. Then he announced to his parents, 'Today I am determined to bring my sister back home. And if I am unable to do this, I swear you will never see me again.'

He took his leave of them, and accompanied by two henchmen made his way to the place where Mr Chang lived. But all he found there was a flat and empty space, a place of desolation. They made enquiries of people who lived nearby, who said, 'Yes, there was a Mr Chang who grew melons here. He had been here for twenty-odd years, but last night there was a black wind and driving rain and today there is no sign of him.'

Astounded, Wei I-fang raised his head to look about him, and saw that four lines of verse had been carved on the trunk of a tree:

Two little cases of a kind unknown to man:
One half my holding in each one lies.
If you wish to know my present address
It is 'Peach Blossom Village, Paradise'.

When Wei I-fang had read this inscription he ordered his henchmen to search all about, and they came back to report, 'Mr Chang on one lame donkey, and the young lady on another lame donkey, with just two little cases, went off in the direction of Chenchou.'

Wei I-fang and his men went straight off after them, and on the way met people who told them, 'Yes, we saw an old man riding a lame donkey, with a young woman on another lame donkey. The young lady didn't want to go on, and wept and pleaded with the old man, "Let me go back to take leave of my mother and father"—but the old man had a stick in his hand and was beating her as they went along, really it was pitiful to see, we had to turn our eyes away.'

When Wei I-fang heard this, two waves of indignation flowed from the soles of his feet through to his forehead, a flame of nameless fire leapt up from his heart thirty thousand feet high, and he was quite beside himself. Still accompanied by his men he continued in pursuit. Another score or two of miles, and still they had not caught them, when they reached the ferry-point of Port Melon,[27] and were told that their quarry had just been seen crossing the Yangtze.

Wei I-fang ordered a boat to be found to carry his party across, and continued his pursuit as far as the foot of the mountain Mao-shan.[28] On enquiry there he learned that his quarry had ascended the mountain. He therefore instructed his henchmen to instal themselves with their luggage in an inn while he went on alone up the mountain. He travelled on for many hours, but found no sign of any Peach Blossom Village. But then walking on he found a broad stream across his path. And this is what he saw:

A stream cool and deep, a murmuring flow of water,
On the icy surface, one's reflection clearly etched,
Foam on distant ripples like welcome winter snow,
Willow branches fold in shade the long ridge of the bank.
For the mortal traveller, this is the end of the world.

There at the edge of the stream Wei I-fang thought to himself,
'I have pursued them all this way, and now how can I return to
my parents if I do not take my sister with me? Best to throw
myself into this stream and put an end to it all.' But while these
thoughts were filling his mind he was taking in the scene, and
noticed a cascade of water down one rocky bank which bore on its
surface a scattering of peach blossoms. 'It is autumn now,' Wei
I-fang wondered to himself. 'Where can these peach blossoms
have come from? Surely that must be Peach Blossom Village up
above there, where my sister's husband Mr Chang lives!'

Next he heard the sound of a flute coming from the far bank,
and raising his eyes he saw a herd-boy mounted on a lame donkey,
sitting there playing his flute. This was the scene:

> *A shade of deepest green over the ancient ferry,*
> *A herd-boy riding back-to-front, his flute held sideways on.*
> *From the flute comes the music of Sheng-p'ing-lo,[29]*
> *Calling a thousand sorrows from the lonely wanderer.*

The herd-boy rode up to the edge of the stream and called out,
'Aren't you Wei I-fang?'

'I am,' replied I-fang.

'By the command of His Highness Chang,' went on the herd-
boy, 'I am to ask you to come across, sir.'

The herd-boy drove his lame donkey across the stream and
led it back again with Wei I-fang seated on its back. Then, the
herd-boy leading, they made their way to a farm. And how can
I show it to you? There is a poem to the metre of 'The Fairy
by the River':

> *For a happy life, there is nothing like a farm,*
> *Quiet, secluded, thatched hut by wattle fence.*
> *Plough in spring, plant in summer, reap harvest in autumn,*
> *In winter, watch the welcome snow*
> *Or lie beneath the bedclothes, drunk.*
>
> *Before my door I will plant more elms and willows;*
> *Already the aspen catkins, falling, cover the stream.*
> *Here is no place for boredom or idle melancholy—*
> *I laugh at the man of ambition*
> *Scurrying round the bazaars.*

When they reached the farm the boy went in, and shortly there emerged from the orchard two attendants clad in red, who greeted Wei I-fang with the words, 'His Highness Chang is engaged on court business just at the moment and is unable to see you, and so he has ordered us to look after you.' And they led him to a great pavilion which afforded vistas on all four sides. On a tablet he read the name 'Emerald Bamboo Pavilion'; and this is what he saw:

> *A lush and verdant grove, a mass of tall bamboos,*
> *Green shade cutting across the screening-mounds,*
> *Packed foliage hiding the balustrades,*
> *By the pavilion wrapped in mist a single crane cries,*
> *From the valley filled with cloud the wild monkeys call.*

Inside the pavilion wine-vessels were laid out ready; outside, hemming it about, were marvellous peaches and luscious apricots, rare and wonderful plants and flowers. The red-clothed attendants invited Wei I-fang to sit down with them and eat and drink. I-fang was several times on the point of asking what kind of man Mr Chang really was; but each time his question was forestalled by a fresh bowl thrust into his hand. At last the drinking ceased and the attendants took their leave and went off, leaving Wei I-fang alone in the pavilion with instructions to wait a little while.

But though he waited for a considerable time nothing happened, and so he allowed himself to stray out of the pavilion. He had walked for some little distance when he saw beyond the surrounding plants and trees a palace, from within which he could hear the sound of voices. Wei I-fang crept up behind a red-lacquered screen, licked a hole in a paper panel, and looked through. And this is what he saw:

> *Lofty chambers, the walls carved and painted,*
> *Flanked by crimson pillars, approached by steps of jade;*
> *Screens open out, cloud-painted or set with pearls;*
> *Jasper towers soar over jewelled halls.*
> *Over paths banked with fairy flowers*
> *Phoenixes, green or red, fly in and out,*
> *In the shade of priceless trees*
> *White deer and black ape play together;*
> *Jade Maiden and Golden Boy wait attendance,*
> *An aura of blessing hangs over all.*

And there, enthroned on a dais, he saw Mr Chang, clad in royal robes with sword and sceptre and with the ceremonial head-dress and boots. The hall below him was lined with crimson-uniformed lictors, each of whom was either a spirit or a demon; and these guarded two figures whose shoulders were weighted down by heavy iron cangues. The first of these, in purple robe and girdle of gold, announced himself as the guardian deity of such-and-such a place; and he confessed his failure thoroughly to investigate the ravages caused in his area by wolves and tigers. The other was a warrior, armoured and helmeted, who announced himself as the mountain-spirit of such-and-such a district. Wolves and tigers had molested the common people of his area, yet his forces had taken no action.

Mr Chang pronounced a verdict of 'guilty' upon each of them. Wei I-fang, watching all this through his spy-hole, could not restrain a cry—'Monsters! Monsters!' The lictors in the hall heard him and sent out two stalwart fellows wearing the yellow head-dress of the Taoist priest. These men grabbed hold of I-fang and dragged him to the foot of the dais. They accused him of scheming to gain illicit possession of divine secrets, and urged that he be punished. In terror, Wei I-fang kotowed and confessed his guilt.

But just as Mr Chang was beginning his pronouncement, a lady stepped forward from behind a screen. She wore the phoenix-decorated bridal head-dress and a diaphanous cape over her full-length skirt, and on her feet were pearl-embroidered slippers —it was I-fang's sister, Lady of Letters!

Kneeling she pleaded before Mr Chang: 'I beg your Highness to pardon him, out of your consideration for me, since he is my own elder brother!'

And so Mr Chang pronounced as follows: 'You, Wei I-fang, were destined to become an immortal; but in contravention of this you struck at me with your sword. Out of regard for the relationship between us I ignored your crime. And now you are back again, spying on my palace and hoping to acquire divine secrets! For your sister's sake I will spare your life. I award you one hundred thousand strings of cash, and I have something here which will serve as a token when you go to collect the money.'

Mr Chang rose and strode off into the interior of the palace.

In a short while he reappeared, holding in his hand an ancient straw hat. This he handed to Wei I-fang, whom he instructed to seek out a Mr Shen, a herbalist, below the K'ai-ming Bridge in Yangchou. There, with the hat as token, he could draw the hundred thousand strings of cash.

'Mortal and immortal travel on different roads,' Mr Chang concluded. 'You may not stay longer.' And he ordered the boy with the flute to take his brother-in-law back, once more on the lame donkey. They left Peach Blossom Village and made their way to the stream; and there, as Wei I-fang sat upright on his donkey, the lad gave him a push and he toppled head over heels to the ground.

As if waking from a dream, Wei I-fang found himself sitting on the bank of the stream: and there in the fold of his robe was the straw hat. How could it have been no more than a dream? He sat there bewildered. But the only thing for it was to set off back, still clutching the straw hat, down the mountain to the inn where he had deposited his luggage the previous day. He looked about for his two henchmen, but the innkeeper came out and said: 'There was indeed a gentleman by the name of Wei, twenty years ago, who left his luggage here and went off up Mao-shan. But he was held up, and his two servants grew tired of waiting for him and went off back. This is the year 606, the second year of Ta-yeh in the reign of the Sui Emperor Yang-ti, and so it's exactly twenty years ago.' [30]

'It's only one day since yesterday, and yet twenty years have passed!' exclaimed Wei I-fang. 'I must return to my parents at the Imperial Stud at Liu-ho.'

He took leave of the innkeeper and returned to Liu-ho. But on enquiry he was told that twenty years before there had been a Counsellor Wei of the Imperial Stud, whose entire family, thirteen in all, had ascended to heaven in broad daylight. The scene of their ascension could still be visited. And he learned that there had been a son who had gone away and not come back.

When Wei I-fang heard all this he raised his face to the sky and cried aloud. Twenty years had passed in a single day, his father and mother were gone and he had no home to return to. There was nothing he could do now but seek out this Mr Shen and ask for his hundred thousand strings of cash.

He travelled from Liu-ho all the way to Yangchou and was directed to the K'ai-ming Bridge. There was indeed a herb-shop there, and it was kept by a Mr Shen. Wei I-fang entered the shop and saw an old man sitting there:

> *An old curiosity to look at,*
> *Dressed in the oddest clothes.*
> *Forked grey beard like a pair of silver scissors,*
> *White hair piled like snow on his head.*
> *Back bowed like a tortoise,*
> *Shoulders hunched like a kite,*
> *Like a star-spirit banished from the sky;*
> *Legs as long as a crane,*
> *Trunk as gaunt as a pine,*
> *Reminds one of Hua Ti or Lao Tzu.*[31]
> *Perhaps Ch'in K'o has escaped from Shang-ling,*
> *Or is this the fisherman of the river P'an* [32]?

'My respects to you, old fellow,' said Wei I-fang. 'This must be the shop of Mr Shen, the herbalist?'

'It is,' replied the old man. Wei I-fang's eyes scanned the herbalist's counter:

> *Of the four baskets ranged there, three were empty;*
> *The fourth was filled with the north-west wind.*

'But how do I get him to give me one hundred thousand strings of cash?' Wei I-fang asked himself. 'Tell me, uncle,' he said aloud, 'may I buy three coppers' worth of peppermint?'

'Good for you, peppermint,' said the old man. 'The *Pen-ts'ao*[33] says it cools the head and clears the sight. How much do you want?'

'Three coppers' worth,' repeated I-fang.

'I'm very sorry, but I'm just out of it,' said the old man.

'Then give me some "Hundred Herbs Syrup"[34],' said Wei I-fang.

'Helps you digest wine and noodles, does "Hundred Herbs Syrup",' said the old man, 'and it moistens the throat nicely. How much do you want?'

'Three coppers' worth', said Wei I-fang.

'I'm so sorry,' said the old man, 'I've just sold the last of it.'

'Then give me some liquorice-root,' said Wei I-fang.

'Very good, liquorice-root,' came the old man's reply. 'Very mild and non-poisonous, mixes well with other medicines, and counteracts poisons, whether of metal, stone, herb or wood. In the trade they call it the Prime Minister.[35] How much do you want?'

'Give me five cash worth, uncle,' said Wei I-fang.

'I don't like to have to admit it,' said the old man, 'but I haven't got any of that either.'

Wei I-fang then looked the old man straight in the eyes and said, 'I didn't really come to buy herbs. A man gave me a message for you—Mr Chang the melon-grower.'

'I trust Mr Chang is well,' said Mr Shen. 'What was his message about?'

'He told me to ask you for one hundred thousand strings of cash,' said Wei I-fang.

'Oh, money is the one thing I *have* got,' said Mr Shen. 'What are your credentials?'.

In response, Wei I-fang felt inside his robe and brought out the straw hat. Mr Shen turned towards a doorway curtained with blue cloth and shouted to his wife to come out. The curtain opened, and out stepped a girl of sixteen or seventeen, who asked, 'Why do you call me, husband?'

'This fellow is just like Mr Chang, picking himself such a young wife,' Wei I-fang thought to himself.

Mr Shen showed his wife the straw hat and asked whether it was the right one. 'Some time ago,' replied his wife, 'Mr Chang came past our door on his lame donkey. His hat was split and he asked me to sew it up. I happened to be out of black thread, and so I sewed it up at the crown with red.'

She turned it over, and the crown was indeed sewn up with red thread. Straight away Mr Shen led I-fang inside the house, where he handed him the hundred thousand strings of cash.

Wei I-fang used the money to repair bridges and to build roads, and the surplus he distributed among the poor. Then suddenly one day, as he was passing a wine-shop, he caught sight of a lad riding a donkey. He recognized him as the boy who had led him across the stream. 'Where is Mr Chang?' he asked him.

The boy replied, 'He is having a drink with Mr Shen just now, upstairs in the wine-shop.'

Wei I-fang climbed the stairs of the wine-shop and saw Mr Shen and Mr Chang sitting there together. He made obeisance before them.

'My real name,' said Mr Chang, 'is Chang the Ancient, Elder Immortal of Eternal Joy. Lady of Letters is the Jade Maiden of the Upper Heaven. But she longed for earth. The Supreme Ruler was afraid of her defilement at the hands of mortal men, and so I assumed this guise to rescue her and take her back to heaven. You, Wei I-fang, are destined to become an immortal, but you are unfortunately over-addicted to violence. Your appointment therefore is only to govern the region of Yangchou as guardian deity.'

His speech ended, he made a sign with his hand, and two fairy cranes appeared. And forthwith Mr Shen and Chang the Ancient, each mounted on a white crane, ascended to the sky. From where they had gone a scroll of paper drifted down, which when opened proved to bear the following lines:

> *Twenty years away from Eternal Joy,*
> *Hidden on earth in the guise of a melon-grower.*
> *Alas, for mortals there is only mortal vision—*
> *Who could recognize me, idling in the dust?*
> *I-fang is appointed and given his domain,*
> *Lady of Letters is borne by a phoenix to the sky.*
> *Henceforth this scene of cranes soaring aloft*
> *Will be remembered with respect in Yangchou.*

Notes

The Lady Who Was a Beggar

1. A man of Ch'in in the Warring States period, who at the age of eleven was ennobled for services to the state.
2. A concubine of the last ruler of the Ch'en dynasty (reigned A.D. 583–9). She was beautiful and intelligent, and her hair was seven feet long. She was executed together with her lord by the troops of the succeeding power of Sui.
3. May be a similar type of song to 'Lien-hua-lo', which was sung by beggars as early as the T'ang dynasty—witness the reference to Cheng Yüan-ho, earlier in the story.
4. To simulate poverty and hunger.
5. Slayer of demons, whose image is posted on festival days to ward off evil spirits.
6. A wife could be put aside for failing to give birth to a son, for adultery, disobedience to her husband's parents, for nagging, stealing, jealousy or for contracting an evil disease.
7. A spur of the mountain Niu-chu which projects from the south bank of the Yangtze and is called the Ts'ai-shih-chi. Its attractions for suicides are enhanced by the legend that Li Po drowned here in the attempt to embrace the reflection of the moon on the water.
8. Six senses (literally, 'six robbers'): sight, hearing, smell, taste, touch and thought. Amida Buddha is Amitābha, 'an imaginary being unknown to ancient Buddhism . . . who has eclipsed the historical Buddha in becoming the most popular divinity in the Mahāyāna pantheon' (Soothill).
9. Sung Hung 'became Minister of State under the Emperor Kuang Wu Ti, and in A.D. 26 was ennobled as Marquis. His Majesty now wished him to put away his wife, who was a woman of the people, and marry a Princess; to which he nobly replied: "Sire, the partner of my porridge days shall never go down from my hall." Five years later he fell into disfavour, and was compelled to retire into private life' (Giles).
10. A man of the Later Han dynasty renowned for his brilliance. On hearing that a man of rank had considered him with approval as a possible husband for his niece, Huang Yün put away his wife. She, in return, ruined his career by giving a party on the eve of her departure, at which she entertained the company with an enumeration of her husband's hitherto-concealed misdeeds.

The Pearl-sewn Shirt

1. The opening chapters of Chang Hsin-chang, *Allegory and Courtesy in Spenser*, offer a translation of a most interesting allegorical treatment of

these four vices in the nineteenth-century Chinese novel *Ching hua yuan*.

2. The 'six preliminaries':
   presents to the home of the bride-to-be;
   ascertaining her genealogy;
   securing a lucky omen;
   sending a present of silk to confirm the contract;
   requesting the naming of the date;
   going to receive the bride.

3. The festival celebrates the annual meeting of the Herd-boy and the Weaving-girl, two stars, lovers, who for the remainder of the year are condemned to gaze at each other across the barrier of the 'River of Heaven', the Milky Way.

4. Hsi-shih is a more frequent object of allusion than any other Chinese beauty. She was born in the kingdom of Yüeh in classical times. Presented to the sensual ruler of the rival kingdom of Wu, with the object of distracting him from affairs of state, she fulfilled her mission with distinction.

5. Nan-wei might have achieved results comparable with those of Hsi-shih had not her master, Duke Wen of Chin, seen the danger and sent her away after three days.

6. A popular mode of portraying the Goddess of Mercy (Avalokitesvara, Kuan-yin) shows her watching the reflection of moonlight on water.

7. Sung Yü: disciple of Ch'ü Yüan, the great poet of Ch'u. P'an An: P'an Yüeh (An-jen), of Chin, so handsome that he was mobbed by women whenever he appeared on the streets of Loyang.

8. Liu Pang founded the great Han dynasty; Hsiang Yü was his chief rival for supreme power.

9. This is an exact translation: the story-teller does draw a veil at this stage of the proceedings. I have however preferred to follow the 1947 reprint of the original in omitting a few phrases, which add nothing but might be found offensive.

10. Conventional allusions to well-known pairs of lovers.

11. See note 6 to *The Lady who was a Beggar*.

12. The story is told in the *History of the Chin Dynasty* of Lei Huan (third century A.D.), who was asked by Chang Hua, Marquis Kuang-wu, to interpret a portent which took the form of a crimson aura in the sky. Lei explained it as the manifestation of the spirits of jewelled swords. The swords would be found, he predicted, at Feng-ch'eng (in present-day Kwangsi province). Appointed magistrate of this city, Lei dug down more than forty feet beneath the foundations of the prison, and unearthed a stone casket which shone with a strange light. Within was a pair of jewelled swords, engraved with the names Lung Ch'üan ('Dragon Spring') and T'ai O—the names of famous swords of the state of Ch'u in ancient times. After the discovery of the swords the aura in the sky was not seen again. Lei kept one sword and sent the other to the Marquis, who predicted that the swords, being of divine origin,

would ultimately be reunited. When the Marquis was at length executed his sword was lost. After the death of Lei Huan his son, Hua, was crossing the Yen-p'ing ford when the remaining sword leapt from his hand. Two dragons coiled up out of the seething waters, and the sword was seen no more.

Wine and Dumplings

1. The staff of the Wen-hsüeh-kuan, instituted by T'ai-tsung to direct the literary work of the administration.
2. I.e. prince and minister.
3. The great T'ao Ch'ien (T'ao Yüan-ming, A.D. 365–427), after less than three months as magistrate of P'eng-tse, burst out before a visiting superior: 'I find it impossible to bend my back to every village lout for five pecks of rice!' That same day he relinquished his post to devote the rest of his days to poetry, Taoism and the contemplation of nature.
4. Right-hand man of Kao-tsu, first Emperor of the Han dynasty (reigned 206–194 B.C.).
5. One claim to fame of Wei Wu-chih was his recommendation to the Prince of Han of the services of Ch'en P'ing, who eventually, in 179 B.C., became Chief Minister.
6. A tsou-ma-teng is a lantern on the top band of which are decorative figures, which revolve as the hot air ascends.
7. The text explains at this point that the word wen, used here for 'woman', is the North China equivalent of the southern word ma. A note of authenticity is here sounded: we are to assume that the story originated in the north, where its events are located, but in its present form reflects the story-tellers of some southern centre such as Hangchow.

The Journey of the Corpse
The Story of Wu Pao-an

1. Chien-men is the name of a range of mountains in Szechuan, to the north of the T'ang town of Chien-chou (present Chien-ko hsien, under the jurisdiction of the prefecture of Pao-ning). Chien-wai, 'beyond the Chien', or Chien-nan, 'south of the Chien' was a T'ang circuit covering parts of present-day Szechuan, Kansu and Yunnan, the administrative centre being Chengtu.
2. Chung Yi was a man of Ch'u in the time of the Warring States, who became Duke of Yün. Previously he had been captured by the state of Cheng and presented to Chin, where he was questioned by Duke Ching. The goodness, sincerity, loyalty, intelligence and courtesy manifested by his answers so impressed his hearers that he was released.
3. Chi Tzu was uncle and Grand Tutor of the Shang Emperor Chou (1154–1122 B.C.). His remonstrances having no effect on Chou's vicious conduct, he put on a wig, feigned madness and became a slave. Chung-hsiang is lamenting that he has no choice and must remain a slave, unlike Chi Tzu who was only playing a part.

4. In the reign of Han Wu-ti (140–86 B.C.), General Su led an expedition against the Hsiung-nu Tartars. Forced to surrender, he maintained an unsubmissive attitude, and was put into solitary confinement in a pit, where he kept himself alive on snow. He was later transferred to the Pei-hai and there made to tend sheep; hence Chung-hsiang's comparison.

5. Li Ling was an accomplished rider and marksman who led a small force of 5,000 men against the Hsiung-nu Tartars, again in the reign of Wu-ti. He was captured by the Hsiung-nu, but his talents led to his being taken into their service. Chung-hsiang here is envying him this favour.

6. This price was already high, as compared with the common ransom (i.e. for 'other ranks') of thirty rolls of cloth.

7. When the general Hua Yüan, in the time of the Warring States, was forced to flee from Sung, Yü Shih ('Father Shih') attempted to prevent his flight. Hua in due course returned to defeat his enemies. Subsequently he was sent as emissary to the barbarians, and had to be ransomed back.

The Journey of the Corpse

8. Yang Chiao-ai and Tso Po-t'ao, a famous pair of loyal friends of classical times, and heroes of *The Battle of the Ghosts*, another of the *Stories Old and New*.

9. T'ao Ch'ien; see note 3 to *Wine and Dumplings*.

10. Chi K'ang, the poet, one of the 'Seven Sages of the Bamboo Grove', 223–262.

11. Kung Yü, in the reign of the Han Emperor Yüan-ti (48–32 B.C.), was called to office together with his friend Wang Chi, and a popular saying about them ran, 'When Wang Chi came to power, Kung Yü flipped his cap'—to remove the dust, in preparation for taking office. The line makes allusion to the friendship of these two men who insisted on accompanying each other in and out of office.

12. Ching K'o was the most famous of the would-be assassins of the tyrannical 'First Emperor', Ch'in Shih-huang-ti. When 'Ching K'o's courage failed', Kao Chien-li proved his friendship for him by himself making an attempt on the life of the despot.

13. Fu Chieh-tzu, at the age of 13, expressed his conviction that 'the man of worth must establish his merit in a remote place'. In the reign of the Han Emperor Chao-ti (86–73 B.C.) he reached high rank and fame in the army. Pan Ch'ao followed his example with the words, 'the man of worth should emulate Fu Chieh-tzu, and establish his merit in a distant place'. He was outstandingly successful as an envoy to the Western Regions in the time of the Han Emperors Ming-ti (A.D. 58–76) and Chang-ti (A.D. 76–89).

14. The usurper, 684–705.

15. Meng Huo, a barbarian chief, after capture by the Chinese, was taken by Chu-ko Liang to inspect the troops. He was surprised: had he known earlier the true state of the Chinese armies, he would have defeated them, he claimed. Chu-ko Liang laughed, released him and challenged him

afresh to battle. Seven times Meng Huo was released, and seven times recaptured.

16. The eastern part of present-day Szechuan province.
17. Ma Yüan, in the reign of the Han Emperor Kuang-wu-ti (A.D. 25–58), wrested regions of South China from the barbarians, and set up posts of brass to mark the extension of the Han dominion.
18. Kuan Chung and Po Shu-ya, celebrated friends of antiquity; allusion to Yang Chiao-ai and Tso Po-t'ao was made at the beginning of the story.

The Canary Murders

1. 'Canary' is used purely for the sake of familiarity to represent the bird *hua-mei*. There are in fact several points of resemblance. The *hua-mei* is a member of the oriole family: it is known to ornithologists as *Oreocinola dauma aurea*. It is 4–5 inches in length. The plumage is greyish-yellow, speckled with black, the breast being yellowish-white. White markings above the eyes give rise to the name *hua-mei*, literally 'painted eyebrows'. The male bird is both a singer and a fighter. The *hua-mei* is commonly found in North China, both wild and as a pet.
2. *Ko-yao*: 'the elder brother's kiln': term used to describe the work of the Sung potter Chang Sheng-yi, whose kiln was at Lung-ch'üan in Chekiang. The porcelain of Sheng-yi's younger brother, Sheng-erh, was known as Chang-yao ware.
3. It would be the gravest of misfortunes for Shen Hsiu in the next world, if his corpse were buried while it was still incomplete. His parents were anxious to postpone the funeral for as long as possible in the hope that the head might be found.
4. Corruption would not set in until the spirit had departed: and the spirit of the murdered boy was waiting for the murderer to be brought to justice.

The Fairy's Rescue

1. A.D. 385–433.
2. A.D. 1036–1101. One of China's greatest poets: subject of an entertaining biography by Lin Yutang, *The Gay Genius*.
3. Literally, 'sweet for whom?'—it was a Chinese habit to take salt not only with savouries, but with such sweet things as oranges, cf. the description, in a poem by Su Tung-p'o's contemporary Chou Pang-yen, of the eating of an orange with 'Salt of Wu, whiter than snow'.
4. See above, note 3 to *Wine and Dumplings*.
5. This was the line Hsieh Tao-yün produced in response to that of her brother, Hsieh Ling-yün (above), at a family party.
6. Ku-she is the name of a mountain in Shansi province.
7. According to the *Shan-hai-ching* or 'Classic of Hills and Seas', a jade-tree grows in the Kun-lun Mountains.

8. There are several mountains bearing the name of Ching-shan, 'Thorn Mountain', in different parts of China, and legends cluster about each. It may be that the writer had one of these in mind.

9. Upright minister of the first century A.D. In his early days of poverty he won admiration for his conduct during a severe winter: found lying indoors half-frozen, he explained that he preferred not to beg, since others were hungrier than he.

10. Hsieh Tao-yün, above.

11. A fabulous beast able to travel 500 *li* in a day.

12. Another magical beast, which answered the questions of the legendary Yellow Emperor about earth, heaven, men and demons.

13. Founder of the Ch'an (Zen) school of Buddhism, who arrived in China in the early sixth century A.D.

14. Boulders on the edge of the lake T'ai-hu are weathered into convolutions highly-prized by the builders of rock-gardens.

15. The *Tso-chuan* records an offering to the king of a tiger carved from salt.

16. At this point the commentator censures Wei Shu's conduct on three counts:

    impropriety number one: a daughter seventeen years old and not yet betrothed;

    impropriety number two: allowing her to take part in the expedition;

    impropriety number three: allowing Mr Chang to sit in the same party with her.

17. Literally, 'single phoenix (male) and solitary *luan* (another fabulous bird —female)': together, these birds constitute an emblem of wedded bliss.

18. The Jade Maiden and the Golden Boy wait on the Taoist immortals at their feasts.

19. The joys of illicit love. This is one of the commonest of allusions, to a hoary legend of a prince who found fairy love on the mountain Wu-shan.

20. See note 3 to *The Pearl-sewn Shirt*.

21. A general who was ennobled by Wu-ti's successor for his part in suppressing the rebellion of Hou Ching.

22. Ao was a hero of the Hsia dynasty (3rd–2nd millennia B.C.) whose strength was such, according to the *Analects*, that he could propel a boat across dry land.

23. The text does not read smoothly at this point, and it seems likely that a further speech by Wei Shu's wife has been omitted.

24. The bringers of rain.

25. Melons of rare quality were grown outside the Ch'ing-men or 'Green Gate' of Ch'ang-an, by, among others, a former marquis of the Ch'in nobility, Shao P'ing—like Mr Chang, no ordinary melon-grower.

26. T'ai O was the name of a sword made for a prince of Ch'u, the 'sword of righteousness' of classical allusion. See note 12 to *The Pearl-sewn Shirt*.

27. What I have christened 'Port Melon' is Kuachou, so called because the local topography recalls the triple-pronged shape of the character *kua*,

'melon'. The story-teller must have chanced with delight on this as the obvious place for Mr Chang to cross the river.

28. In Chekiang, named after three brothers surnamed Mao, who in Han times went into seclusion on the mountain and 'attained immortality'.

29. A song by this name is recorded in Sung sources.

30. The reader will remember that the story began in the year 525, so that in fact some eighty years have passed. The traditional system of numbering years worked in cycles of sixty, and one can only suppose that the story-teller in calculating his dates has missed a complete cycle. The T'ang version of the story, in Li Fu-yen's *Hsü Hsüan-kuai-lu*, omits entirely this 'Rip Van Winkle' episode, and the blame must therefore be borne by the author of our prompt-book version.

31. In the text, Hua Hu. *Hu* and *Ti* have the same meaning, 'barbarian', and I therefore read Hua Ti, the legendary inventor of boats. Lao Tzu was the founder of the Taoist school of philosophy.

32. Wang, Grand Duke of Chou, who according to tradition met Wen Wang (father of the first Emperor of the Chou Dynasty) when fishing in the P'an, a river in modern Shensi.

33. A work on herbs and medicines, dating from the Han period.

34. *Pai-yao-chien*, a decoction efficacious against scrofula.

35. I.e. 'king of herbs'.

Religion & Philosophy Titles
From Grove Weidenfeld

___ BIALI	0-8021-3146-8	Aberbach, David BIALIK	$6.95
___ BIALIC	0-8021-1062-2	Aberbach, David BIALIK	$15.00 (cl)
___ ALONE	0-8021-5127-2	Batchelor, Stephen ALONE WITH OTHERS: An Existential Approach to Buddhism	$8.95
___ ANTHO	0-8021-5038-1	Birch, Cyril (ed.) ANTHOLOGY OF CHINESE LITERATURE, Vol. 1	$17.50
___ ANTH2	0-8021-5090-X	Birch, Cyril (ed.) ANTHOLOGY OF CHINESE LITERATURE, Vol. 2	$14.95
___ MING	0-8021-5031-4	Birch, Cyril (trans.) STORIES FROM MING COLLECTION: Art of The Chinese Story-Teller	$9.95
___ ZENTEA	0-8021-5092-6	Blofeld, John THE ZEN TEACHING OF HUANG PO	$10.95
___ KISSI	1-55584-194-5	Calisher, Hortense KISSING COUSINS	$14.95 (cl)
___ CRUCI	0-8021-1094-0	Fricke, Weddig THE COURT-MARTIAL OF JESUS	$18.95 (cl)
___ BANKR	0-8021-3184-0	Haskel, Peter BANKEI ZEN: Translation from the Record of Bankei	$9.95
___ BANKC	0-8021-1211-0	Haskel, Peter BANKEI ZEN	$27.50 (cl)
___ ANTHJ	0-8021-5058-6	Keene, Donald (ed.) ANTHOLOGY OF JAPANESE LITERATURE	$14.95
___ MODJAP	0-8021-5095-0	Keene, Donald (ed.) MODERN JAPANESE LITERATURE	$14.95
___ ZENTR	0-8021-3162-X	Kraft, Kenneth ZEN: Tradition and Transition	$8.95
___ FRONPA	1-55584-197-X	Levi Peter THE FRONTIERS OF PARADISE	$16.95 (cl)
___ LIVIN	0-8021-3136-0	Linssen, Robert LIVING ZEN	$9.95
___ SIMON	1-55584-021-3	Miles, Sian SIMONE WEIL: An Anthology	$8.95
___ DROPP	0-8021-3052-6	Mitchell, Stephen DROPPING ASHES ON BUDDHA: The Teaching of Zen Master Seung Sahn	$11.95
___ CRAZY	0-8021-5184-1	Oe, Kenzaburo THE CRAZY IRIS AND OTHER STORIES OF THE ATOMIC AFTERMATH	$6.95
___ CRAZYC	0-8021-1212-9	Oe, Kenzaburo THE CRAZY IRIS AND OTHER STORIES OF THE ATOMIC AFTERMATH	$22.50 (cl)
___ PERMAT	0-8021-5061-6	Oe, Kenzaburo A PERSONAL MATTER	$7.95
___ TEACH	0-8021-5185-X	Oe, Kenzaburo TEACH US TO OUTGROW OUR MADNESS (The Day He Himself Shall Wipe My Tears Away; Prize Stock; Teach Us To Outgrow Our Madness; Aghwee The Sky Monster)	$9.95
___ RASHI	0-8021-3147-6	Pearl, Chaim RASHI	$6.95
___ RASHIC	0-8021-1063-0	Pearl, Chaim RASHI	$15.95 (cl)
___ WHATBU	0-8021-3031-3	Rahula,Walpola WHAT THE BUDDHA TAUGHT	$8.95
___ HEINE	0-8021-3148-4	Robertson, Ritchie HEINE	$6.95
___ HEINEC	0-8021-1064-9	Robertson, Ritchie HEINE	$15.95 (cl)
___ PALAC	1-55584-068-X	Shahar, David THE PALACE OF SHATTERED VESSELS	$22.50 (cl)
___ TRAIN	0-8021-5023-3	Singh, Khushwant TRAIN TO PAKISTAN	$5.95
___ WORBUD	0-8021-3095-X	Stryk, Lucien (ed.) WORLD OF THE BUDDHA: An Introduction to Buddhist Literature	$12.95
___ ZENPOE	0-8021-3019-4	Stryk, Lucien (ed.) ZEN POEMS OF CHINA AND JAPAN	$7.95
___ ESSAY	0-8021-5118-3	Suzuki, D.T. ESSAYS IN ZEN BUDDHISM	$13.95
___ INTRO	0-8021-3055-0	Suzuki, D.T. INTRODUCTION TO ZEN BUDDHISM	$4.95
___ MANUA	0-8021-3065-8	Suzuki, D.T. MANUAL OF ZEN BUDDHISM	$10.95
___ BUBER	0-8021-3149-2	Vermes, Pamela BUBER	$6.95
___ BUBERC	0-8021-1061-4	Vermes, Pamela BUBER	$15.95 (cl)
___ BOOKSO	0-8021-3021-6	Waley, Arthur (trans.) THE BOOK OF SONGS	$9.95